SOLO BY GASLIGHT

a psychological suspense
by
TIMOTHY
REYNOLDS

cometcatcher
press

First Edition: 2024

Cover Image: iStock: B Nattasak & Gabink

Cover Design: Cometcatcher Press

Library and Archives Canada Cataloguing in Publication

Reynolds, Timothy G. M. 1960 -

Solo by Gaslight

Psychological Suspense/Timothy G. M. Reynolds

ISBN: Paperback print: 978-1-7380328-3-9

ISBN: eBook: 978-1-7380328-4-6

1. Fiction 2. Psychological Suspense I. Title II.

Title: Solo by Gaslight

Cometcatcher Press

Calgary, Alberta, Canada.

For Stephanie Rozek...
musician, singer, animal lover,
and wonderfully bright light;

and for the late Stephen Krawetz...
the kind, patient, and dedicated teacher
who first put a cello in my clumsy hands.

"'Hell is other people' has always been misunderstood. It has been thought that what I meant by that was that our relations with other people are always poisoned, that they are invariably hellish relations.

But what I really mean is something totally different.

I mean that if relations with someone else are twisted, vitiated, then that other person can only be hell. Why? Because...when we think about ourselves, when we try to know ourselves...we use the knowledge of us which other people already have.

We judge ourselves with the means other people have and have given us for judging ourselves."

~Jean-Paul Sartre

Chapter One

Elteen stood at the stained, chipped, brown-muck-filled sink, doing her best to ignore the stench in the vending machine-sized service station bathroom. Time was short, so she thumb-typed as fast as she could. *Auntie Jubilee! I tried calling. Turn your damn phone on. My news feed lit up with the Butcher's latest victim & I know her! We know her!! It's Gemma we went geocaching with, in Fish Creek, so I searched for a picture of the first victim & she was part of our group too. WTF??!! He's hunting the Knightly Girls of Cache-a-Lot! Stay safe! I'm—"*

A fist pounded on the flimsy door and startled her. She dropped her phone.

"Time's up!"

oOo

There was a bench. I sat. If there hadn't been a bench, I still would have sat, down in the mud, slush, and Calgary's typical late-season snow. I just couldn't stand any longer. I'm not squeamish, though. The sight of blood has never bothered me, until now, even though my doctor-prescribed Happy Pills were working overtime. I even took an extra one half an hour ago, knowing I was coming here. But the blood...

There wasn't much of it—just a couple of crimson flecks—but back when I signed the release forms so my twisted car could be put on display, they promised they'd scrub it clean. Apparently, their definition of 'scrubbed' and mine wasn't even on the same planet. To be fair, though, if you didn't know where to look, you wouldn't even see the spots. But *I* knew where to look: the passenger-side window, at the bottom, near the wide black doorpost. Yeah, I knew *exactly* where to find those two little flecks that were all I would ever see again of Vivaldidog—my best friend, my precocious, milk-chocolate-brown poodle.

My dog was dead, but I didn't want to run and hide, scream and wail, or pull my hair out like a normal person would. That double dose of Happy Pills made sure of that. I also definitely couldn't stand. Not yet. I looked away from the specks, taking in the rest of the carcass that had once been my trusty PT Cruiser, *Muse*. Yes, I named my damned car. I name everything. My car is "Muse" and my beautiful Sderci cello with its Voirin bow is "Gavroche". Or it *was* Gavroche. If I climbed up on the flatbed trailer and peered into the crushed and mangled mess of Muse's back seat, would I find splinters that used to be Gavroche's perfect amber-yellow top? Or maybe just my one forest-green leather glove that the paramedics couldn't find.

At the wandering thought of the paramedics, some of the scars on my left hand began to itch. The plastic surgeon said the surgery was mostly a success. I asked if I would be able to play cello and he laughed and asked if I could play *before* the accident. *I* didn't laugh. A nurse whispered to the doctor that I was a concert cellist. He apologized. I told him to go fuck himself. I didn't actually use those words. Or *any* words. I just lay in the hospital bed and stared at my destroyed hand, the way I was now sitting on a bench two weeks later, staring at the wreckage on display in front of Bishop Something-or-Other High School. The sign mounted on the trailer said "Texting Kills". I rubbed the little scar that divided my right eyebrow in half. It was an old scar my sister had given me and rubbing it was an old habit.

My heart rate was disgustingly steady and calm. My breathing was distressingly slow and sure, puffing out in long steamy cloudlets in the mid-April chill. My life was shattered, mangled, shredded, and dead...and I should have been a hell of a lot more than numb. I suppose numbness is better than Depression, though. I knew Depression. She'd sat on my shoulder more than once in the last year and whispered her dark, suffocating words in my ear. She may have dropped by to visit once or twice before that, but I first noticed her just after breakfast last Thanksgiving, the day James looked at me across the kitchen table and dropped his "I-can't-do-this-any-more-I'm-sorry-I'm-moving-back-to-Vancouver-Island" bomb. Fucker.

He moved into the spare room right after he cleared the table and loaded the dishwasher. I'd sat there staring into my half-empty coffee cup, not giving a shit about the dishes. Depression moved in that afternoon and stayed for a week. She wouldn't let me eat, wouldn't let me sleep, and wouldn't let me get any damned work done. It was a good thing we owned our own business and worked from home writing and editing technical manuals, but that didn't mean the work didn't pile up. The only thing Depression *did* let me do was shuffle along behind Vivaldidog on the other end of the retractable leash with a pink baggie of shit clutched in my hand. I guess the Bitch Queen of mood disorders didn't want V-Dog to suffer, too.

James packed all week, loaded his van on Saturday, and drove off that night. He said that he wanted to catch the 10 AM ferry to the Island. I didn't care.

"Are you OK, lady?"

Suddenly I wasn't at home, I wasn't walking the dog, I wasn't even depressed. I was back on the bench, next to the wreckage, stoned, looking up at a pretty, fortyish Filipina wearing purple scrubs under her long, puffy winter coat, worried about me, a complete stranger.

"Yeah. Sorry. That's my car."

"That big fat mess? *Your* car? And you live?" She sat beside me.

"Yeah. *Yes.* I guess."

She leaned and read aloud the sign on the trailer. "'Texting Kills.'" She put her hand on my forearm and squeezed. "Someone die?"

"The other driver. And my dog, my cello...my *soul*."

"That's no good." She looked at me then, and it was such an honest gaze that I couldn't help but look back. She smiled and held her palm over my heart, not actually touching my chest. "No, your soul is no dead. It is here, hiding deep."

It was *my* turn to squeeze *her* hand. "Thank you," I whispered. I didn't know what else to say. The same drugs that kept me from imploding also kept me from articulating any deep thoughts. But she didn't need me to say anything. She understood, probably better than I did.

A siren approached fast from behind us and a black police truck flew past with its lights flashing, slowing just enough to make sure two pedestrians cleared the way. My new friend pointed after the vehicle. "Hope he catching that evil killer!"

"The Geocache Butcher?"

"Yeah, him. The... Butcher. What is this 'jee-oh-cash'? I don't know that word."

Good question. "In simple terms, it's an outdoor activity where people hide containers and others use a GPS to find them. Like a treasure hunt."

"Like the Butcher hide his victims! One hand *here*, one hand *there*, the head in another place. Evil. He is *pure evil*. How many victim now?"

"Two." The sick bastard had been terrorizing the city for months, all over the news. He had sent the coordinates for one body part to the spouse or a friend of each victim and then led the police on a merry chase through the city's various parks, as they searched for hands, feet, and eventually the heads of each of the two women. The Butcher was gutting the geocaching community with the bad press and the darkest possible association. "They don't even have a clue who they're looking for." And worst of all, my goddaughter has been missing for a week.

"Yes, they do! Alert came out today. Police post pro-file." She pulled out her phone and in a moment opened X and showed me the press release, except that it was an actual Police Service tweet, not someone else's post of what they said the police were saying. Typical social media. The entire city was so on edge that people were hooked into updates from any source possible.

I squinted down at it in the bright sunlight. *Male. Caucasian. 25-45 years of age. Physically fit. At least 5'10"/175 cm in height.* Shit. That described *James* and tens of thousands of men in the city. "He should burn in Hell." But after we find Elteen, safe and sound.

"Hell is exactly for him. *God* will punish him."

I had no reply to that. Would someone that evil even care about whatever the mortal courts threw at him?

We sat like that for who knows how long. I didn't really notice the cold and she didn't comment on it, so maybe she didn't notice it either. Eventually, I squeezed her hand one last time and stood. I wobbled for a beat, then my legs remembered their job and I was good.

"I'm OK now." I wasn't, but I had to move. She stood, too, and I finally noticed that she was taller than me, though not by much. I'm pretty short.

"No, you not. But you *will* be. You are strong. I know strong, and *you* are strong." She peered up into my eyes. "Let the pills do their job, but don't let them take over. I see too many get taken over. Most not as strong as you."

"Thank you."

She squeezed my hand with both of hers and smiled one last, wide, warm smile. She was beautiful in so many ways, inside and out. My saviour-of-the-moment crossed the street to a waiting bus, turned back, and wiggle-waggle finger-waved at me. Then she was inside and the bus was gone in a hiss of brakes released and engine revving.

For the first time since the accident, I was something other than numb and weak-kneed. I almost smiled. I had no idea how I was going to wade through the shit-show my life had become, but I was damned sure I needed to kick the meds before I could do it. This not feeling anything sucked.

My bus came down the steep little hill to the west and turned into the bus loop. I kissed my cold fingertips and touched them to Muse's door. I needed to cry or scream or something, but the drugs nixed the idea and told me to get my ass home. I crossed at the light and shuffled over to the bus. I almost turned on my phone, just in case the family had heard from Elteen, but I didn't, afraid that the news might not be good.

o0o

"You have a one-cup coffee maker but no K-Cups! How retarded is that?"

I wasn't even through my own front door before my older sister, Joyce, started in on me. Even medicated to mellowness, I often regretted giving her a key to the house, but after the accident, it had been either her or my parents. That's the problem with having even a wee bit of a concussion—the doctors pretty much insist on somebody being able to look in on you. Joyce took the job willingly, but only so she could raid my once extensive wine cellar. She's always been a bully, but she became a world-class bitch after I stopped restocking the empty slots in the three big racks in the basement.

"The drawer next to the fridge. I use reusable ones. The coffee is in the freezer."

"You freeze your fucking coffee? And Dad says *you're* the smart one."

"Juice, is there a particular reason you're here?" Joyce hated that nickname, but she was getting on even my medicated nerves.

"Yeah, *JuJube*, I came to get some money for Mom's birthday present, but you weren't home. I've been here an hour." She examined a reusable K-Cup like it was a Rubik's Cube and she was colour-blind.

"You should have called." She *always* called. She also always set an exact time for her visit and then didn't even come close to the time. I rarely waited for less than an hour for her to 'drop by'. "I was out," I said.

"No shit. Trying to get your shrink to fix your crazy?"

Wow. She was really pissed. She didn't usually play the 'crazy card' until were at least fifteen minutes into what passed for conversation between us. "I was looking at my car. They finally put it out on display at the school." I hung my coat up in the entry closet and fumbled out of my boots one-and-a-half-handed.

Joyce gave up on the little plastic cup and tossed it in the sink. "You went to look at that wrecked piece of shit? Why? It's just a damned car. I don't need you tripping over your self-pity and doing something stupid so they have to call me."

"There was some of Vivaldidog's blood. They were supposed to scrub it."

"A little blood is good. Maybe if they see some gore, it'll convince people not to text. Too bad there wasn't fur and brain matter."

"You're talking about my dog, Juice." Dear Happy Pills, why won't you let me kick her hard and low, just once?

"Yeah, a dog. It's not like it was a baby, or someone important."

Did she just say what I think she did? *Enough was enough*. Her coat was tossed over the back of the leather couch beside me. I picked it up and shook it, listening for the tell-tale jingle of keys. I retrieved them from the right pocket, found my house key next to her 'I-got-drunk-and-laid-in-Puerto-Vallarta' brass key fob, and slipped it around and around the split ring until it popped off in my hand. I dropped it in my pocket and returned her keys to her coat.

"Right? Just a *dog*." She rooted through the freezer.

"Get out, Joyce. Go." My voice was low as I tried to stay calm.

"Make us some coffee, for Christ's sake."

"No." I held her coat up at arm's length. She started toward me as if she was going to punch me like she did when we were kids, like when she gave me the scar on my eyebrow. I took a step forward, too. She was only half a head taller than me, but my slim muscle had never been a match for her pure fury.

To my surprise, she accepted her coat, so I picked up her purse from the couch and handed it over, too. The house was so quiet I could hear my pulse surging in my ears. She wasn't used to me saying 'no'. She slipped silently into her coat, so I stepped out of her way and she went to her little tan ankle boots on the entry mat. I stayed back a few feet, out of reach of her fast hands, because thirty-four years of experience taught me that when my big sister got quiet, she was just planning her attack.

She opened the front door, and then the storm door, but all she fired back was "You're a bitch."

"Yup." I had no witty comeback or zinger, so I just watched her go. I bolted the door behind her, closed the blinds on the bay window, and then dropped onto the couch. I curled up in a ball and let the agony roll up and out of my gut in shuddering sobs, weeping for Vivaldidog and how empty and hollow this house felt without him. Without James, there was less anger, but without V-Dog, there was less heart, and that hurt *so* much. He wasn't just a faithful companion--he'd been my best friend. It was as if God reached into my heart ten years ago, took a little piece of it, and formed it into a tiny, curly-haired, chocolate-brown bundle of love who would spend the next decade wanting nothing more than to wait until I sat down and crossed my arms so he could climb up and fall asleep over my heart.

As much as I'd loved James, I never felt more whole than when V-Dog settled in. And now he was dead and I didn't know how I was going to make it without him. The back of my useless hand began to itch and I scratched it. My broken, torn, ripped apart, put-back-together-but-never-going-to-be-the-same-again hand. No, I'll never play cello again. If it was my bow hand—my right hand—then *maybe* rehab would work; but my *left* hand? My *fingering* hand? With practice, I think the doctor said, I would be able to hold a fork and catch a ball, but Chopin's Cello Sonata in A—fuck no.

I don't know if I'd label myself as a virtuoso, but I could hold my own in first cello chair. I was supposed to return to Vienna for three performances in November, but that's gone now. *Gone!* Suddenly I couldn't breathe. My pulse hammered in my ears, my hands shook so badly that I jammed them under my armpits so I didn't have to watch them freak out.

Oh God... music was my soul. There's been music coming from me since forever, and now I had nothing, just... *drugs*. I couldn't do this alone. Between Joyce and this other shit... I slapped the pocket of my jeans because I didn't trust my eyes to tell me that the bulge was Happy Pills in my pants and not a wad of snotty tissues. The tiny clicky-clicks of pills in a plastic bottle convinced me. I dug at them. Please don't be aspirin, I pleaded. They weren't. I dropped back on the couch, popped the hinged cap off with my thumb, dumped the pills onto the coffee table, and grabbed one. You don't think about how tough it is to take pills with only one hand until the other one is pretty much useless. Thank Christ it wasn't a childproof cap.

I chewed the pill, regretted it almost immediately, then sock-shuffled across the hardwood to the fridge and washed the bitter powder down with Coke from the small bottle. With a smashed heart and a severed soul, I returned to the couch, climbed under the big green afghan, and curled up in anticipation of my medicated rescue.

At some point during my weak-ass pity party, I fell asleep and stayed that way for a helluva long time. When I finally stirred and uncurled from my Ball of Protection, the house was dim. The setting sun lit up a bit of the west-facing kitchen in soft gold, but the east end—the front of my small duplex—was darkish and cool. I got up, stretched out some of the kinks, and wandered over to the kitchen. Now I *really* needed coffee, because even though I'd finally purged Joyce from my sanctuary, I was still over-medicated and a long way from clearing the cobwebs in my head. Coffee became a priority, but first, I had to eat. I don't do well with coffee on an empty stomach.

While I choked back coleslaw from the tub at the back of the fridge, I turned my phone on and checked for messages. There were three texts: one from Joyce, one from Mom, and one from a client. Nothing from anyone who would have news about my goddaughter, Elteen. At some point in time, I had to get my ass back to the task of paying the bills, so I quickly read the client's *Please give me a call about a change to the project* message.

The call was important, but could wait until I finished with the food and caffeine. I took the tub of coleslaw and returned to the island to read the other texts. My sister's came up first and was typical Joyce in its simplicity. *Fuck U, Jujube.*

Chapter Two

Now I *did* laugh, finally. My big sister was making it really easy to not feel guilty about my decision. So, what did Mother dear have to say? I was sure it would be related to Joyce's because that's who Juice always ran straight to. Sure enough... *Jubilee Jayne, what on earth did you say to Joyce? You really need to get help for your anger. You just haven't been the same since your little mishap on the highway. Is it true that now you're not coming to my birthday? What on earth would possess you to make such a hurtful decision?*

Mom didn't even hesitate to take Joyce's side in this, but I wasn't surprised. The two of them had been double-teaming and gaslighting me for as long as I could remember. Mom was the queen of making me think I was exaggerating or misremembering or even outright making shit up. After even a short conversation with her, I usually came away confused and feeling guilty as hell. I picked up the coleslaw tub and stumbled back to the couch where I dropped into my spot.

o0o

If it sounds like all I did was feel sorry for myself, take pills, and sleep, that just about sums it up. It wasn't very suck-it-up-Buttercup strong, but I just didn't have the strength to do much more.

I did eat—mostly veggies and rice—and I kept myself clean, but only because my other go-to cocoon was a soak in a hot bath with lavender, Epsom salts, and flickering candles.

Online, I was no better than dead. I let my music blog slide—what was the point? No Gavroche-cello, no skill, nothing to say. I stopped posting tweets to X, but to be honest, I rarely tweeted anyway because I find that X is nothing more than a right-wing orgy of self-promotion or pithy poser wisdom, and I had nothing to promote and no wisdom that I was aware of. Instagram was completely out of the question. I finally pried myself off the couch and started up my laptop, just for the hell of it. I was really worried about my twenty-year-old goddaughter, though. Elteen usually sent me a text updating me on her latest adventure, but there'd been nothing from her in over a week. She came to see me in the hospital, and that was the last I saw of her. Unfortunately, I'd been so caught up in my misery that I hadn't noticed anything but the mess in my own head, but now I checked all of her various social media feeds. Her last post anywhere was ten days ago, just after she visited me. Damn.

I quickly scanned my emails to make sure there was nothing urgent, work-wise. There wasn't. Then I remembered the call from the client, found my phone, and called her back. I got her voicemail and left the requisite phone tag-you're-it message. Finally, I clicked the Facebook tab—three friend requests, six messages, and fifty-two notices. I wasn't in the mood for new friends, so the six missives seemed like a good place to start.

My cousin, Lisette, meant well, but five words into her message I knew she'd crossed over to the Dark Side and joined the 'I Know How to Fix You' Club. *JJ, here is a survivors group I think you should join. They help people who've lost pets under traumatic circumstances.* There was a link to some stupid-ass Facebook group with puppies and kittens with angel wings all over the neon-pink-background cover photo. I shit you not. I got up, poured myself a mug of grapefruit juice, and returned to my desk.

The next message was from Karl, Elteen's uncle-in-law, the symphony's first violin, and one of my best friends. He wanted me to check out a PTSD Music Therapy group. This one was no surprise, though, because Karl and his husband, Reggie—Elteen's actual uncle—had looked out for me since James and I had our first argument. It was sweet of Karl and Reggie to worry about me, but *music therapy*? I knew music therapy. I'd recorded a number of tracks for a health firm out of New York, and the last thing I needed or wanted was to be told to kick back and listen to some mellow cello. With *my* luck, the tracks would be my own. I typed a quick note, *Thanks, Lads. I love you, too. BTW, have you heard from Elteen lately?* and went to the next message.

The third message was a characteristically short one from James. *I'll be in town at some point in the next three weeks. We need to talk.* Since he didn't actually ask a question or say something I needed to respond to, I closed the message and moved on to the fourth one. It was from Mom, time-stamped the night before, close to midnight. I didn't have the patience for her shit. I closed Messenger without reading any more and took a look at my News Feed, hoping that somewhere in the posts by my two or three hundred Facebook 'friends' was good news to distract me from my own life.

A quick scroll down revealed baby pictures, pet pictures, witty musical memes, not-so-witty political memes, endless sharings of two or three Geocache Butcher updates, the usual rants on gun control or climate change, and far too many "please say a prayer for me" posts.

I wasn't sure whether to mock those last ones or add my own to the list. I suppose we don't appreciate the crap people are going through until we wade through our own steaming pile of it. I took a sip of juice, revelling in its tartness but wishing it had a little—or a lot—of gin in it, then I exited the browser and closed the laptop. My short-lived desire to try and relate to the rest of the human race today was done. My brain was trashed, my heart was hollow, and my feet were itching to move even if only a shuffle. I couldn't sit still, but I hardly had the energy to walk further than the mailbox around the corner. What I really needed was to *clean*. I hated to clean, but I hated the sight of two weeks of dust and crud even more. It was something I was sure I could do one-handed. Well, except maybe using a dustpan, and vacuuming the stairs, or...oh, what the hell—I was even procrastinating procrastinating.

I grabbed the lemony spray cleaner, gave the orange tentacles of the mega-duster a good spraying, tucked the can into the pouch of my hoodie, and started with the two-inch-wide wood blinds in the living room bay window. It has always amazed me how quickly the damned blinds got dusty, but I needed something mindless and simple.

Lemoniness on, dust off. It was almost distracting enough to keep me from noticing the seriously heartbreaking lack of dog nails click-clacking back and forth on the hardwood. Happy Pills and housecleaning... my evening in a nutshell. If any of the neighbours were wondering what the hell I was doing cleaning at this hour, I didn't give a damn.

oOo

The three blinds of the bay window surrendered without a single curse being uttered or shot being fired, though I needed a couple of trips to the kitchen for coffee refills and to shake out the duster over the big stainless garbage can James had insisted was the only one both big enough and streamline enough to fit our kitchen. He was like that—probably still is—rarely compromising, getting his mind set on something and then only accepting that for the result. The real end result was that he often paid too much for Product A when the Product B alternative was less expensive and just as effective.

I thought about James and the stainless-steel garbage can every time I stepped on the pedal to pop the lid. *Every damned time.* That's one of the joys of my meds. They won't let me get all wound up or spun down, but I often get stuck in what I call "thought ruts". The ruts aren't quite obsessing, but more like being half asleep and reflexively spooning sugar into your coffee over and over, not realizing with your mind what your body is doing—at least it *is* for me. A half-step-to-the-left "disconnect".

To be honest, some days a little disconnection is perfect, and this was one of those days. But that's OK. I just couldn't let it become a habit or an addiction. Or I *shouldn't* have let it, but one foot in front of the other, plodding forward, free of pain and sorrow, had its attractions. Of course, I was sure that in about half an hour enough of the medicated blanket would have slipped off and exposed me to a hint of the chill of reality, so the remaining numbness would be what irritated me, not what comforted me. Then I'd look down at my dead hand, remember reality, and need the medicated numbness again. Yeah, I know. I'm seriously screwed up.

Happy Pills or not, numbness or edge, the task of cleaning made a difference. I shuffled along, floating serenely in the sea of not-giving-a-shit riding the wave of a clean-gasm. You know what I mean. That almost pelvic rush when a long-dirty or untidy thing finally gets done through nothing more complicated than elbow grease and determination. When the procrastination finally fucks off.

After the blinds, I attacked the tall, thin, right speaker. There used to be a serene white-porcelain Indian Buddha on the speaker, but James absconded with it. Sure, he was the one who bought it, but I'd always found an odd peace in that enigmatic smile when the two of us stood on opposing sides of an issue, like his smoking. Although he was smoking less and less at the end, we both always seemed to find something to snarl about. I missed Buddha.

The single set of bookshelves was half-empty of movies—I still hadn't gotten around to filling the many gaps left after James picked and chose from our Blu-Ray collection. Music had kept me so busy for so long that I never really got into plopping down on the couch and wasting an entire evening staring at the big screen. I guess I'd better change my attitude and get used to binge-watching *Witcher* or all ten seasons of *Friends* or whatever. Maybe I'll finally get around to watching *Sherlock*.

I kept going… Lemony on, dust off. I glanced back at the empty space on the speaker. I really missed that Buddha, which was easier than missing Vivaldidog. There was hope I could find another Serene Being to feed me peace and truth, but another V-dog? Never. To misquote Sean Bean, one does not simply replace a heart-dog. Not overnight or overmonth, or maybe ever. If James were here he'd know the perfect words of comfort to embrace me with. For all his faults and his occasional angry outbursts, his words could cradle my heart and make me feel safe. Sometimes I missed him, too. Not often or for long, but once in a while, for a few beats.

I finally took a break, dropped the duster on the kitchen island, and heated my coffee. I could clean all night, and probably needed to. I had nothing on my calendar tomorrow until seeing Dr. Ella at two, to 'fix my crazy', so I'd get back at it after a quick break. The coffee smelled great, punching through the dusty mustiness while the hazelnut creamer tickled my nose. I sipped, and the brain cloud parted just slightly, allowing me to feel like there was hope, somewhere, waiting for me to be ready.

o0o

I cleaned for another hour, finally calling it quits after polishing up the little two-piece powder room opposite the basement stairs. It needed minimal attention, mostly because I seldom use it. It's really for guests, though it was so close to the dining room table that most of the guests opted to use the bigger one upstairs. After folding the little gold hand towel and sliding it back onto the wall ring, my body's battery level was in the red. I stumbled upstairs, where I managed to at least brush my teeth, but when I stood up from spitting watery rinse into the sink, my head spun and my knees wobbled. I could have opted for a bath, but the tub took so long to fill that I'd probably fall asleep before it was done, and then it would overflow and run all night, spinning the 'my-life-is-screwed' meter right off the dial.

I did manage to wash my face at least, take my little ponytail out, and give my shoulder-length hair a bit of brushing, but as soon as I put the brush back down on the vanity the bed beckoned.

Lights out, socks and bra off, I crawled between the crimson Egyptian cotton sheets. Their sensual coolness caressed my bare skin so delicately that an unexpected shiver rolled up and back down my spine. I was asleep before the shiver was done.

My relationship with Captain Happy Pills was a love-hate one. I love that he keeps me from going over the deep end with pain and the blues I'm mired in, but I hate that he doesn't let me feel much of anything. He also shuts my dreams down damn effectively, though, and when I say 'dreams', I mean nightmares. In the beginning, I relived the accident a dozen different ways every night and always woke up screaming and sweat-drenched. I used to sleep like a peaceful rock, through James's snoring—back before he abandoned his side of the bed for the Island, through V-dog's sotto voce snore-snort combination—before his spot by my feet went cold and lifeless; and through phone calls, early morning Jehovah door knocks...*the works*—before I got so messed up that I couldn't even use work to pound my brain into numbness. Thanks to Captain Happy Pills, my restless sleep was dream-free, though I still woke up sweat-soaked. As irritating and uncomfortable as all of my pleasureless sweaty wetness was, though, the true tragedy was that Captain Happy Meds had pulled a runner and slipped away before I woke. He can be such an asshole sometimes.

I'd neglected to set the alarm, but the clock on my phone claimed it was 9:12 am, so it was all good. Well, not *good*, but acceptable. 'Good' would have included a certain little poodle curled up and doing his best to convince me to stay right where I was, and a text from Elteen to reassure me she was safe. My post-sleep, early-morning mind could feel V-Dog at my feet, and smell his 'dogness' right there with me, but intellectually I knew it wasn't true. He was gone and his little blue blanket would forever be empty and limp and stinky. *Stinky?*

Of course! I jumped up, whipped open the door of the walk-in closet, and found V-Dog's blanket and bed right where I'd thrown them how many weeks ago. I snatched up the blanket and buried my face in it. Oh shit! It was my boy! It was his sweet, curly coat, his often-sour breath, and the once-fresh-cut grass he'd rolled in on our last walk! It was...the end of me. I slumped back to bed, the blanket still clutched to my cheek, all surrender and no willpower. I wanted to scream and die and wail and hold him and join him and turn back time and kill the other driver *before* he killed the only being who had ever loved me unconditionally with every fibre of his soul.

Somewhere in the mess that was my swamp of self-pity, the phone rang. They could wait. They could leave a message. Or they could go screw themselves. Answering the damned phone wasn't even on my fuck-it list. I squeezed my eyes shut tight to make the rest of the world go away, and once again I wailed and wailed and wept like I had forty days and forty nights of tears to flood away humanity because if I couldn't save my Vivaldidog, the rest of the world could go to Hell.

Chapter Three

S ometime later, after my emotional symphony wound down, the phone rang again. Again, I didn't answer it, but I did look up at the digital clock on top of my dresser. It was late. The morning was almost gone, ripped away from the shore of sanity by wave after wave of my pain and self-pity. I had two hours to get cleaned up and all the way downtown to Dr. Ella's office.

I didn't want to wash V-Dog's scent off me, it was so damn comforting, but I definitely needed to wash my own scent away. I didn't exactly stink, but there was no way I was going to subject my therapist to forty-five minutes in a closed office with my dried-sweat-covered self. I was depressed and unsteady, but I wasn't completely ignorant.

Carefully, lovingly, I folded the little blue-with-white-bones fleece, and placed it on the bed, on James' side. I wasn't done with it yet, and I sure as hell wasn't going to wash it. As I peeled off my still-damp pyjamas I had the horrifying thought that Joyce would drop by while I was out and wash it, erasing the last vestige of Vivaldidog I had. She wouldn't dare! *Yes*, she would! She'd do it just to spite me! But she didn't have a key, anymore, because I took that. But was the front door locked? Shit!

Completely starkers, I thumped downstairs and turned the deadbolt. But both Joyce and Mom knew I kept a spare under a broken flowerpot in the dirt beneath the lilies under the front window. Well, I wasn't running my bare ass out into the yard to fetch it. I could lock the storm door, though. No one had a key for that except *me*.

I unlocked the front door, opened it a crack, and peered through, looking up and down the cul-de-sac as far as I could without flashing the world. No one. There looked to be a big kid in the shadows of the slide in the little playground across the street, but I was pretty sure they were looking the other way. I yanked open the inner door, spun the latch to lock the storm door, then slammed and locked the big door again. "Nekked as a jaybird", as Granny used to say. A bloody *cold* jaybird.

Back upstairs I finally showered the sweat away and brought my core temperature back up. As the heat sluiced my stress away, I was pretty sure this six-setting shower head was the best invention in the whole damn world. It pulsed out an energizing beat, a firm, fulfilling tempo. I hummed along, no particular song, just bits and pieces of whatever came to mind.

I was dried, dressed, medicated, caffeinated, and out the door in record time. As I shuffled to the bus stop I spotted a neighbour walking his dog. Oh shit. I took a deep breath and kept walking, hands jammed in my pockets, staring at the sidewalk in front of me. I could do this, dammit. Then there were two more dogs, and as they passed by me, a hound in a nearby house started barking. Then I spotted another neighbour walking his Bijon-poodle, Obi-Wan, who just happened to stop and sniff at the same post-V-Dog always did. 'Checking for pee-mail' I used to call it.

That was more than I could handle. I fumbled the pill bottle out of my pocket, opened it with my teeth and my good hand, fished out a make-me-happy pill, tossed it back, chewed it, and then rinsed it down with spit. I stumbled to the bus stop bench where I began obsessing over the time, waiting both for fixes of drugs to kick in and the bus to arrive. I didn't give a shit about the sunshine or the sour, chalky residue in my mouth. I cared about the scuff on the left side of the toe of my left boot that I would have to polish out. I cared about the tiny, meandering crack in the sidewalk between my feet and whether or not it would eventually become a big crack.

I was saved from caring about the particular shade of green of broken glass to my right, though, by the arrival of the bus. Being midday, there were plenty of empty seats, so I didn't have to care about crowding in next to some chatterbox on their phone, or worse, one who wanted *me* to be the other half of a conversation from Hell. I hid behind my big sunglasses, staring out the window as the world blurred past. My breaths were quick and ragged but settled down a bit after the bus merged onto the short stretch of highway linking my beige, vinyl-sided subdivision with the rest of the city. Since no dogs were ever walked along the highway shoulder, I tuned it out. Letting my vision zone out, seeing everything but registering nothing.

Eventually, we reached the southernmost station in the line. I let my fellow passengers drag me along in their wake. I stared at the puffy, rust-and-brown-quilted back of the jacket ahead of me. She walked, I walked. She stopped, I stopped. This may sound a little extreme, seeing as how the dogs were gone from sight now, but this wasn't just a train station, it was the station across from Bishop Whatchamacallit High School where a certain shattered PT Cruiser looked down from its high Trailer of Accusation. I couldn't afford to even *glance* in that direction right then. Until Captain Happy Pills swept me off my feet, I was teetering on the edge of the Nasty Cliffs of Despair, or the Black Bluffs of Now-You're-Screwed. Sometimes it's damned hard to tell the difference.

Along the sidewalk, up the ramp to the platform, I followed close on the heels of my unsuspecting guide. A train was already sitting in the station, so we shuffle-jogged to reach the doors before the driver locked them and departed. Once on the train, I found a window seat, leaving my unaware guide to join people she knew, judging by the hugs and cheek kisses they exchanged. I claimed a seat, wrapped my arms around myself, and let my mind flit away, trying to ignore a nerdy, balding guy who rushed to get on the train and then glanced my way, twice. Jerk. I considered putting my earbuds in and letting music block out the universe, but most of the music on my phone was classical, and I just couldn't deal with it now. Maybe never.

A couple sat down on the bench ahead of me, excited or upset about something. "Don't tell me it was an honest mistake, Lenny. How do you mistake a homeless indigenous man in his fifties for a white serial killer in his thirties?"

"They thought he was geocaching another victim."

"Bullshit! Look at the article!" She held her phone up, nearly shoving it in Lenny's face. "He was bottle-picking. His old grocery cart was full of 'stuff', not body parts! It was nothing more than a couple of drunk racists using a helpless man as a punching bag."

"They're scared, just like the—"

I couldn't listen to them anymore. I slipped along and off the vinyl seat and shuffled to a quieter part of the train where I tucked myself into another window seat and closed my eyes.

o0o

When I awoke, the train was packed with commuters, and a petite Asian senior sat beside me. I had no idea where I was, but it wasn't like this line of the two-line train went anywhere but up and back. We pulled into a stop and I caught a glimpse of the sign, "University Station", but the train was too packed for me to have simply slept through the downtown stops. It was also a little darker. I couldn't see the train's digital clock for the packed bodies, so I fished my phone out for a time check.

It was...15:42. Damn. I missed my appointment by a long shot. Just lovely. That's $150 I'll never see again. There were two missed calls, one from Dr. Ella's office, about the missed appointment, no doubt, and one from some 'Det. K. Marlin, CPS'. There were also two voicemails, presumably one from each of them. The train was still northbound, so I had almost ninety minutes before I was back at my end of the city. Screw it. The appointment was already missed and it's not like my social schedule was packed, or even existed. I wasn't up for talking to anyone, so I ignored the messages for the time being. I went back to sleep, helped by the murmured conversations of a hundred passengers.

oOo

It was the best sleep I'd had in a year, or at least since the accident. No lingering scent of James' Players Light smoke, or the comfy memory-full blanket of V-Dog's, and no wax and rosin from Gavroche's bow. I woke up four stops before the bottom of the line and surprised a slender middle-aged man across the aisle who had been watching me, with his phone in his hand. I raised my eyebrows in my best "what-the-hell-you-lookin'-at" expression and he looked away. I went back to staring out the window. I would have been more than happy to ride it around at least one more time, but as we approached the final station the announcement came over the speakers that this was the end of the line and this train was out of service for some mechanical issue.

Once I got back out onto the platform into the cold, I had to pee so badly that I thought I was going to have to duck behind the shrubs next to the three newspaper boxes, but there was a Tim Hortons/Wendy's combo half a block away and I was sure I could make it in time, with luck. There was no sign of Nosy Staring Guy.

As I stumbled through the double doors, I realized that I'd been so busy trying not to piss myself that I hadn't even looked over at the wreckage of Muse. Well, that's one way to deal with it, I suppose; though I'm pretty sure if I walked around all day with a full bladder in order to distract myself, I'd end up either with one mean infection or soiling myself—or *both*.

The little bathroom was surprisingly clean, so when I was done and felt like my teeth weren't going to float away, I wasn't grossed out or needing full-body decontamination. By the time the bathroom door swung shut behind me, I was so famished that a fast-food burger, fries, and iced tea were the perfect solution to world hunger—or at least for my pending first-world starvation.

In between bites, I checked my voicemails and sure enough, the first one was from Dr. Ella's office. It was her receptionist, Song, simply and politely letting me know I'd missed my appointment. No reprimand or admonition, just a request to reschedule. Of course, I would—sometime in the next few days. In the meantime, the sea-salt-sprinkled fries were all the therapy I needed. There was also the message from the detective whose tone was more concerned and frustrated than angry. He needed to speak with me urgently. Please call him. I promised myself I would, but right then I was starved.

I'm sure there were other people in the place, eating, chatting, refuelling, but I didn't notice. I started thinking about what the detective might want, though and had no idea. Finally, with the grease lining my stomach, and the cup with the last of the sweet tea and ice clenched in my good hand, I returned the detective's call, suddenly afraid that it might be about Elteen.

"Ms. Krawetz. Thank you for getting back to me. Would you be available to come in and talk to me about a case I'm working on? I'll have a uniformed officer pick you up wherever you are."

"Right now?" I just wanted to back home, and maybe call Karl and Reggie back.

"Yes, please."

Damn. "OK." I told him where I was, which turned out to be only five minutes from where he was. I said I'd meet his officer in the parking lot, and she did indeed arrive quickly, thank God without lights and sirens.

Ten minutes later I was sitting at a conference table opposite the detective, in a room without the expected mirrored wall and heavy steel door. Windows on two sides looked out into the open-concept offices.

"This doesn't exactly look like the interrogation rooms on TV."

"It's not. It's just a meeting room. Thank you for coming in. Do you know who Bill Watson is?"

I did. "He's that investigative reporter. There was an article about him a couple of weeks ago."

"He's been missing for a few weeks and the article was in the Journal-Times—the paper he works for."

"I don't think much of him as a journalist."

"Neither do I, but he's still missing. Have you ever met him?"

"No, I don't think so. Unless it was at a symphony event."

"That's odd because your name was found scribbled on a piece of paper in his house, the house of a missing reporter who was looking into the Geocache Butcher. I was brought onto the case a few days ago."

What the hell? "*My* name? In his house?"

"Yes. We have no idea if it's connected to the Butcher, but your name was there with another name. Do you know an Elteen Sanders?"

"She's my goddaughter. I haven't heard from her in a few weeks."

"Neither have her parents."

"And her name was on the paper with mine?"

"Just your two names, nothing else. We're treating her as a missing person now, possibly related to the case. Bill Watson may have thought you two had information, and now I'm thinking the same. But before we get into that, I need coffee. Can I get you one?"

With the meds still fogging me up, more caffeine was a brilliant idea. "Sure. Black, please."

He stood. "Give me a minute or two and I'll get us each a cup. I'm interested in hearing about Ms. Sanders. Think about it and I'll be back shortly."

He left me alone but didn't close the door behind him. I was still in the middle of a police station, though, surrounded by cops. I suppose it was a good thing I wasn't guilty of anything more than missing my appointment with Dr. Ella, and maybe taking a few too many Happy Pills than I should have. I'm pretty sure there was a statute of limitations on my two shoplifting incidents when I was in my early teens.

Was I a Butcher suspect, though? Or was I a potential victim? If this Geocache bastard had Elteen, was he after me next? If he's done anything to that sweet girl, stalking *me* would be fucking stupid. I might not show it to my friends and family, but I was bottling up a hell of a lot of anger that started back when James quit on me, or maybe before. I clenched my fist-and-a-half and growled, low and angry. Then I laughed at the absurdity of myself. I've never hit anyone in my life! Not even to defend myself against Joyce when we were kids. I was still smiling at the idea of me as an avenging angel when the detective returned and put a big white mug of caffeine in front of me.

"You've remembered something funny, Mr. Krawetz?"

"No. Just an absurd, random thought. Please, call me Jubilee."
I sipped the hot generic roast and dropped my stump self-consciously to my lap, out of sight.

"So, Jubilee, tell me about Elteen, please."

"I've been her godmother since she joined the church about ten years ago. Her Uncle Reggie is one of my best friends. His husband is a violinist I work—*worked*—with." Damn. I had to get used to the past tense.

"That's at the Calgary Symphony?"

He'd done his homework. "Yes. Both in the CSO and in our little quartet." My gut churned and my scars itched, just thinking about music. I flexed what I could of my useless appendage and rubbed it on my jeans to banish the itch, but with only coffee in front of me, there was very little I could do about my churning gut.

"Do you spend a lot of time with Ms. Sanders?"

"Since October, yes. We hiked Banff and Lake Louise areas a lot with my dog." *Damn.* My gut and my heart both wanted another Happy Pill. "Last fall she took us along on a geocaching treasure hunt course her group was doing. Here..." I took out my phone, opened the photos, and... let out a sob. They were all photos of V-Dog! Shit.

"Are you OK?"

"My dog." I tilted the phone so he could see V-Dog's goofy grin. "He was killed in the crash that did *this*." I lifted my stump from my lap, shook the two floppy fingers at him, and dropped it back down out of sight.

"I'm sorry."

"Me, too." I returned to scrolling through the photos until I found the one I wanted. It was Elteen and me in our hiking gear of solid boots, fall jackets, knit caps, and light gloves. She was holding a map and her GPS, I was holding V-Dog up to smile like a furry toddler, and I had my other arm around her shoulders.

"That's a great shot."

"One of her teammates took it with my phone. It was the week before Thanksgiving." The week before James ran off to his future without us.

"Would you mind emailing that to me? It looks like Fish Creek Park." He slid his business card across to me so I could read it.

"It is." I took a moment to send the image.

"So, now we have your missing goddaughter and a missing reporter who wrote your name and Ms. Sanders' down on a piece of paper, and a photo of the two of you geocaching in Fish Creek Park, where a serial killer hid parts of his victims."

Holy shit! "Are you trying to scare me, detective?"

"Only if it shakes free some memories, anything that can help us solve what is looking more and more like one big case instead of separate smaller ones."

"Memories of what?"

"Have you seen anyone following you?"

"Like a stalker? No, I don't think so." Or was there? Was the jerk staring at me on the train a stalker or just an asshole? He hardly looked menacing, just a loser. I'd feel pretty stupid starting a manhunt for a man that I only remember as balding and white.

"Do you remember anything strange about the day this photo was taken?"

I took another look at the photo. "It was cool weather. There were eight or nine of us." I sipped more coffee to push back the fuzziness in my memory. Some memories from before the accident still eluded me. "We spent the day all over the park."

He alternated writing in his notebook and drinking from his mug, but he remained silent, letting me remember at my own pace.

"We laughed a lot, just being silly, but also because the other girls were mocking the amateurish simplicity of the geocaches, the clues, and the hunt. I got the impression they're all pretty experienced competitors and whoever designed this particular treasure hunt was a clumsy poser full of their own intelligence. I was just along for the fresh air and exercise with V-Dog."

"We're now pretty certain that the killer is a white male, aged 25 to 45, strong enough to overpower his victims. Do you remember any man fitting that profile, anywhere near you folks that day?"

"I remember the park being busy. We'd had two weeks of cold rain and even a couple of hours of snow a few days before that, but there could have been a dozen guys like that and I wouldn't remember. I'm sorry." Now, if he'd whistled a tune, I'd remember every note of the tune, but that's just how my mind works with music.

"Don't be. You've already given us some links that we didn't have before. You've been a big help. I'll get an officer to take you home now."

"Thank you. I'm sorry I wasn't more help."

"Well, there's no solid connection between you and the two victims other than both the missing reporter and your goddaughter being geocaching enthusiasts. You mentioned that there were others in the group. Do you remember any of their names?"

"No. Sorry. I just met them the one day." I'd check my emails from Elteen when I got home, just in case.

"That's OK. Starting now, we're going to treat your goddaughter's disappearance as if it were connected, and I'm hoping we can find Bill Watson soon so he can tell us what he wanted to speak with you about. We may have to look at him as a possible victim as well, especially if he got too close to uncovering the killer's identity. Members of the media can be a big help in an investigation, but their need to get the scoop and write an exclusive can sometimes do more harm than good."

"And it's not like the Journal-Times is much more than a tabloid." The paper was trash. A few years back they even promoted the idea of drinking triples, seeing double, and acting single during the ten-day Calgary Stampede party season.

"True enough." He hesitated, seeming to collect thoughts together. "You've got my number if you remember anything else, or hear from your goddaughter."

"Of course." I took a final sip of brew, stood, and tucked my phone back into my pocket. "Are there any other women missing?"

"Too many, especially when we include the missing aboriginal women along the Highway of Tears in British Columbia."

"Damn."

"Yeah."

o0o

A different officer drove me home and watched until I got inside the house before driving off. No doubt that would start the neighbourhood rumour mill grinding away. At least Mom wasn't around to tell me I was just doing it for attention.

I made myself a mug of hot chocolate with a shot of maple whisky and took it out onto the back deck. It was dusk, and there were a few clouds, but I could see glimpses of the three-quarter moon. Wondering why the hell some trash reporter had my name with Elteen's, I stared at the moon. As I stared, Mozart's Piano Concerto #21 in C ran through my head, and I finally let it. In reality, my left fingers were as useless as shit, but in my head, they flew up and down the fingerboard. They hopped from string to string, bringing Wolfgang's incredible piece to life. My right hand gripped an imaginary bow and made little hops back and forth, drawing remembered rosined horsehair across the strings of my mind.

If there were any hope at all that more surgery would give me back my music, I would take it. I would bust my ass to play again, but right now I was starting to get freaked out that we hadn't heard from Elteen.

Chapter Four

I spent a chunk of the morning travelling to and then struggling through physio, distracted by worry. The physiotherapist, Hussein, was impressed with the quality of the surgery, but not with the mobility of my fingers. I told him I'd been doing the exercises, but after five minutes of work, he could tell that I was a lying bitch. He didn't call me that outright, but his one raised eyebrow and dark stare sent the message loud and clear. He was right. For someone so traumatized by the loss of dexterity, I was doing fuck-all to improve it. He gave me a fist-sized blue foam stress ball, showed me a range of stretching and strengthening exercises, and handed me a two-page printout as a reminder. The second page ended with a list of things I had to do to keep my scars supple and healing properly.

"Will I be able to play cello again?" Don't judge me! I had to ask.

"If you learned to finger with your right hand, probably. But you've spent a lifetime learning to play with your left hand, so it could take another lifetime to teach the right. But, yes, you will be able to hold the bow in your left, eventually."

That was the first honest answer anyone had given me since this whole shit wagon got rolling. I was so relieved that I hugged him. He gave me a polite squeeze and then broke free, which was the smart thing to do. Right about then honesty in a man threatened to break through my desire to mope forever. Then again, so did extra caramel in a Frappuccino. I left Hussein with a little hope. There were brilliant, beautiful, gifted disabled musicians around the world, and I *knew* the music—it was all stored away in my head. Maybe I *could* learn to do it in reverse—after we get Elteen home safe and sound.

o0o

I stopped by the little sandwich place in the sports complex and picked up a soup and a wrap. While I ate, I checked for any reply text from Reggie, but there was nothing. I went online and once again checked Elteen's social media accounts, hoping there had been something since I last checked. Nothing. Eventually, I drifted into the public library down the hall and spent far too long staring at the latest issue of the local papers. I didn't so much read the words as stare at the patterns the type made. I wandered out to the bus stop.

By the time I was home, it was rolling on evening and I was a bit less worried about Elteen, who preferred to wander the world free of commitments, and back to obsessing about my claw. I considered going out back to my deck but ended up just sitting on the swing in the cold, empty park across from the house. I didn't swing so much as I twisted back and forth, facing away from the house, staring through the fence at the highway that ran north forever, and south pretty much down into Vegas and beyond. If I got onto the shoulder of that highway and started walking now, would I end up in Mexico for Christmas, eight months away? Did they maybe have miracle surgeons in Mexico who could do what the local surgeons couldn't, and fix my hand? Or maybe I'd find a chapel dedicated to the patron saint of lost musicians and I could pray for healing. Having grown up in a household of hard-core "casual drinkers" I hadn't spent much time in church so I'm not the religious type, but maybe I needed to remedy that.

Canvas strap under my ass, one mitt clenched on the chain and the other in my lap, this was the kind of deep thinking I did on that swing, for minutes or hours or whatever. Of course, if I *did* try to climb the fence, my useless claw would probably foul me up and I'd get stuck hanging upside down by my pants. My death would be a result of hypothermia and humiliation.

At some point, I realized how damned cold I was and abandoned the little playground. I shuffled through the gravel, down the paved path, and across the street to the house. The motion sensor on the entry lamp detected my sluggish dawdle and welcomed me home. I'd love to say that it was better than nothing, but the dark, dog-less hollow space beyond the front door was just enough of a kick in the gut to suck my little bit of energy away. I got my gloves and boots off, but just stumbled around the couch to curl up in my coat and hat. Before I fell asleep I had just enough time to acknowledge that I needed help. Dr. Ella, Karl and Reggie, someone...

o0o

There's a lot to be said for the comfort of winter clothes when a person can grab eight hours of sleep right there on the couch. Sometime before sunrise, a thumping car door out on the street stirred me and I managed to strip out of my Gortex-fleece combo and climb the stairs to flop on the bed. When my phone rang and vibrated my butt cheek sometime later, I was rested enough to answer in the requisite four iterations of Beethoven's Fifth. The caller ID said it was Dr. Ella's office. I started off contrite.

"I'm sorry I missed it. I can explain."

"Good morning, Jubilee." It was the doctor, herself. Oops. "I have a cancellation at 11:15 this morning. Can you make it, please? That's two hours." Her voice was calm and soothing, just like during our sessions. She didn't sound angry at all. Calm and soothing was just what I needed.

"Yes. Toast, juice, gargle, and out the door."

"Excellent. I'll see you then. Thank you, Jube."

She hung up and I wondered why *she* was thanking *me*.

o0o

Believe it or not, I got through the various tasks with the floppy stump and I even got to her office on the fourth floor of the Tower Business Centre on time. I loved this place. It was shades of chocolate and large woven fabrics. There was even the world's softest Angora blanket that drew me to it the moment I stepped across the threshold and nodded a greeting to the receptionist, Song.

Song waved at me and smiled as I settled in with the blanket. This was a warm, positive place, and Song's beautiful smile, framed by her dark, South Pacific Asian face made me wonder how I could possibly ever miss an opportunity to be here. I wanted to redecorate my entire home to be this comfortable, and put framed photos of Song's smile on every wall. I know how creepy that sounds, but until you've been down at the bottom and found that the way up out of the darkness started with the light of a sincere, honest, caring face, you'll have no idea what I mean. If I were gay, I'd propose to her every time I stepped through those doors. Hell, I'd make appointments just to see her smile.

The door to the inner office opened and there was Dr. Ella, with her arms open, waiting for the requisite hug. In a world of don't-touch-me distancing, this was a place where the hug had once again become sacred, warm, and healing. I favoured my stump but didn't scrimp on the squeeze. Around here, you got more than you gave, and today I gave all I had. I gave so much that when I finally let go, my knees wobbled a bit. Dr. Ella caught me, easily. She was only three inches taller than me, and slender, but ten years as a corrections officer and an adulthood spent training and running marathons packed a lot of power into her unassuming frame.

"Whoa! Easy, Jubilee. Song, can you give us a hand, please?"

Song was out from behind her desk and steadied me before the doctor even finished speaking. The two of them gave me a moment to steady myself, then I let them walk me into Dr. Ella's office. Once I was settled into the big, generously padded chair I preferred, Song left us without a word, closing the soundproof door behind her.

"Thank you for coming, Jubilee. I appreciate it." She sat in her favourite chair, which was simple, comfortable-looking, and not at all imperious or authoritative.

"Why are you thanking *me*? I'm the one who missed the appointment. I'm the crippled screw-up."

"Excuse me? You're a *what*?" A calm question, not an attack.

"A crippled screw-up." I knew she heard me the first time, so I suppose she was wondering if I had the nerve to repeat it. Of course, I did. This was the place I could safely speak the truth, and *that* was the damned truth. "I have a semi-repaired, forever-damaged left hand, making me a 'cripple', and I'm developing an unhealthy relationship with my anti-depressants, which is known in some circles as 'screwing up'.

"Not in *my* circle, but first things first. What did the physiotherapist say about your hand?"

"I'll be a cripple forever and it's no better than a stump."

"Ah. I see. The words 'cripple' and 'stump' were both used? That's pretty serious."

Really? She was pulling this shit? "You're patronizing me."

"And you're lying to me in this place of Truth."

"I'm not lying."

"Yes, Jube, you *are*. The physiotherapist did not use those terms. That's how you feel, but it is not what was said to you. I'm not negating your feelings, I just want to get the facts out of the way first. Please repeat as best you can recall, what the physiotherapist said, m'Dear."

Anyone else calling me 'Dear' would have chased me right out the door. Even James had known better. But Dr. Ella meant it only with true affection. We established this in our first session two weeks ago, when she told me about her Prince Edward Island roots and down-home approach. Her accent was thin, but she'd kept some of her East Coast expressions, which I found endearing and pleasant, even when she was implying I was a lying bitch.

So I told her what Hussein said about the transverse ligament, carpal bones, tendons, and nerve damage. I told her that I just might get forty-percent use of my hand. Forty percent of *normal* usage. Normal wasn't good enough for me. "Maybe hold a bow" wasn't good enough. It was seriously substandard. It might as well be a stump. As I ranted, she listened. She didn't take notes, clean her nails, or do anything but look directly at me and listen to every word. Near the end, I got up and paced, and she just smiled warmly and kept listening.

When I was all done reiterating the physio-speak, I found myself standing in front of a large photograph of an odd-looking owl that wasn't there last session. "This is gorgeous. Did you take it?" It was *stunning*. The detail was exquisite, revealing the fine brown-on-white chest feathers, the mottled brown head, the bright yellow claws, the beak, and the piercing eyes that ensnared me. This beauty was looking directly into the camera and had one claw up as if it were waving. I got a chill.

"It was a gift from a patient. It's a Northern Pygmy Owl."

"He must have waited for *hours* just to get this one, perfect photograph."

"*She* said that this little one was in the trees twenty feet from the parking lot. She admits she got lucky this time. She's told me a few stories about sitting for hours or hiking ten kilometres just to get a glimpse of a bird she'd heard a rumour about."

"*That's* dedication." It was crazy.

"Really?" She said it quietly, almost whispering, which hooked my attention.

"Of course. To sit and wait for hours for the sake of one's art."

"Very true. It *is* art, isn't it? The art of timing to capture light in a scene, and compose the final image."

"It's not painting, requiring dexterity with brushes, but, yes, it's art."

"Just like music is art."

"Of course. Audio art or performance art, but music is definitely art. Was this in doubt?"

"Not at all."

"But you're leading the conversation somewhere in particular." She was sneaky that way.

"Just nudging one you started."

"About art."

"More about the artist—you."

"My art is music. I've never used anything more complicated than my phone to take pictures."

"Everyone has to start somewhere, but that is a conversation that can wait until early next week."

"Next week?" So soon?

"You have something else planned? I'm not being sarcastic, m'Dear. If you have plans, then we'll work around them. I'd much rather you were out doing something fun than in here."

"No plans." Which was the truth. There was a little wine and cheese birthday thing in a day or two, and Mom's party next weekend, but even that was on the 'Are they even talking to me?' list. "Nothing important. I do have to get some work done at some point, but that's as flexible as always."

"Good. Set something up with Song, please."

I'd been so caught up in the ambiance of the place and blowing off self-pity steam that I nearly forgot to tell her the big news. "Have we still got a few minutes left? I should probably tell you about my chat with a police detective yesterday."

"Um...'probably'?" She leaned forward. "Yes, please, Jubilee."

I told her everything I could remember about the conversation, about Elteen and the reporter both being missing. I showed her the picture of the two of us with V-Dog. When I was done, she was uncharacteristically quiet for a moment, before she finally decided what to say.

"It does sound like an odd coincidence."

"Maybe. I think the reporter just wanted to ask me about my goddaughter since we're in a bunch of each other's photos." I smiled and looked back to the owl on the wall. "Speaking of photos, do you think she would sell me a copy of this picture? I have a perfect place for it over my desk."

"She might. I'll ask her and have an answer for you when you come in next."

"Thank you." I left her then, in her place of Truth and Comfort, made an appointment with Song for Monday, after morning rush hour, and went back out into the harsh, hide-no-secret sunlight.

It was midday, downtown, I was hungry, I had nowhere to be in a hurry, and with a quick look around I determined like the smart ass that I am that no stalker was watching. Also, for the first time in weeks, there was only a trace of meds in me, and I felt OK. Sort of functional and almost human. I still wasn't the Queen of Decision-making, but across the street, there was a high-end steakhouse on the left and the Marriott Hotel with its lounge on the right.

I caught sight of a member of the orchestra's horn section go in through the hotel's revolving door, and in a moment of panic, I decided that there were plenty of restaurants back in my end of the city that weren't a block away from our rehearsal space. I pulled my hat down, kept my eyes forward, and walked the two blocks to the train station as fast as I could without looking as suspicious as a thief.

By the time I reached the front end of the train platform, the next train was arriving, so I was able to tuck into a seat, pull my hat down further, and feel stupid and childish without anyone recognizing me. I guess I wasn't quite as ready to join humanity as I thought I was.

My phone beeped with an incoming text. Reggie said that Elteen's brother—Kenny—was the last to hear from her, in a text sent from Banff. The message was a short 'howdy' note and a picture of his sister in a bar, sticking her tongue out at the camera and holding up a shooter glass. Kenny didn't seem as worried as his parents or uncle since Elteen had hinted at a trip to the West Coast with friends. I was tempted to tell Reggie about the conversation with the detective about the reporter, but if Elteen had been in Banff and was off to Vancouver or Victoria, she was hardly at risk from a serial killer in Calgary. I relaxed. There was no point in freaking Reggie out.

Chapter Five

I stepped into the house but couldn't shake the feeling I was forgetting something, something lost in the fuzziness in my brain. All along, I've been describing what I was going through as 'depression', but to be honest it was more like PTSD. Or most probably a combination of the two, with a hint of anxiety. I've avoided saying that it's PTSD because it seems that every dysfunctional twerp and his cousin has jumped on that diagnostic wagon and it has lost its 'power'. Someone gets yelled at by her boss—PTSD. Someone falls off his eScooter—PTSD. Someone watches FOX News—PTSD.

So, being someone who lost her dog *and* her art in an accident that ended the other driver in a gory splatter, I don't fancy being lumped in with idiots crying PTSD because they can't handle everyday life.

Also, I'm not a war veteran or an emergency responder who gets overloaded daily with harsh, bloody, dark input. Sure, I have bad dreams, and I have an occasional flashback to the accident, but I could never look a war vet in the eyes and say "PTSD? Yeah, me, too. Stay strong, Brother." But while Depression is even more universal, there's no 'coolness factor', so it's not a wagon as many people willingly jump onto. Sad but true, in my experience.

Inside, I shed my winter clothes, finally hanging or stowing them as needed. I wandered to the fridge for some juice. I could have gone for some wine, but thought I'd better start slowly. Juice first, then some food, and maybe a glass of simple, cheap California white. I learned from Dr. Ella that alcohol and Happy Pills aren't particularly good together, but everyone is different, so maybe I'd be OK in moderation.

I took my juice over to the couch. I needed to eat, but I just wanted to put my feet up for a couple of minutes and close my eyes without having to worry about missing a train, bypassing a bus stop, or watching over my shoulder for some ass-hat who wanted to saw my head off and hide it in the park. I promised myself that after taking a break with the juice I'd dig into the big chest freezer to see what delicious treats lay buried beneath frozen peas and never-to-be-used pucks of frozen raw dog food.

I closed my eyes—

—and woke up two hours later.

This was all bullshit. Sleeping my miserable life away sounded like a viable choice after what I'd gone through, but part of me just couldn't get on board with it. Before, when I was bored, I would walk V-Dog or play some Brahms to relax, but neither of those were options anymore. If I didn't do *something*, though, I was going to snap.

I chugged back the remainder of the now-warm juice, and suddenly I knew *exactly* what I could do. I sock-skated into the kitchen where I placed the dirty glass in the sink, grabbed a pair of heavy-duty orange garbage bags out of the box on the pantry cupboard floor, and marched right upstairs to my music room. No, my *former* music room. That's what it was and what I'd better get used to calling it until I repurposed it—maybe a self-flagellation room where I can go and whip myself one-handed into a punishing frenzy every time the meds don't do the trick.

The door was closed, as it had been since the day I got home from the hospital. I took a breath and barged into what had once been the sanctuary of my soul, where I once upon a time coaxed Liszt and Chopin to fill the house; where I often sat on the love seat, reviewing arrangements with V-Dog curled up beside me; where *I* curled up on that same love seat with V-Dog and sniffled my way to sleep after my first, second, and third fights with James. After the third one, I just stopped fighting. I couldn't handle living in a war zone, even if it was a beige, suburban, voices-barely-raised war zone. By then I was sure he was planning to leave and was picking arguments intentionally, but it didn't hurt any less.

The air in the room was stale and thick with olfactory triggers. Rosin, wood polish, more V-Dog—I stumbled in the doorway and grabbed the doorframe for support. This was a stupid idea. It was a punch in the gut, a kick in the groin, and a hammer to the face, all at once. This room had once been my sanctuary, and now it was apparently the least safe room in the house. But I had to face this shit. If I let it get the better of me, I might as well wash down the month'sworth of Happy Pills with a mickey of tequila and call it my last night.

Fuck it. I was alone, so I could weep like a basket case through the job at hand and there was no one to 'tsk tsk' me. I *needed* a purge, a cleansing fire, and this was it. My sheet music was kept in a pair of beautiful, dark oak, two-drawer file cabinets. There were also a half-dozen short stacks of music books and random sheets of scribbled notes from back when I fancied myself to be a composer. I started with the cabinet on my right, with the file in the front of the top drawer. I didn't even read the file name, just grabbed it, made sure it was music and not my late grandmother's letters, and then dumped it in the bag at my feet. Next file, same routine.

In the beginning, I could barely see through stupid tears, but file by file my resolve strengthened. Well, I don't know if it was actually resolve. It could have been anger, because with every sheet of Ravel, Rachmaninoff, and Paganini, I got more and more pissed off at the universe, and more and more pissed off at the texting asshole that tried to pass me and ended up ruining my goddamned life. If he hadn't died, by the time I got to the file of eighteenth-century sonatas I was ready to kill him with my bare hand-and-a-half.

How fucking *dare* he! It was a winding two-lane snowy country road with barely enough room for one car in each lane, let alone for one to pass another while sending a goddamned text to his wife, boyfriend, or boss. He didn't even give me a chance to react and avoid him. If my dreams were accurate, he pulled up beside me, his head down, thumb-typing. Then another car or truck came around the corner at us and ass-hat suddenly swerved into my lane, and all I could manage to say was 'Oh shit' before he shoved Muse right into the ditch. At least, I think it was. My memory is still spotty. There was snow. Maybe. And although it was night-time in my nightmares, I'm sure it was mid-afternoon.

He was yet another man tearing out a chunk of my heart and snapping my life in two. Once upon a time, I thought Dad was a destroyer by siding with Mom and drinking instead of supporting me; then James swept me off my feet, spun me around for all those years, and finally ruined Thanksgiving forever by picking *that* weekend to sauté my heart and serve it up with the breakfast omelette. I survived Dad and I've survived James, but this latest asshole who had the indignity to die before I could kill him myself...

And *that's* when I found the divorce papers. Shit. I swiped at the tears with my sleeve. I was served with the papers three weeks after James left. As glad as I was that I was free of the crumbling marriage, it was still such a slap to get the formal request to sever the bond that I'd stuffed the papers in the file cabinet, had a strong drink and a good cry, and went about my new half-life, ignoring his calls, texts, and Facebook messages. Eventually, he was down to one call a month, on the fourteenth, the *monthiversary* of our first date. The last call had been a polite one from his lawyer.

I opened the green envelope with my name and address neatly typed on the front and the law firm's imprint in the top left. I half expected it to be 'Dewey, Cheatham, and Howe" from the Three Stooges, but it was three bland names and their 'associates'. Being a technical writer and editor, I'm more than a little familiar with legalese, so I reread and understood the document sealing the end of that part of my life, and reached for a pen.

I couldn't bring back Vivaldidog, Gavroche, or Muse, and even if I could bring back James, I had no desire to. At the time his leaving hurt like hell, but compared to everything I was trying to deal with after the accident, his abandonment was just a missed beat or a change in tempo. I signed both copies of the writ, folded them up, and slipped them back into the envelope. Tomorrow was soon enough to get them to my lawyer. Hell, I wasn't even sure what more needed to be done, though the title of the house was probably at the top of the list. That's probably what James wanted to talk about when he arrived later in the month. I put the envelope on my chair.

That, too, could wait. Finally signing the damned divorce papers made me both nauseous and energized. For whatever it was worth, it was *done*, and I now wanted to finish what I'd started in this music mausoleum.

Chapter Six

I used to be pretty good at quickly getting focused and relaxed.
You can't play for royalty or bounce around an Offenbach duet
with Yo-Yo Ma and not be in a deep Zen chill, focused only on
the world at your fingertips and ears. My old calming centre was
achieved by petting V-Dog when I was at home or pulling up a
vivid memory of petting him when I was elsewhere. At least for the
time being I needed to find another calm focus. I took one more
long, deep, diaphragm-expanding breath, and let my mind grab at
any images it wanted to.

Maybe not so oddly enough, the first and strongest image that
popped up was of that owl photo in Dr. Ella's office, with the
calm expression and the yellow toes and razor-sharp talons raised
in greeting. I could see so clearly in my mind the black-on-yellow
eyes looking laser-direct back at the camera. A feathery warmth
settled down on me. My breathing slowed, and then a sudden
shiver shook me right down to the soles of my feet. After it rolled
through me, I relaxed two keys lower. I was ready.

Looking around the room I could see that I needed at least
four more garbage bags—two for the remainder of my music and
two to double-bag the too-full pair beside me. I could also use a
damned drink. Not coffee or tea, though. Something stronger, but
not heavy, which eliminated my rum. What I *did* have, that I'd
managed to hide away from Joyce's thieving fingers, was a bottle

of honey wine—my cousin Tereasa's homemade raspberry-mint mead, to be precise. Made from her own bees.

The good news was that it was hidden here in this very room, behind the loveseat. The bad news was that it was room temperature and it was best chilled. Yeah, I know, beggars can't be choosers. I crawled awkwardly around the end of the mini-couch and reached back into the shadows with my good arm. It was exactly where I had left it. I retrieved it and wiped off the thin layer of dust.

"Hello Sweetheart. You wanna par-tay?" He was the strong, slightly sweet, silent type, so I just kissed his label, thankful for this respite, and headed down to the kitchen for the corkscrew, a large glass, and the garbage bags that sent me off on this unproductive tangent in the first place.

Five minutes later I was back up upstairs with a full wine glass in my useful hand and the garbage bags draped over my stump. Now that there was no risk of Joyce getting her pilfering mitts on it, the open bottle was ensconced in the freezer for a quick chill. Just the thought of my sister no longer having a key to my sanctuary gave me an added little boost.

Somewhere in the house, my phone rang, but with the glass in my hand and my butt firmly entrenched on the loveseat, it could ring all it wanted to. It wasn't Elteen's *Addam's Family* ringtone, so it didn't matter. Nothing could be urgent in the evening, and I would check the messages later. I looked around the room. There wasn't that much to do at this point. I had a plan now, and the first stage was to get rid of the sheet music I would never need again. I had a small collection of rare original sheets in a glass case in the corner, but their value spared them from the purge, for the time being.

A sip of mead was followed by a dumping of sheets. A sip...a dump...and so it went. By the time the glass was empty, the garbage bags were ready to go. I grabbed the first one by the collar, twisted it around with my useful hand until I had a good grip, and quite unceremoniously dragged it bouncing down the stairs like the body of a sibling I'd shot in the act of robbing me of my wine. Then along the slick hardwood to the back door, where, with some manoeuvring, I got the door open and dragged the bag out onto the deck. The motion sensor security lamp flooded the yard like an LED welcome. I smiled, then returned upstairs and repeated the process with the second and third bags in turn. When I was done, the deck looked a little junky, but I felt *great* and was ready for Phase Two.

The mead was a little cooler now, so I filled a big coffee mug and dressed for the cold outdoors. I expected to be out for a while, so I slipped my feet into my big, white, astronaut-looking snow boots, worked my way into my hooded parka, and grabbed a toque and old mitts. Clomping comically with big moon-walking steps from the front door to the back, I detoured around the kitchen island to grab the long-necked candle lighter from the twist-ties-and-old-pens junk drawer next to the fridge. The dollar-store fire stick went into the coat pocket and the mug of mead into my good mitt.

I hadn't used the little metal fire pit since before the accident, but it waited, clean and ready under its vinyl cover. I placed my mug on the patio table and dragged the bags of my past one at a time out to the pit next to my little reading gazebo and garden. Tied down to keep it from blowing away, the cover was a pain in the ass to get off, but once I took off my mitt I managed to squeeze the toggle and loosen the string enough to slide the cover off. I then spent ten minutes one-handedly crumpling papers and making a burning bed on the fire pit's grate. Maybe it was the mead in my belly, but I started to get excited for the coming purge. Well, excited *and* nauseous.

Logic told me that destroying my music was rash and ill-conceived, but emotions told me to screw logic and let it all burn. If I couldn't play music, then what was the point of wasting the space? It's like keeping a bicycle after going blind. I wasn't famous enough for my scribbled notes in the margins to have any collectible value, and the music itself was available online or in music stores. Earlier I'd thought I could learn to play again, but after going through the cabinets I was sure I was done as a musician and needed this closure to move on.

I stuck the fire stick into my crumpled past, pulled the safety switch back, and clicked the trigger. For a split second, I felt like I'd put a gun against my temple and fired a final shot. It took a moment for the flame to get a purchase, and in that second-and-a-half, I changed my mind. Then the fire caught. The inferno spread slowly, gradually, deliberately, turning to ash and smoke the notations of Anatoly, Frédéric, Carlo, Ludwig, Wolfgang, and so many others who wrote for the singularly wonderful voice of the cello.

I placed the mesh dome over the pit to keep the sparks and burning floaters from getting free and attacking me and the surroundings, then I leaned back in my red, plastic Adirondack chair. I wanted to just close my eyes and let the smoke swirl around me, but I couldn't. I couldn't *not* watch this ending. Of course, tears appeared, but there was something deep down inside my gut that forced me to witness my past vanishing and my future stepping in as the flames chased each other and danced and leaped and attacked the crumpled sheets and each other.

The fire finally got a solid grip and burned quickly. I lifted the mesh off with the iron wood-stirring rod, and crumpled more sheets, trying desperately not to look at any of the details... but that one was *Andante Pathetico*, this one was *Dances of Galanta*, and that was one of the many *Sonatas in G Major*. Having not taken any Happy Pills all day, I was finally able to sob, laugh, and whimper while I crumpled sheets and hummed snatches of the pieces as I mangled them and fed them to Jubilee's Inferno.

I sat back, letting the smoke swirl around and periodically drift over to taunt and tease me. With my stump cradled in my lap, every once in a while I would lift the screen, add a few crumpled balls, then poke the whole mass to get air into the middle to keep it raging. I quickly discovered that paper doesn't burn quite as steadily as wood and needs to be tended more closely, but it's not like I had anywhere else to be. Me and my not-so-towering inferno.

The smoke, the cool not-winter-not-spring April air, the mead, the purging of the past...what more could a girl want—except maybe her dog, her cello, her car, her *hand*, a call from her god-daughter, and a man who didn't abandon her and move west, or even one who called after a missed date to see what had happened. I'd done my best to not think about blind date Niko in the after-math of the accident, but now I was pissed off that there'd never been even one message from him since my life went to shit and I stood him up.

He probably read about my accident in the news and decided that a broken, ex-musician divorcée wasn't what he was looking for. Joyce took great pleasure in telling me how much the accident was all over the news and even suggested that it was a ploy for at-tention on my part, but I've read very little about that day. Why see someone else's summary of the worst day of my life, accompanied by the grisliest photo of the accident they could find?

Thinking about this shit was harshing the mellow mood of the fire, so I imagined all of my thoughts of Niko as confetti, bundled them up in—I took a look at the next sheet in my hand—the Brandenburg Concerto—and tossed it into the blaze. I cracked a weak, half-ass smile, but it was still a smile. A long chug of mead widened the smile, so I closed my eyes for a moment and felt the cleansing scorch of the blaze on my face and the fire of the mead snaking down into my belly. My life was shit, but if I could string together enough peaceful moments like this, then maybe, one day, the shit would thin out, dry up, and blow away.

It took a half-mug more of mead to finish the sacrificial pyre of days gone, and when it was done, I was exhausted—and more than a little drunk. After dousing the fire, with a final look up at the handful of stars judging me from between the clouds, I shuffled back inside, shed my smoky winter gear, dragged myself upstairs to the bathroom, and eventually stumbled into bed. I was asleep before I could even set the alarm—not that I had anything I needed to be up early for, I think.

oOo

I was up early to pee, of course, dragged from some quickly dissipating Matthew McConaughey dream involving bongos and a Sailor Moon costume.

The bedroom stank of fire pit smoke, which was a helluva lot nicer than the old James-smoked-a-pack-with-his-buddies-while-playing-poker stench. The living parts of my left hand hurt like hell, so I must have slept on it. I'd have to wash all the linens and my clothes to rid them of the fire pit smoke, but that could wait until I had a nice, long, hot bath avec candles, salts, etcetera.

oOo

An hour later, I was scrubbed, dried, wrapped in my oversized, forest-green, terrycloth robe, with a freshened cup of coffee in my hand, chilling in the big comfy chair, gazing absently out the bay window at the empty, partly snow-covered playground across the street.

A muffled beep of a message poked at my awareness with a finger of sound, but for the moment I was too damned comfortable. Despite my Zen-like chilling in the chair, though, I knew that a proper breakfast and digging back into my actual job was where the morning had to go. Of course, the best-laid plans oftentimes go awry, as I knew only too well. I seriously think that 'go awry' is Latin for "get fucked up", when applied to *my* life and plans.

I finished the coffee, right down to the last life-affirming drop, and closed my eyes, letting the sun do a little of its magic on me. I imagined it burning away layer after layer of emotional crap, and as it did so, I was lighter and clearer than I had been in weeks. Then the fucking phone beeped again and I stumbled into a very un-Zen place in a hurry. I levered myself up and out of the chair and went in search of my electronic leash.

The last place I remembered seeing it was when I slipped it back into a coat pocket, so I went to the front hall closet. If the message was from my mother or my sister, I was ready to flush the damned phone down the toilet, which of course made no sense because it was hardly the phone's fault; but since I couldn't reach through the phone and punch the texter a couple of times with my stump, threatening the phone would have to do.

Sliding open the bi-fold doors, I couldn't remember which of my three winter coats the phone was hiding in, so I went through each of them, pocket-by-pocket, striking oil in the last one, of course. The little banner on the lock screen simply said *Missed Call: Karl & Reggie*, and there was a little '1' next to the voicemail icon. It was kind of the boys to call, especially since it was the...I squinted at the date. The twenty-seventh. But that had to be wrong because Reggie's birthday was the twenty-sixth. Oh. *Fuck.* I missed Reggie's birthday party. I mean, it's not as if I was in any shape to be around people anyway, but I should have at least called. Shit, shit, shit.

Better late than never, I suppose. The fingers of my right hand started to tingle in a weird not-right kinda way but I ignored it as best I could. I tapped the phone icon next to the number, peeked at the time, did a semi-quick mental calculation, and realized two things just as the call went straight to voicemail. One—the boys would be at Friday yoga class; and two—I hadn't even listened to the voicemail they'd left.

I hung up. I felt stupid enough missing the party, but I wasn't keen on compounding it with further stupidity by leaving a weak "I'm-sorry-forgive-my-idiocy" apology without even hearing what they had to say. I logged into my voicemail.

"We missed you tonight, Jubidoo." It was Karl. "It's not a celebration without you. We worry, so sue us. Give us a call or we'll drop by unannounced. Yes, that's a threat! Love you." Despite my guilt, I couldn't help but smile. I saved the message for no other reason than it was a friendly voice I could replay any time I needed a boost. I used to have one of James' messages for when I was away on tour and missing him, but that got deleted sometime between when I stopped missing him and when he left.

What I loved about Karl and Reggie was their lack of judgment. There wasn't even a hint of a guilt trip in their words, just love and caring. The same couldn't be said about any messages ever left by members of my family. Even Dad, when he deigned to leave a message at all, always had a veneer of guilt laid on top of even the nicest message. Somehow he always made it sound like I missed his call on purpose, but the real difference between him and Mom was that I could see through his clumsy attempts at being nice.

Mom is so smooth that I get sucked into whatever story she's spinning before I realize she's lying through her ass and turning the confusion up to eleven. She even manages to make me think that whatever the problem is, it's *my* fault. Every damned time. She's the Evil Red Queen of Gaslighting. I guess I hadn't realized how much my music had been my coping mechanism until it was ripped away and I stopped coping.

But I was now determined to get my shit together, and though Captain Happy Pill was wonderful, I just didn't see our relationship being a good long-term investment. With Karl and Reggie's sweet message still echoing in my ear, I clomped over to my desk, flipped open the laptop, and turned it on with the intention of at least reviewing where I was in my workload and whether any deadlines were looming. While it booted up, I returned to the kitchen sink where the dishes had been piling up. They needed to get into the dishwasher and this was a good time.

As usual, the dishwasher was still full of the dishes from the last cleaning, so I started one-handedly putting everything away, beginning with the cutlery. Fork by fork, spoon by spoon, tediously one at a time, because all the stump was good for was holding the cutlery basket steady on the countertop above the open drawer. Eventually, the empty basket went back into the machine and I started on the plates. During such simple daily tasks, we take having two good hands for granted. I found out *very* quickly how much I relied on the second hand when I tried to lift a stack of four heavy dinner plates with just my right one. I struggled with the weight until they were about a foot-and-a-half above the lower rack, then they tipped over and the top three crashed down on the rack, smashing wine glasses, cereal bowls, and the glass lid of the rice cooker.

"Fuck! Fuck! FUCK!" I threw the remaining plates down into the mess and a couple more things broke. "Fuckety fuck! Goddamned fuck!" I dropped down right there on the floor next to the open dishwasher. There was broken shit everywhere, but I didn't care. I tipped over and curled up on the mat in front of the sink.

Broken shards of something poked my arm, but I truly didn't give a crap.

My mind tried to spin and I fought the urge to reach for the drugs. I couldn't risk becoming dependent on them, but maybe a drink would be good. A rum and Coke would not just do the job, it would do it with a smile, a kiss, and maybe a friendly pat on my ass.

Joyce hated rum, which is the only reason there was any within a hundred yards of the house. I had to get my damned head back on straight, or at least straight enough to get some work done, so at *eight in the freaking morning*, I rolled over and got myself to my feet. I searched the cupboard and found one of the crystal rocks glasses James missed in his rush to quit our life. Since I hated drinks watered down with ice, I kept the rum in the fridge, right next to the Coke, handily enough. I noticed that there were some juice drippings from some long-gone casserole, so I reached for a paper towel. The roll was down to its last piece and I kept new rolls down in the laundry room, so I put the rum back and went in search of paper towels. The drippings couldn't stay.

I froze at the top of the basement stairs. *What the hell was I doing?* I didn't need goddamned paper towel! I didn't need to clean the fridge. I didn't need to clean up the mess in the dishwasher. I needed a drink. I needed a *big* drink, and I needed to *focus* and get some goddamned work done. No more cleaning, no more moping. *Alcohol and work.* And if Happy Pills and alcohol were a bad mix, then no Captain Happy and only Captain Morgan would be commissioned. Nothing too serious, just a bit more to slow the spinning.

I returned to the kitchen and poured a two-fingered fix into the glass, then I topped it up with Coke. The foamy beige head settled and I took a sip, letting loose a brief but honest-to-goodness snicker when the rum-scented bubbles hit my nose. This plan just might work, I thought.

The first sip was an elixir to my soul, so another followed, and it felt *so* good. I settled down and sat in front of the computer. Even the tingling in my fingers faded. With only a hand-and-a-half to type with, I fumbled along, opening the worksheet and seeing that I had five clients in the queue, with the work started on four of the jobs. They were straight edits of the client's drafts, so the rum shouldn't interfere. Though if it did, I would do it like my English Lit professor had done and write drunk then edit sober. It sounded like a good start for getting my head on straight without stripping the threads. I shifted my chair so that I couldn't see the dishwasher out of the corner of my eye. *That* damned mess could seriously wait for another day.

The fifth job was the update of a manual based on a handful of chicken-scratch notes, and only sober and clean would do for that. I opened the file for the oldest job in the queue and got to work cleaning up a short article about refinements in crude oil processing.

Chapter Seven

Two hours later, what nerves still worked in my left hand were bitching and whining, but the first of the four jobs could be filed for "next day review", which was something every piece of work eventually got. My biggest rule was to sleep on the final draft and give it the stamp of approval after a good night's rest, with fresh, caffeinated eyes.

The next project wasn't a tough one, but I needed a break, so I pushed back from the desk and stood up. My back was a bit sore from sitting so long, but without the rum, it would have been impossible to sit up at all. I shuffled into the little bathroom, did what I had to do, and wandered back to the desk. I wobbled a bit as I sat, and concluded that maybe, just maybe, work was done for the night.

I knew I should just log off, shut it all down, and get some sleep, but I was as curious as the next cat and just had to take a quick look. I logged on to my eRomance account and checked my inbox. Messages were supposed to be forwarded to my personal email, but after the twentieth "Hey Gorgeous! S'up?" message last month, I turned off the redirect.

The website's summary bar showed sixteen matches of 75% or higher, 104 matches of 50-75%, and eleven messages that had cleared the hurdles I'd set using the filters. The filters weeded out any message that didn't mention dogs, cats, or music. Those three were all in my profile, so any man who couldn't bother to at least *mention* one of them, was separated like chaff from wheat.

The senders' handles were all visible in the message summary so I quickly saw that none was from Niko. Right up to that moment, I hadn't realized just how much I wanted to hear from him, despite my attempt to burn thoughts of him away in the fire pit. In the last two months, he'd been a friendly texting 'voice' amidst the post-divorce anger, confusion, and guilt. Right then and there, staring at the laptop's screen, I didn't care if his message was a perfunctory *Screw you, bitch, for standing me up*. At least it would have been honest, deserved, and something I could reply to.

But there was nothing. The real bitch of it was that I *liked* Niko. He was someone I'd easily envisioned myself spending time with—sampling foreign foods, trying our hand at homemade wine, listening to music, and walking the dog. Of course, these days I could probably do with *less* wine, couldn't give a C-major crap about music, and, well, there's not much point in walking an urn containing a dog's ashes. But maybe Niko would have understood. Maybe he would have just hugged me and let me cry on his shoulder. Maybe.

I wrote him a quick note. Just a short one to say hello and maybe we could talk, so I could explain why he hadn't heard from me. I know. Pitiful. I didn't do anything wrong and I was hoping *he* would forgive *me*. Of course, after that much rum, I was lucky I didn't sign off with "Please, please, please!" Begging was beneath me, but mostly because I was too drunk to get down on my knees without tipping over and hitting my head on something hard.

The eleven messages sat waiting for my tender loving replies and suddenly, out of the blue, I needed to reply to these men, needed to create a link with other human beings.

I hold no illusions that there's a Mr. Perfect out there for me, nor do I hold to the school of thought that people aren't complete unless they're part of a couple. That's just bullshit perpetuated by people who don't like themselves enough to be alone—says the girl currently logged onto eRomance-dot-ca.

Just before noon, moderately drunk and seriously silly, I fired off notes to each of my eleven would-be suitors. Actually, I penned one brief but hopeful "Write-back-because-who-knows" note then cut and pasted it to the other ten. I'm pretty sure I corrected the name in all of them, but that close to a drunken nap I couldn't be sure. Getting a name wrong would piss off a woman, but a man probably wouldn't give a shit if it meant he might get laid.

I saved all my files and sent copies to my external drive, but before I could log off, a news alert popped up on my screen. It was the Internet's version of an emergency broadcast and I subscribed to get reports of extreme weather for when I'd had to perform out of town, but this was an unusual one from Calgary Police Services. I opened it. It was brief and to the point. The severed hand of a brown-skinned woman had been found in one of the city's parks and they were looking for anyone who may have seen a man fitting the following description in the area. What followed was the same description the detective had given me: a white male, aged 25 to 45, medium to heavy build, and physically fit.

Shit. A third victim. I said a silent prayer for her but was relieved that it wasn't Elteen. Shutting down the laptop, I clomped back up to bed for a nap. My phone sat on the bedside table, plugged into the charger so I set the countdown timer for two hours, just before the double waves of physical and emotional exhaustion hit me. Maybe Elteen was safe, but maybe not. Maybe I was doing OK and recovering, but maybe not. Drunk and crippled? I was not OK. I resisted sleep, though. There was one thing I had left to do. I sent a short text to Karl and Reggie. *I'm sorry. Not doing so well.*

o0o

The alarm went off and I woke up clueless. My brain was still fuzzy from the rum, but I knew I was ready for food when my stomach let loose a nice rumbling vibrato. I had expected to dream about either my mess or the latest victim, but whether because of the rum or because I was so damned tired, dreams had eluded me, thankfully.

Halfway down the stairs—my footsteps absorbed by the plush carpet—my hackles jumped up. I wasn't sure if I heard the sound of fabric sliding across leather first, or the soft cough, but I stopped short and peered around the wall where it sloped down from the ceiling of the main floor.

There was someone on my goddamned couch, which I suppose is better than God damning my couch, but *still*!

"Coffee will be ready in a minute, Sweetie. We didn't want to wake you."

Shit! It was Karl and Reggie. "You scared the crap out of me, boys."

"*We* scared *you*? You don't show up at the party of the year *or* return our calls, then when you finally text us it's a distress call from out of the blue."

"I texted?"

"You don't remember?"

Damn. I laughed, but only because I was scared and didn't want to cry. "I guess I was a little drunk and a lot tired. Or possibly the other way around."

Big, bearded Reggie guided me to the couch where he sat me down, draped the Afghan over me, and sat with me. Karl returned to the kitchen and popped a reusable K-Cup into the machine. Two half-full mugs on the coffee table told me they'd been here for a while.

"How long have you two been camped out in my living room, and how the hell did you get in?"

Reggie leaned forward and picked a mug. "Since one, so about an hour." He sipped. "We know where you keep the spare key because you made sure we knew, right after he-who-shall-not-be-named moved out."

Karl arrived with my cup, handed it to me, and then plunked himself down on the other side of me. "We checked on you, heard you snoring like the cute little kitten you are, then came down and did a little cleaning. You know, Jube, if you're going to smash the dishes, you should save on water and do it when they're dirty. Just saying."

I kissed him on the cheek. "You're such an asshole."

"Guilty as charged. Now, tell this asshole what's up. Talk to us."

"No." I put my steaming cup down on the table. This was something I needed to do now.

"No?" I'm pretty sure that wasn't the answer he was expecting.

"No. Not until I give Reggie-Dad a big birthday crush." Only a little hampered by the Afghan, I gave Reggie the biggest hug and wettest kiss on his hairy cheek I could manage. I would have made even Dr. Ella flinch, but Reggie squeezed back and kissed the top of my head.

"We missed you, Jubidoo."

"I'm sorry." And I truly was. Maybe I hadn't been up for human company, but maybe human company in a light social setting was just what I needed. We broke from the hug and I reached for my coffee. I was still half asleep.

"Ahem!" Karl flicked my leg with a long finger. "If you haven't got the energy for *two* hugs, then we're taking you to the ER right now."

I leaned into his open arms and... fell asleep.

The delicious aroma of pizza dragged me up into the real world, and there'd been no pizza when I'd conked out. I don't think Karl had moved a muscle after I tucked myself in, but Reggie was gone from the couch and I could hear him puttering around in the kitchen.

I stirred and Karl gave me a quick squeeze and let me sit up. "Never let it be said that Jubilee Krawetz slept through pizza," he quipped.

I was starving. "Tomato, mushroom, pineapple?"

Karl boosted me up off the couch with a push on my butt, then levered himself up and followed my shuffling self to the kitchen. "Would we *dare* order anything else?"

"But you two love sausage."

"True, but that's beside the point." They both laughed, and I belatedly caught the unintended double entendre. "Doctor's orders, Jubidoo. No more preservatives."

"Smart doctor."

"Smart *sister*."

"Stephanie's your doctor? She *must* be smart—look who she picked for a brother."

"Haha. I'm pretty sure Mom and Dad didn't give her much of a choice. 'Here's your baby brother, Stephie. He'll be slower, taller, and will want to date the same boys you do.'"

"How much older is she?" I'd met Stephanie only once before, briefly, after a concert, but we were Facebook friends.

"Twelve minutes."

"You're twins? You never told me that. Or maybe you did and my mushy mind let it slip away, like last night's party."

He squeezed my forearm. "So, what happened with that? We were worried. Still are."

"I'm really sorry, guys." I took a deep breath, for strength. These two lovelies weren't Dr. Ella but they were just as important to me, if not more so. "You *should* be worried. I'm so screwed up it scares me."

Reggie arrived back on the couch with three plates of pizza, handing Karl and me each one. "We're here for you. Let it all out."

"I'm done. No more music." I held up my claw for them to see.

"No!"

"Yes. The nerve damage was too extensive. With physio I'll be able to use it again, but not for much more than picking my nose." They both gave me a little hug and I drew as much strength from them as I could. Hugs were what the three of us did best.

I held my good hand out and Reggie gave me back my pizza. I ate, and between mouthfuls filled them in on the details I could remember from the last few days. I sort of avoided the interview with the detective until I had food in my belly. I chewed the last bite, swallowed, and placed the plate on the table.

"You know that missing reporter? The one from the Journal-Times?"

Karl growled. "The homophobic prick with the cheesy soul patch?"

"That one. Bill Watson. Apparently, he was investigating the Geocache Butcher when he disappeared."

"After his nasty article about the Pride Parade, am I wrong in hoping that the killer got to him?"

"Yes!" Reggie and I both said at the same time.

"Sorry, not sorry."

"While they were searching his house, they found a piece of paper with both Elteen's and my names on it."

Reggie let out a squeal. "*What?* She's in Banff. I think."

"Hopefully, but her parents reported her missing and until she calls or shows up, they're now investigating her disappearance like she's a possible victim." Having said those words aloud, I realized that reassurances from her brother weren't the same as personal communication from her.

"It's about damned time!" If the Butcher hurt little Elteen, her kind, loving, gentle Uncle Reggie would hunt him down and tear his heart out with his bare hands, and I would hold the murdering bastard down while Reggie did it. "Then why did he have *your* name written down?"

"I have no idea. All I can think of is that he wanted to talk to me about her disappearance."

Karl growled, again. "Or he thinks that you might be at risk from the killer?"

"I hardly think so."

"Have they found any more of this latest victim?"

"Not that I've heard." Reggie was so worried about Elteen that he got news alerts if there was anything about the Butcher on any of the news feeds. "The latest hand belongs to a dark-skinned woman and was found in Nose Hill Park. The most recent alert I got said that the next clue led them to Edworthy Park, so they have the whole place cordoned off."

The Butcher was insane! "He's all over the place."

"And so are his victims. The first one was from B.C. and the second from Saskatchewan. Regina, I think. Or Moose Jaw."

"And the missing reporter who was hunting him had your and Elteen's names written down?" Reggie's voice rose with his panic.

"So the detective said."

"Well, Missy Miss, maybe the odds are slim that a serial killer is after you, but you still need us. Come stay. We insist. At least for a few days to refresh your batteries and get out of that house full of emotional triggers. We can all worry about El together."

"Thank you. Just for a few days. So long as I can bring my laptop and get some work done. I have to pick up the tempo or leave the orchestra pit, so to speak. I'm fed up with the snivelling mess I've become and am so ready to move on that I signed the divorce papers."

"*What?*"

"I'm done. James and I are over, and until I lost V-Dog I was OK with the break-up and some days even happy about it. But just because V-Dog is gone and my heart is hollow doesn't mean James and I would be less toxic together than we were, or that our relationship is salvageable." My stomach growled rather rudely. "Is there more pizza?"

Reggie hopped up and retrieved the entire box from the kitchen. He doled out three more pieces.

"Thanks, Hon."

"Thanks, Reg." I continued, finding strength in the words even as I said them. "I may be a walking disaster, but it's time to let James go. In our last email, he told me how hurt he was that I didn't fight for him or beg him to stay. What I couldn't admit to him then but now can to myself, is that we'd been having trouble for a few years, the kind of deep trouble that time transposes into bone-tired discontent that can't be healed by love. No matter what the greeting cards say, love is *not* enough." I chomped away at the pizza. It was perfect. We all ate in near silence. Reggie refilled each of our plates in turn, as needed. Eventually, I was bloated full.

"James's coming to town in a few weeks and wants to talk, but I want the papers filed before then. I have an appointment down-town on Monday to see my therapist, so I'll drop the papers off at my lawyer's then."

Karl shook his head. "Nonsense. They have Saturday hours until noon. I'll drop them off tomorrow when I go in for... when I go downtown."

He'd almost said 'for rehearsal', I'm sure. "You don't know where the firm's office is. I can take care of it on Monday."

"Silly girl. Did you forget who referred you to the firm? Remember? They handled Mom's estate." He stood awkwardly. "Damn! My leg's asleep." He shook it and banged it with his fist to get the blood flowing again and Reggie and I just watched and snickered. "Laugh it up at my expense, you two." He took a couple of tentative steps. "Where are the papers, Jube? I'll fetch them right now so that we don't forget."

"In the music room. Green envelope."

He limped up the stairs slowly and Reggie stirred off the couch with the dishes and pizza box in hand. I freed myself from the Afghan and followed him into the kitchen. I reached for the carafe of coffee, but a short scream from Karl upstairs stopped me.

Chapter Eight

"**Y**our music! What have you done?" He clomped back downstairs to meet us at the bottom as we were rushing up. "Your sheets, your music... the cabinets are *empty*." He handed the green envelope to Reggie who slipped it into his coat hanging on the foyer tree.

"I had a fire sale. Or rather, I had a fire."

"You burned it? *All* of it? Oh, Jube..."

"Karl, sweetie, I had to. I didn't touch the collectable ones, but I have to face the fact that music and I are *done*. I can't even play timps. Drumming with one hand doesn't work. It's better this way, not having false hope. Besides, it felt *great* to just let it all go."

He hugged me. I didn't blame him for being upset. To a classical musician, sheet music is more than black notes and lines on white paper. There were performance memories in each symphony, each sonata, and each *phrase*. But I wasn't a musician anymore and it was a waste of space and emotion. If Gavroche hadn't been crushed in the accident, I would have sold him rather than have his lonely presence looming over me every day. "It's done and I have to move on." Even if it shredded my heart

There wasn't much he could say—I was right. We returned to the kitchen and poured three fresh cups of coffee. It was great to have the two of them there. The comfort I gleaned from them was wonderful. I climbed up on a stool and sat at the breakfast bar on the far side of the island, alternately blowing on the still-hot coffee to cool it and sipping it to test the temperature. "But I sure as hell miss V-Dog."

"That beautiful pup was part of your soul, and your music was your soul's voice. You've been kicked in the face and it's normal to feel smashed down and just wishing you had someone to take some of the weight off once in a while." Like I said, these two were good for me. "Are you sure you're *both* gay? I'm willing to work around the whole 'married thing', but gay doesn't work for me. Even bi would be fine."

Reggie gently lifted my chin with two fingers so he could look me in the eyes. "We need to get you laid, Jubidoo."

"I'm working on it."

The phone rang. Without even looking at the caller ID, Karl picked it up off the counter and swiped the screen to answer it. Instead of saying *anything*, though, he simply handed it to me, the asshole. This whole sequence couldn't have taken any longer than a couple of seconds, but it was too long for the caller. As I raised the phone to look at the screen I could hear my mother starting into her rant. Shit!

"Mom!" I interrupted her. "What a surprise. Unfortunately, I have company over, so can I call you back a bit—"

"*Really*, Jubilee? You have company?" And the gaslight was lit. It didn't sound like much to anyone else, but Mom could sow doubt with just the slightest change in tone or inflection. If I couldn't see Karl and Reggie right there in front of me, she'd have me believing I was imagining them.

I must have gone pale because Karl snatched the phone out of my hand and disconnected the call. "Whatever she said to you, Missy, you do *not* need that shit right now."

"It's Mom. I really should talk to her." I reached for the phone but he took a step back from the counter and I didn't make any effort to go after him. He won.

"Your family is a big part of your problem. How do you expect to recover and get your wonderful self back together if you keep letting those toxic people pollute your self-esteem?"

"I know. You're right." And he was. "I might need some help," I mumbled.

"What took you so long to ask? Anything you need, Jube."

"I don't *know* exactly what I need. That's the problem." I was too screwed up to be able to specify how I was screwed up. How screwed up is *that*?

"Then let's pack you a weekend bag and get you out of here. There's a desk in the guest room for you to work at, and we'll both be out until around two tomorrow afternoon, so you'll have the place to yourself. No V-Dog or James reminders. No family dropping by to throw toxic words in your face. I'll drive you to your appointment on Monday morning, and you can call Karl to come pick you up afterward. Won't you, Hon?"

We both looked to Karl who nodded and smiled warmly. "Of course. There's still half a birthday cake and two bottles of Icewine in the fridge. We'll keep it simple and throw some steaks on the grill tonight, then tomorrow we'll figure out something more interesting." He looked directly at me and raised one sharp, greying eyebrow as only he could. "Does that meet with Your Highness' requirements? Hmmm?"

"What kind of Icewine? Not a bottle of Royal DeMaria Chardonnay I suppose?" Ha! It was $30,000 for a *half* bottle.

"No, we drank all that last night, but you missed it Smarty-Missed-the-Party-Pants. You'll have to be satisfied with Northern Ice Vidal Blanc."

The gold medal winner? Nice! "I *suppose* that will do. We can make slushies."

Reggie laughed. "I like how you think, Sweetie!" He squeezed my shoulder affectionately. "Now let's pack you a bag and sweep you off your feet!"

We were out of the house in record time.

o0o

Even though we took our time cooking the steaks and vegetable skewers, sipping as we supped, we finished both bottles of the delicious, sweet, fruity wine without much effort. Of course, it helped that Icewine bottles were half the size of the usual wine bottle, and the alcohol content was a bit lighter. By the time Karl placed fresh cups of decaf in front of each of us, I was done. We retired to the couches and finished off the evening with an episode of the rudely hilarious "Mrs. Brown's Boys". I managed to last to the end of the opening credits before drifting off. Not long after, the boys walked my dozy butt up to the spare bedroom.

o0o

I woke in the middle of the night in response to sharp pressure on my bladder and I knew immediately that something was wrong. The room was dark, but it was *too* dark. Even with the heavy blinds, there were always slats of light on the ceiling of my bedroom, but there were no slats now, just impenetrable shadows. For a moment I imagined a man standing in the darkest corner, watching me. There was a familiarity about his face, someone I had seen recently. I stared, trying to remember. When I blinked, he was gone. But the pressure on my bladder was still there and now I was finally awake enough to remember where I was. I found the bathroom right where Karl and Reggie had left it—the first door on the left. When I was finished, I returned to the embrace of restless sleep.

o0o

I finally crawled my Icewine-addled ass out of bed a little before ten. The condo was nearly silent. Even in the downtown core where traffic was thin but steady on a Saturday, it was still quieter than my house overlooking two highways with no sound barriers. There were as many advantages to living in the core as there were to living away from it, but the cost of a nice downtown condo crushed the core's advantages down to dust. As much as I would love to live back in the heart of the city, I wasn't even sure how long I was going to be able to afford my suburban duplex without my music revenue. It looked like copywriting was my new life, but I hoped it would be enough. There was no time like the present to find out.

Ten minutes later I was camped out in the executive-sized desk chair at the little pine desk in the guest room. My laptop was warming up, a hot cinnamon bun was dripping in creamed cheese on the plate to the right, and a mug of fresh coffee was sending curls of fragrant Guatemalan roasted steam up to lure me in for a sip. I decided to forgo my daily Happy Pill. I was done being numb. I could handle the heartache. I *had* to.

I had four hours to get some work done, which was likely going to have to include updating my company's website with a discount for new clients and an email to existing clients with a special discount for their next job. I had a few emailed queries that would hopefully lead to more work, but the best source of work for us had always been word of mouth and returning customers, so there was nothing to do but dig in and impress the hell out of the clients I already had.

Unlike yesterday when I was drunk, today I was dead sober, so trying to type with the stump drove home how useless I was. I had one good finger and a thumb, one slightly wonky finger, and two floppy, half-curled-up sticks of flesh on my left hand but I wasn't going to give up. I was going to push through and get this shit done. I was slow as Mozart's Requiem in D Minor, but I wasn't giving up. I ate, I worked; I sipped, I worked; I dabbed my damp eyes, I worked. Tears were OK. They were part of the healing process, Dr. Ella said. Wallowing in self-pity wasn't, though, and I was done with wallowing. I still had enough strength in my bad hand to take life by the balls and squeeze.

Two o'clock must have snuck up on me like a damned ninja because Karl whispering my name sotto voce from the doorway scared the shit out of me. I jumped in the chair and threw a handful of still somewhat tear-soggy tissues at him. "You asshole!"

"Sorry, but what was I supposed to do? We made enough noise coming in that I didn't think you could possibly miss that we were home." He stepped into the room and hugged me. "Would you have preferred me to sneak up on you and flick your ear with my finger?"

I covered my ear reflexively. "Hell no! Reggie would be a widower if you did that. No flicking the Jube. Or tickling or flurping or—"

"Flurping?"

"Like with a baby. You put your mouth on their belly and blow so that it sounds like sloppy farting."

He wrinkled his nose in disgust. "Sloppy farting? Lovely!"

"Tell that to James. Some people give hickeys. James liked to flurp. It was cute for the first month or so of dating, but it got old pretty damned fast."

"I would think so."

"Ancient history. I might as well go through menopause now for all the good my sex drive is doing me." If I could have gotten my music back, though, I would have given up sex forever. No contest.

"Then let's forget about that stuff and go for a stroll down Seventeenth Ave. We'll grab dinner, then join the candlelight vigil in the park for the Butcher's victims and all missing women. We'll even light some candles for Elteen, and say a prayer or two. This city needs hope and love, especially after some street preacher on a soap box downtown was stirring people up with a sermon about how greed, gluttony, and sexual deviants have invited Satan to walk our streets."

"I've heard him. He's an idiot, but he draws a crowd. The last thing we need is another homeless person getting hurt by a city of vigilantes. I have about half an hour's worth of work to do if that's OK."

"Get back to work. I'll let Reggie know what we're up to. Just come down when you're ready."

I put that half hour to good use, finishing the rough draft of my discount ad and digging up a couple of punchy but not overwhelming graphics. I slipped my jeans on over my yoga tights, swapped my light hoodie for my heavy Merino wool turtleneck sweater, and joined the boys out in the living room.

Reggie smiled and stood. "There she is! Shall we pick up a few truffles at the shop around the corner, to fortify us?"

"Your sweet tooth hardly needs fortifying, Reg, but it sounds good. Is it cold out?" I could have checked the weather app on my phone in my hand, but I prefer the opinion of someone who has been outside recently.

"Jacket, light gloves, hat. Most of our snow is gone here downtown."

"Perfect. Where will we eat? It's been years since I lived in this area and have no idea what's still around."

"What are you in the mood for? Thai, Greek, or a soul-anchoring, belly-grabbing Alberta beef dip?"

Until Reg rattled off our choices, I didn't think I was that hungry, but the more I thought about a juicy, tender, beef dip with au jus for dipping, the more intense my hunger got. "Belly-grabbing beef dip, please. I don't know about soul-anchoring, but I'm willing to give it a try. God knows I need an anchor."

"You've got *us* for that." He kissed the top of my head and turned away to fetch our coats from the entry closet, so he didn't see my eyes mist up.

Karl came out of the bathroom. "Decision made?"

"The pub." Reggie handed him his coat. "I'm curious to see what they have on tap this week. That wheat ale last week was delicious."

"Agreed!" Karl slipped into his coat, then helped me into mine, since I was struggling. The fingers of my left hand kept catching on the lining of the sleeve. "By the way, Jube, I have the receipt from the lawyer. Annette at reception even called the courier while I was there, to pick up the papers today."

"Thank you." I'd forgotten all about the divorce papers. I considered sending James an email, telling him that they were signed and en route, but it's not like he gave me much notice when he fucked off in the first place, so I didn't. We were over and done. He'd moved on and now it was my turn, though to be fair, my *not* signing them had been more lazy stubbornness than any hope for reconciliation. Of course, he wouldn't see it that way when he arrived in town. "I hope this pub of yours serves good whisky because I think it's George Thorogood time."

"One bourbon, one scotch, and one beer? Really?"

"Hell yes. It's not every day one gets divorced. I don't need to get drunk; I just need to mark the occasion."

"That's a hard-core mark." Reggie led us out into the corridor and Karl locked up behind us.

"Damned straight it is, and it's all Karl's fault. He introduced me to the Thorogood during our guest week with the Nashville Symphony."

"Don't blame—". He paused and smiled. "Oops. My bad. It *was* me. But it was only because you got me hooked on double-vodka paralyzers."

That was a great week! "OK, so we're even." It was just one flight of stairs down and out to the street and I was glad for my sweater. Maybe I should have checked the weather app after all because the chilly breeze was a shock. Once we got moving it wasn't too bad, and I got caught up looking in all the shop windows that I hadn't seen in ages. Of course, the raspberry-and-blood-orange truffle I'd picked at the chocolatier helped immensely. The Mount Royal/Beltline area is a nice one, within walking distance to the business core of the city where most of the office towers belonged to oil and gas giants, banks, or telecoms. Covid layoffs had hit the city pretty hard with thousands gone from the core alone, but here, just on the edge, there was still some life. Even with a serial killer possibly amongst them, there were couples out strolling, bundled against the spring chill, and rowdy fans heading to bars to watch hockey, according to the conversational snippets that came our way. There were plenty of dog owners out with their besties, but I kept my chin up and concentrated on the truffle's aftertaste. I couldn't cower in my house forever, and if I kept telling myself that, then maybe it would become the truth.

Karl made some wisecrack about a polka-dotted dress in the window of a retro shop so we stopped to check out the display. I turned to say something about a pair of glossy pink pumps but someone coming along behind us caught my attention. It was the guy from my dream or nightmare or whatever it was! He was walking straight toward us! I grabbed Reggie's arm and squeezed, panic rising fast. Then the man strolled past without even acknowledging our existence and I suddenly doubted my sanity. Who the hell was he?

"Ouch. I love you, too, Jubidoo, but you don't have to dig your fingers in."

"Sorry. I thought I saw someone."

"You probably did. It's Seventeenth Ave on a Saturday night and there are someones everywhere. You've lived in this city your whole life, so you can't but help see people you know."

Now I felt crazy *and* stupid. "True enough." I patted his arm gently and started on down the sidewalk again. I saw the stranger ahead, his non-descript dark bomber jacket standing out for one final moment before the crowd swallowed him up. For a split second, it looked like he glanced back at me, but between the dark and distance, I knew I was wrong.

Karl continued to stroll and we followed along. He checked his FitBit. "We have two hours to eat, drink, and make our way back to the vigil in the park by 8ᵗʰ Street."

"Do you have candles?"

He patted his pocket. "Right here. Tinfoil, too, to keep the wax from dripping on our hands."

"You've thought of everything."

"This is hardly our first vigil. We have a little one during Pride Week every year, and one after the ladies do their Take Back the Night walk."

"We're here."

And we were, wherever 'here' was. Karl held the pub-standard heavy wood door open and we left the chill of the street for an establishment that looked, sounded, and smelled like every other pub I've ever been in, including the ones in Dublin. Low lights, dart boards, a pool table, sports-filled flat screens hanging from wooden ceiling beams, female servers in cleavage-showing black leotard tops and leg-baring short skirts, while the male bartender was in khakis and a pub-logoed golf shirt. I shook my head to no one in particular. Some things never change.

Chapter Nine

"Well, at least it's not Hooters," I pointed out as I followed the boys to a table in what passed for a quiet corner. "Hooters isn't exactly our style." We sat.

"James's tried to get me to go there a few times, saying that the food was pretty good, but one night we were at a restaurant owned by the same people as Hooters and they had all thirty Miss Hooters Canada contestants there for a group dinner. James graciously sat with his back to them, so I got to watch them coming and going to the bathroom in groups. I think it was the sight of two skirts so short that I could see they were panty-less that turned me off of the whole 'Hooters is a family restaurant' thing."

"That's just wrong!" Karl was the more prudish of the two. "I'd have walked out right then and there."

I laughed. "They weren't the *servers*, K. They were just customers. I'm not criticizing their fashion choice, but I just couldn't shake the mental image connected to a restaurant."

"But still..."

"It could have been worse. My late Uncle Fred used to take his wife to strip clubs for dinner. I didn't know they even served food at those places."

"Just finger food," Reggie chimed in and smirked at me.

The server arrived right then and saved Reggie from a smack from Karl. She introduced herself as Brianna, placed three menus on the table, and asked us for our drink orders. As expected, Reggie and Karl each ordered pints of the Barman's Special of the Week.

"And I'll have one bourbon, one scotch, and a pint of the Special, please."

She laughed and gave me a thumbs-up. "Girl, I *like* your style! Two pints of the Special for the gents and a Thorogood for the lady who knows how to kick off a Saturday night. I'll be back in a jiff with all that while you folks decide on nibblies." She swing-hip *sashayed* back to the server's data terminal at the end of the bar, and I picked up the menu to see if maybe they had something even more tempting than a beef dip.

"Looks like you might have a new BFF, Jube." Karl teased.

"I think she'll be disappointed to find out that this isn't how I spend every Saturday night." The next moment I completely forgot about the beef dip. This cookie-cutter pub had Yorkshire puddings stuffed with shaved roast beef and horseradish! That was a culinary cut above the beef-on-a-bun combo, and I *love* my Yorkies!

Brianna arrived not only with our tray of drinks but with the tall, wide, surfer-looking hot bartender. "Your Thorogood is on Levon here, Miss."

Levon flashed a thick, gold wedding band and an even shinier smile. "I'm sorry. I'm not flirting, I promise. I just haven't had anyone order a Thorogood in years, and even then it was always sales-creeps trying to impress the boys."

"Thank you, Levon. It's just something I drink when I celebrate the really *big* events in my life."

"Twenty-fifth birthday?"

Oh, bless his heart! "Divorce." There were two beats of awkward silence around the table and then stumbling laughter.

Levon nodded and eventually smiled, obviously caught off guard. He must really love his wife if he was uncomfortable with the idea of celebrating divorce. "Well, enjoy your evening, folks. Um, congratulations."

"Thank you, Levon. And thank you for the Thorogood."

"My pleasure, Miss."

He left, and then Brianna took our orders and moved on to the next table. I raised the shot of bourbon and tipped it slightly. "To the only direction worth living—forward."

The boys joined me. "To forward."

"Onward and upward."

It was simple bourbon, probably Jim Beam, and it burned in the best way, straight down my throat and into my gut. I swear I heard the crash of cymbals when the shot hit the bottom and knocked my breath out. "Whoa! Now *that's* what I needed!" I licked the inside of the shot glass, gently banged it down on the table, and picked up the shot of scotch. "If it don't burn, you won't learn." I hammered back the bar scotch, and it hit me hard, lacking the smoothness of the bourbon and having an aftertaste like peat soaked in tobacco. I coughed and gasped for air, shaking my head as if that would clear the fire that I'm sure just incinerated my tongue and tonsils. To hell with breathing—I took a quick gulp of the beer to keep my head from exploding, and things calmed down a bit. I carefully placed the glass down on the Guinness coaster and looked up at Karl and Reggie.

I managed a grin. "Damn!" I felt like I was back in college, making impulsive, stupid, drinking decisions during Frosh Week.

"You going to live, girl?" Karl tried to smile and failed. He was worried.

"I am *now*." I took a ragged breath, then another sip of beer. "That's it. I'm cut off for the night. I think there's still some Icewine in my veins and it just got together with the whiskies and decided to kick my ass."

"Hopefully food will help."

"If it doesn't, I'm going to be in *big* trouble." My phone picked that moment to ring, but when I got it out of my pocket and on the table, the screen read "Unknown Caller." I ignored it. "Another one. That's the third one today."

"Why not answer it and find out?"

"Anyone I want to talk to is in my contacts list and their names would show up. No, it's just some telemarketer, survey, or fake Revenue Canada scam."

Brianna dropped off three glasses of ice water with lemon wedges, and not long after, our meals. Reg's quesadilla was big enough for two, Karl's half-order of nachos was the perfect size, and my three huge, puffy, baked, beef-stuffed Yorkies looked like they were sent down by pub angels to wrap themselves around me and carry me to a world of pure bliss. Or maybe it was the booze talking. Probably the booze.

Between the smell of the Yorkies, the two-punch of the liquids, and a day of really digging into my work again, I felt, if not invincible, then at least capable, and capable wasn't something I felt a lot of lately. Then I tried eating.

Ever since the accident, I'd limited myself to soups, stews, pizza, sandwiches, sushi—anything I could eat one-handed. But the Yorkies were another matter and in my excitement to savour the flavour and textures, I hadn't thought it through. My left thumb and first finger had most of their strength and dexterity, so I was at least able to pick up the fork. I got my knife with my right hand and realized that both Reg and Karl were watching me, probably waiting. I'm not even sure they knew they were doing it.

"Let's give this a try, shall we?"

I positioned the fork tines-down with the end of the handle butted up against my palm. Slowly, gently, like the opening notes of *Bach's Suite For Cello Solo #1*, I speared a corner of a Yorkie and held it down while I sawed at it with the steak knife. The puffy pastry slipped and I pressed down harder. It stayed put, but the butt of the fork dug into my scarred palm, revealing that there were still a few pain receptors working at full tilt. Surprised, I dropped the fork.

Karl reached for it but I let out an unintentional growl and he jerked his hand back as if I'd bite it off. I took a long, slow breath, picked up the fork in what I now was starting to think of as my claw, and tried again. I'm not stupid. I know that the Thorogood made me sloppy, so I slowed down, concentrated, and did everything with deliberation.

Physio was going to give me more strength and control down the road, but if I kept quitting when I fumbled, I was really and truly screwed. I cut off a chunk of pudding, speared some of the shaved, rare beef, dipped it in the gravy on the plate, and managed to get it all into my mouth without jabbing myself in the eye or shoving roast beef up my nose. My teeth and lips hurriedly clamped down on the forkful and I slid the utensil out. I chewed just as slowly and swallowed deliberately. I realized I was still holding the fork in my claw and placed it back on the plate.

I smiled at the boys. "There. That wasn't so damned difficult, was it?" Then I saw their tears and felt like shit. "It's OK, you two. It's only Day One, sort of. I know, though. From Tchaikovsky to tweezers." I pinched my left thumb and finger together for emphasis. "It's seriously messed up, but I'm determined to make it work. With the help of Dr. Ella, of course."

"And us."

"Of course." I dabbed the paper serviette at the gravy on my lips. "Now let's eat."

The remainder of the meal was uneventful. I still struggled a bit with the fork, but with two shots and a beer in my gut, I stopped caring somewhere into the second Yorkie. The food balanced the alcohol nicely and it all gave me just the boost I needed for the candlelight vigil.

Tomkins Park was a full block long, but couldn't have been much wider than fifty feet between 16th and 17th Avenues. We stayed on the roadside sidewalks as we made our way around the growing crowd, to get closer to the tiny red-domed bandstand at the west end of the mostly paved century-old urban park.

As we walked, Karl deftly wrapped a simple white taper with a tinfoil wax-catcher and handed it to me. Booze-fuzzy and distracted by the crowd, wondering where the Butcher was hiding, I nearly dropped the candle. Reggie reached in and gently clamped my hand around it.

"Hold tight, Jube."

"Of course." I looked at him and smiled. "Thanks, Reg. Thank you, Karl."

"What's up, kiddo? The Thorogood not sitting too well?"

"Hmm? No. Well, maybe a little. Not much." I looked around us. "I just can't shake the feeling that he's here, watching it all, hiding in plain sight."

Reggie abruptly stopped walking and followed my gaze over the crowd. "Here? Now? You're sure?"

"Of course, I'm not sure. I just feel like I'm being watched and followed. Who else would it be? The only jilted lover in my life is on the West Coast, and to be accurate, *he* did the jilting."

Karl turned back to us, handing Reggie a wrapped candle, too. "Keep your voices down," he whispered. "If people think *he* is here, in the crowd, they could get nasty. The city is scared and on edge. It wouldn't take much of a spark to get even this sombre crowd to turn ugly. Do you see the police? At least a dozen uniforms stand with us. If you see someone truly suspicious, go talk to a uniform. Don't be a hero, and don't start a riot."

"Good thinking." And it was. I was a little drunk and a little wound up. "Let level heads prevail." I don't know why I was getting all freaky about a guy who may or may not have looked at me strangely.

"REGGIE!" An amplified woman's voice shouted over the crowd noise. The three of us looked toward the little bandshell where a curvy brunette with hair and makeup like a very sexy forties poster girl waved in our direction while shouting into a microphone. "Reggie and Karl! Get up here! Let them *through*, people!"

Once the crowd figured out where she was pointing and whom she was referring to, they gladly parted to let Reggie and Karl pass through, with me in tow. The bandshell was only raised a foot above ground level, so it wasn't until we got close that I could see a poised, pretty blonde girl about nine standing at her side. The identical broad red-lipsticked smiles told me that they had to be mother and daughter.

Reggie reached them first and when she saw him, the young girl opened her arms and ran to meet him. "Uncle Reggie!"

He swept her up and spun her around, laughing like I hadn't seen him laugh since my accident. "Ivy-Ivy-Bo-Bivy! Girl of my dreams, if I dreamed of girls!"

Karl took the mother into a huge hug. She snuggled in tight and looked like she was going to crush him with love. When they pulled apart, Karl leaned in for a kiss but she turned her head and presented her cheek. "Not on the lips, darling! This luscious red will smear all over!"

He kissed her gently on the cheek and then turned to me, his arm still around her back. "Jubilee, this voluptuous hot mama is Tanya. Tanya, this is Jubilee, Elteen's godmother."

I awkwardly shifted the candle to my claw and extended my good hand to Tanya. She flashed a perfect white smile, batted huge dark lashes, and looked right into my soul with light blue-green eyes. She took her black leather glove off and shook my hand in a way I can only describe as firm but cool to the touch. "Cold hands, warm heart."

She laughed kindly and gave my hand a final squeeze before withdrawing it. "Oh Jubilee dear, you have no idea." She looked up to Karl. "She's sweet. Can we keep her?"

Karl reached out and took young Ivy from his husband. She gave him a big smooch on the cheek. "She's already family, missy. She's not going anywhere."

Reggie and Tanya exchanged hugs, and when Karl lowered Ivy so that her feet touched the stage, she stepped up to me, extended a white-gloved hand, and curtsied. "I'm Ivy. It's nice to meet you, Miss Jubilee."

I shook her hand. "Call me Jube, Ivy. It's a pleasure to meet you, too."

Tanya cleared her throat for our attention, then motioned us to either side of her. I ended up on her left, with her daughter. I was going to say something banal and dorkish about the weather, but Tanya raised the microphone to her Rita Hayworth lips.

"Ladies and gentlemen, while you're getting your candles ready, let me unnecessarily introduce you to two denizens of the Belt-line and Mount Royal. Not only are Karl and Reggie two of the founders of Pride Calgary, but they are also here tonight because one of the missing women is none other than their niece, Elteen." A sigh swept through the gathered throng. "And on this side is Jubilee, Elteen's godmother."

A few quiet voices said "Hi Jubilee" in the warmest, most sincere tones I could imagine and I nearly lost it. From the moment we left the condo, I had been able to distract myself and keep my thoughts from drifting into the darkness but standing there in the bandshell, holding a candle, preparing to join in prayers and songs for three murdered women and so many missing women, including our dear, sweet, Elteen, the weight was almost unbearable. If I'd had V-Dog with me, it might not have hit me as hard, but I didn't, so it did.

The microphone appeared in front of my face, out and below my chin in a polite, non-obtrusive way. "Jubilee, did you want to say a few words?"

Speak? Me? Right now? Fuck no! All I could do was shake my head. A tear escaped my eye before I could catch it with my sleeve and Tanya graciously withdrew the mic and offered it to Reggie.

"Reggie, can you tell us about your niece, about Elteen?"

Reg nodded and took the mic. He started by telling us about how gifted and beautiful Elteen was, and I had to turn away from the crowd. The lights weren't overly bright, but I'm not one for crying in public. A tissue was suddenly stuck in my hand and I looked down to see Ivy had turned with me.

"Tears are good, Jube. They remind us that we're still alive and that there's hope." She held up a lighter as if waiting for me to hold up my foil-handled candle, so I did. She lit the taper, then pulled a similar candle from her coat pocket and lit it. I turned back to face the crowd and the sight took my breath away. There had to be a thousand candles flickering back at us from across the long park. While Reggie spoke about Elteen, Ivy lit first her mother's candle, then Karl's, and finally Reggie's.

Tanya reached up and took the microphone from Reggie when he was finished, and read a brief poem of remembrance for the two victims. My thoughts spun, though, so I didn't hear her words.

I started remembering Elteen like she was gone, even though she wasn't. Not yet. We didn't know where she was, but she had to be *somewhere*. I prayed silently that if the Butcher had her she was locked up in a cellar somewhere, waiting for the police to track her down and rescue her, like an episode of *Criminal Minds*.

Lost in my own little reverie, I didn't notice Karl move to the upright piano at the back of the little stage until he laid down the opening notes of *Let It Be*. Within seconds a thousand or more voices were singing along, holding their candles high, their hearts open and their eyes moist. During the bridge, someone in the middle of the crowd joined Karl with a violin and he looked up at me, tears flowing. A cruel, inhuman son-of-a-bitch was taking the lives of women in the city and Calgarians were coming together to support each other.

Karl segued into Clapton's *Tears in Heaven* and Reggie gently took the microphone from Tanya and sang like I'd never heard him sing before. This wasn't karaoke night in the privacy of the condo, it was a hearts-on-sleeves for the world to hear. Halfway through the song he held up his candle and spoke Elteen's name. He then continued singing at a lower volume and someone loudly spoke the name of the Butcher's first victim. Someone else added the name of the second victim, and it got rolling from there. People throughout the crowd called out names of missing loved ones, and the list was just too damned long. I stepped back into the shadows of the bandshell and sat on a chair next to the piano. I was done. Whether because of the heavy food, the excess of alcohol, the overwhelming emotion of the vigil, or just thinking about how much my life sucked, I was toast. I closed my eyes and drifted off.

I didn't sleep so much as I zoned out. Ivy came over and took my hand for a while, then Tanya slipped back and gave me a soft kiss on the top of my head, before joining Reggie and holding his hand while he said a prayer to close off the gathering. We weren't too far from the condo, so the three of us parted company with Tanya and Ivy, sharing hugs and cheek kisses and then walked home. The lads tucked me into the spare bed with hugs. I was asleep before they closed the door.

o0o

I woke up with the sun the next morning, flipped open the laptop and forced work to clear my sleep-and-boozed-crusted mind. Accustomed to typing at a moderately high rate of speed, being reduced to hunt-and-pecking with my left pointer finger pissed me off, but the more I did it, the better I got. It was like playing Chopin with only two strings—it was tough, but it was possible. By the time my hosts were up and about, I felt like I'd made a dent in my do-it-now-dammit list. I saved the files to the cloud, shut the computer down, and wandered downstairs.

"Good morning, Sunshine. You're looking quite a bit more bright-eyed and bushy-tailed than we expected."

No doubt. "I've been up for a few hours, working. Sorry about last night, I was a bit of a mess."

"That's life. Messy, crazy, honest, painful, but full of shits and giggles." Reg always had a way with words. Karl poured me a coffee and passed it to Reg who handed it to me.

"Thank you. I need more shits and giggles, that's for sure."

"First, food. Eggs Pacifica for breakie. Smoked salmon and fresh Hollandaise. Also nitrate-free bacon, hash browns, and fresh fruit."

"Sounds like breakfast at Denny's." My stomach growled.

"It only *sounds* like Denny's. It's our Sunday morning tradition when we're both home."

I sipped the coffee. Mmm... Ivory Coast Robusta. Perfect. Black. "How can I help? I'd like to do more than eat your food, drink your alcohol, and cry on your shoulder."

"You're our guest. Sit back, relax, and shut up."

"Shut up?"

"At least about helping. Sunday mornings is Karl's."

Karl shooed us out of the kitchen. "You two sweeties go stream something. If I need help, I'll scream."

"Yes sir!" Reggie took me by the elbow and led me to the couch. "Like I said, I stay out of the way. Your taste buds will thank you."

"Why don't I know anything about this Sunday tradition?"

"It's new. We started it after your accident. I was a mess, and that Sunday Karl whipped this up for me, to cheer me up. We do it to remind ourselves how precious life is. We've been wanting to include you, but..."

"Have I been that bad?"

"No. It's us. We almost lost you but we didn't want to get pushy. We kind of hoped you'd call us. We gave your family our numbers, just in case there was anything we could do to help."

"My family?" That explains a lot. "Maybe you should have contacted someone who gives a shit. Hell, I should have had *you* two be my lifeline."

"Except we're not always in town."

"True enough." Captain Happy Pills had been my go-to, but I suspect that Super Karl and the Amazing Reggie were going to be at the heart of my healing process.

Reggie turned on Netflix and quickly got me hooked on "The Morning Show", a police procedural set in Scotland's Shetland Islands starring the oh-so-lovely Douglas Henshall.

Halfway through the pilot episode, a light, silver, high C silver bell sounded from the kitchen. "Five-minute warning. Tinkle if you have to, because once you're at the table there is *no* leaving."

I stood up and waited for him to shut the system off with his convoluted three-remote system. "He's that strict?"

"No, it's that *delicious*. The timing of his serving is perfect. If you don't have to pee, go sit, and I'll be in in a sec."

Reg disappeared into the bathroom so I joined Karl. I stood silently in the arch between the kitchen and the dining room, out of his way, but able to observe every aspect of his solo performance. He looked up and blew me a kiss while not missing a beat from gently whisking something on the stove. I blew him a kiss back and went to my seat at the handsome Art Nouveau brass and glass dining table. A moment later Reggie joined me, took the carafe of what looked to be fresh-squeezed orange juice out of its bed of shaved ice, and filled three tall glasses, slowly, ceremoniously. With anyone other than these two, I would have laughed at the degree of silly pomp, but I know how much they love each other and how much it kills them when they're apart, so I accepted the solemnity and let myself be swept away by such a positive, gentle, nourishing tradition.

o0o

Breakfast wasn't just as good as Reggie claimed, it was so much better that something inside my heart went 'pop' and as I drained the dregs of my third glass of sinfully-good juice, tears poured out. I first dabbed my mouth with the linen napkin, and then my eyes, trying to dry them before I got caught. I was too slow.

"Oh no, Jubilee! What is it, Sweetie? What's wrong?" They each reached over and took one of my hands, Karl being extra gentle with my claw.

"Nothing's wrong. It's just so perfect. I have never, in my entire life, had a meal reach me on so many levels, and that includes homemade pasta and wine on our honeymoon on a villa terrace overlooking Lake Como and the time Michael B. grilled the perfect Kobe steaks for everyone after the concert in Nagasaki."

"Michael B.? As in 'Bublé'?" Karl swooned.

I shrugged, keeping the mystery a mystery. "My point is, this wasn't just a perfect meal, it was a perfect *experience*. Maybe it's the juice talking, or the fact that I haven't had today's little pill to suppress my emotions, but..."

Karl beamed. "Thank you. You're welcome back any time—*every* time."

Reggie patted my arm. "Now, will you ever doubt anything I tell you? He's a maestro."

Never! "Not a chance. He definitely *is*." I leaned back in my chair and sighed. "I think I'm ready to face the world, even with a deranged killer stalking the streets."

"What shall we do, then, Missy?"

"I'm horning in on your weekend, guys. You deserve time together without a third wheel. I should get home."

"Bullshit." Karl actually looked ready to slap me. "You're here to heal, so heal. You're family and you know it. We've had this conversation before, Jube. Get it through your thick skull—you're our little sister, whether you like it or not."

Like it? I love it! "What's that homily? 'Friends are the family we choose'? Thank you. I choose you right back, especially after thirty years of having my blood family disappoint, ignore, and criticize me every chance they get."

Reggie stood and took my dirty plate. "You two go relax while I clear the table, load that old dishwasher, and pray it works. There's one of the lesser home and garden design shows this weekend.

Maybe we should go. Get distracted—and maybe a new dishwasher."

That sounded good. "I'm in. I want to change up a few things in the backyard, so maybe I'll find some inspiration."

"Then that's the plan." He picked up his husband's plate, kissed him on the top of his head, and disappeared into the kitchen. Karl and I moved to the couch, where he sat close beside me and took my good hand in both of his. They were strong and warm and soft and seemed to draw stress right out of me.

"We're all worried that something bad has happened to Elteen, but we're worried about you, too, and I know you know that, but what we don't know is how we can *really* help you."

"Didn't we have this conversation after I woke up in the hospital?" My memory was fuzzy, but I did remember their tears.

"Sort of. We said we're here for you, no matter what, but no one knew what that was going to mean at the time. We had no plan. I think it's time for a plan, to orchestrate your recovery."

I squeezed his hand, afraid to speak for fear of weeping again. I needed one of the pills I was trying to wean myself off of, so instead I let Karl talk because he seemed to need to, and I probably needed to listen.

"We'd have you here even if there wasn't a serial killer loose, you know that, I hope. Weekends like this are delightful, but it's the day-to-day stuff that weighs so much and takes strength to slog through. We're not going to tell you what is going to happen, we want *you* to tell *us* what you need. Buying groceries, cleaning the house, cooking meals to freeze, yard work, whatever."

He was right. I needed someone to kick my ass. I used to do it to myself by talking it all out with V-Dog, but that was no longer an option.

"How about appointments, Jubie? Therapist, physio...?"

"Public Transit is good. Dr. Ella is downtown at the Tower, and physio is at the sports medicine clinic right on my bus route."

"Good. When are your next appointments?"

"Dr. Ella tomorrow and my next physio is Tuesday."

"Will you agree to send us a text after each one, just to keep us in the loop?"

"Of course. I think it'll help me find a rhythm, too. Doctor's orders had me keeping in touch with Joyce after the accident, but no matter how much or little information I gave her, either my mother would make me doubt that anything I experienced was real at all, or Joyce would find a way to tear my head off and shit down my neck."

"Wow. That's a helluva an image."

"Sorry. Every time I talked to them I came away thinking I was making it all up." Talking about my family got me wound up, even in such safe company.

"It's OK because I know exactly what you mean. I'm sorry you had to go through all that."

"It's been my life for as long as I can remember, so I'm used to it."

"No, you're not. I can see it in your eyes."

I wiped away a traitorous tear. "Maybe."

"No 'maybe'. We're here for you. End of discussion."

"Thank you." I lifted his hands and kissed the back of the top one.

"Now, how about money?"

Chapter Ten

"I'm OK for a while."

"Good. But we'll help there, too, if you need it."

Reggie reappeared from the kitchen and handed us each a fresh coffee. "What did I miss?"

"I've just hired you two to babysit me."

"Sounds like fun! Then shall we take little Jubidoo for a walk to the Home and Garden thingy? After the coffee, of course."

"Of course."

"Definitely."

o0o

It may have been one of the smaller trade shows but it still took us two hours to wander through it, what with all the stopping, chattering, flyer-grabbing, and free-pen-snatching we did. By the time we were done, I had some landscaping ideas and a bag of info and freebies. The boys, on the other hand, had bought all new appliances at an amazing show-special price, booked an appointment to have the window treatment people come and measure the condo windows for new blinds, and had entered every single free draw they came across.

"You two do know that those draws are just fishing for sales leads and that not only will you be getting sales calls for the next six months, but one or two of them will probably sell your contact info and your email will get packed with electronic shit, forever?"

"Or we could win a trip to Cabo San Cabo and it'll all be worthwhile."

"Maybe."

"Why are you so cynical about it? A free trip together would be lovely."

"It would, I agree. But one of my clients is a company that mines sales leads and I edit their quarterly in-house newsletter. It's all very rah rah rah and doesn't contain anything incriminating, but after two years of newsletters I've put together a pretty good idea of their business model."

"Ouch. Too late now."

"It is. So, let's cross our fingers that you win something big."

"Cabo San Cabo..."

"Is that even a real place?"

"No. I think it's from the original 'Night Court'. The trip is to Cabo San Lucas. Cabo San Cabo just sounds better."

It did.

We had an early dinner of stir-fry, and then my sweeties drove me home. They wanted me to stay and I wanted to, but I needed clean clothes, a proper bath with my too-expensive soaps, and a night in my own bed before my appointment with Dr. Ella. The whole police questioning and a serial killer on the loose seemed silly after a wonderful weekend with the boys, but I peeked out all of the windows to make sure there was no one watching me. To be honest, though, how would I see him if he were hiding? There was no one out there, though, and it felt good to be home. I was OK. Not perfect, not brilliant, but definitely OK. I was even leaning toward the idea that Elteen was off exploring, not chained in a basement. I still sent her a text telling her to call ASAP, though.

First thing Monday morning I had that bath, broke fast with supplies Karl had insisted on buying for me on the way back south the night before, and was out the door with something akin to energy in my stride. I gave myself two hours to do a forty-five-minute trip, and if I got downtown early enough I intended to grab a coffee and a croissant and relax before the inquisition.

I was in such a good mood that I almost didn't notice the gold minivan with the tinted windows parked where my next-door neighbour usually parked. I could see her white Honda over on the cross street, which meant that the van had been there since sometime yesterday evening because she always went to the late church service. I took out my phone and snapped a quick photo of the vehicle while I walked, hoping that the license plate was clear. I'm sure it was just one of the contractors working on the house three doors down, but maybe not entirely sure. The tempo of my heartbeat quickened just a little.

Throughout the six-minute walk to the bus stop, I couldn't help but look back over my shoulder every so often. There was the usual traffic, but no sign of the van. Still, I couldn't shake the feeling that there was something *wrong* with the van being there. Once the bus arrived, I relaxed, though I said a quiet prayer for the Butcher's known victims and the too many missing women. I closed my eyes for the remaining ten minutes of the ride to the station, thinking about the vigil and the tears and love and songs of people shaken to their core by the bastard terrorizing the city.

By the time I'd ridden the train north into downtown, sat, enjoyed a croissant and coffee, and walked the four blocks to Dr. Ella's office, thoughts of the Butcher made me feel silly and paranoid. I'm pretty sure if the Geocache Butcher wanted me as a victim, he wouldn't follow me around the city, waiting for me to spot him.

Then again, I'm not a serial killer and have no damned idea how they think. James did, though. His brother once gave him a signed copy of a book about humans hunting humans or some such, and he said it opened his eyes about 'those psychos'. I wondered if that book was still on the shelf in the basement.

Thoughts of serial killers vanished in a puff of mist in a breeze when I opened the door and stepped into the reception area ten minutes early. Song waved to acknowledge me and continued with a sotto voce phone conversation. Between the height of her desk, the plush carpet, and the wool hangings on the walls, sound didn't travel far in this antechamber to healing. The coffee gave me a nice little pick-me-up, but I still closed my eyes to find my center and shed the shite of the outside world, at least until Dr. Ella brought it up for pick-at-and-purge time.

I must have dozed off because a gentle touch on my forearm woke me. Song knelt next to me.

"Dr. Ella will see you now, Jubilee." I nodded and smiled, so she stood and returned to her desk.

Shaking off my stupor only took a moment and as I approached the door to the place of healing, it opened and Dr. Ella and her hug greeted me. It felt great. I managed to not collapse this time. It had been less than a week, but after my weekend of Karl-and-Reggie-care, I felt a thousand times better than the last time I was here. So *this* is what healing felt like.

"You look terrific, Jubilee." She closed the door behind us and we found our places.

"Between my power nap in the waiting room and a great weekend with Karl and Reggie, I feel a bit more solid, like my life is less of a solo effort and more of an ensemble."

"I love that analogy. May I use it?"

"If it helps."

"I'm sure it will." She smiled and asked what was so wonderful about the weekend.

I gave her the Coles Notes version, fleshing out the breakfast and the vigil. My mood shifted to the blue end of the spectrum when we discussed Elteen and not knowing where she was and if she was safe. I felt so useless. When I told her about feeling like I was being followed, though, her eyebrows lifted and her smile faltered. I described the incidents and added the van this morning. "It's never the same man, and to be honest I didn't notice anything until after I spoke with the detective. Do you believe me?" My mother wouldn't have.

"Of course, I believe you, Jubilee. Even if you *are* being paranoid and imagining it all, there is still a psychopathic serial killer on the loose so no limit to the caution we can all take. How did the photo of the van turn out?"

"Blurry." I took out my phone and showed her. "I was in too much of a rush, I guess. I assumed it was a contractor working in the area and people don't take kindly to strangers taking photos of their license plates."

"I understand. If you see the van again, use video—it's easier to isolate a single frame."

"You know about this stuff?" She was always full of surprises, but I guess I wasn't there to learn about *her*.

"A little." She stood again. "Speaking of photography, there's someone I'd like you to meet. First, though, I want to tell you that I'm really happy with your progress, Jubilee." She held her arms open so I stood and stepped into a quick hug. "I've had Song put aside some time next Monday. I don't want to delay too long when you're doing so well but also so worried about Elteen. Your inability to rush off and go to her rescue is going to weigh heavier and heavier each day. Let's keep on top of it. Song will confirm the time with you." She turned around to face the owl photo. "You asked me if the photographer would sell you a copy, and she said yes, but under one condition."

"A condition?"

"Only that she wants to deliver it to you herself if that's OK. She needs the validation that she did something good."

I could understand *that* need. "Of course."

"Excellent." She checked her watch—something she rarely did. "She should be here by now."

"Now?" Coming out of these sessions I'm not exactly ready to meet new people, but what the hell.

"Only if you're comfortable with it. Otherwise, I can arrange another time."

"Now is OK. But I don't have any cash."

"That's not a concern. You can do it all through Song if you wish." She reached for the doorknob but hesitated, waiting for my decision, watching my expression.

I smiled and took another quick look at the owl. I was excited to have one for the house. "Sure. That's fine." She opened the door and returned to the hushed reception area. A woman about my age, with a long, chestnut-brown ponytail with gold highlights, rose from a chair like a panther rises from a spot in the sun, with power, confidence, and grace. She wore a slightly fitted plaid flannel shirt, straight-leg jeans, tall, espresso-brown Westport riding boots, and a brown Carhartt jacket. She was at least a head taller than me and I suddenly felt like sidekick Gabrielle next to L.L. Bean Xena, Princess Warrior. Then I saw something very unXenalike in her eyes. Hesitation? Fear? I held out my hand and she shook it, firmly but gently.

"Hi. I'm Jubilee."

"Hi. Charlene—*Charlie*. You're a birder?"

I chuckled. "Hardly. I barely know a chickadee from a sparrow, but I *do* love them. That owl..."

"The Northern Pygmy. Yeah, he's a beauty. It was a lucky shot."

"A *stunning* shot." Joy pushed fear out of her eyes and she picked up a big manila bubble pack on the coffee table. She opened the flap and slid out a matted copy of the photo. My stupid eyes got moist. "I feel like he's looking right into my soul and waving, telling me to take a deep breath and it'll all be OK."

"Me, too. Owls are my second favourite bird. Solid, steady and strong—even the little ones."

"Your *second* favourite? What could be better than owls?"

"Hummingbirds. They're almost the complete opposite of owls, but watching them flit and feed, their wings a blur, it's surreal. My cousin, Deb, and I spent one Sunday afternoon sitting on the deck of her farmhouse, drinking tea, eating home-baking, and watching them zip back and forth to her feeder. It was a perfect day, except that it was before I got into photography, so no pictures."

"Sounds like a perfect day." I could use a day—or a *year*—like that.

"Then dusk rolled around, the hummers went to sleep, and the baby bats came out, flying straight at us, then veering away, probably learning to echolocate. We were out there for twelve hours, all told." She sighed, and so did the three of us listening.

Dr. Ella placed a gentle hand on my arm. "You two figure out payment and I'll get back to work. Jubilee, I'll see you next week. Charlie, thank you so much for coming in, and Song, please send Trey right in when he arrives." Then she smiled, waved and was gone.

Charlie handed me the envelope. "Would you like to grab a coffee?"

Her voice was casual and controlled, but her eyes darted from me to the door, like a long-legged deer trying to decide if I was a wolverine or a bunny. Coffee with a human being who wasn't connected to my pain? I could go for that. I can't remember the last time I had coffee with someone who wasn't James or from the symphony. "That would be nice. Talk birds, bats, photography..." I could text the boys from the coffee shop to let them know how the appointment went.

"How about Starbucks across the street, in the Marriott?"

Shit. That's where the orchestra refuelled. But it was Monday and they rehearsed on weekends, so it should be safe. "Terrific. For some reason, I'm in the mood for a caramel Frappuccino..."

"With extra caramel?"

"Of course! But let's settle up for the owl, first."

o0o

I confirmed my 10 am Monday appointment with Song, and then she credited Charlie's account for fifty dollars and charged mine for the same, which worked just fine all around. Starbucks was busy so we took our decadent Frappuccinos to a pair of comfy chairs and a low table in the Marriott's lobby, right by the fireplace. Charlie lowered her long frame down into the low lounge seat, took a sip of her liquid sugar, and sighed. It was as if she hadn't relaxed in a long time. I knew the feeling. I plunked myself down, sipped my dessert, and let go of the last little bit of stress I had left over from seeing Dr. Ella. I glanced around for members of the orchestra or my stalker, but more out of reflex than anything else. The lobby was quiet, with just the occasional suit exiting the elevator with a briefcase in hand and a purposeful stride out the revolving doors to the queue of taxis on the street.

"So, where do we have hummingbirds in Calgary—I mean, other than people's yards? I used to see them at my aunt's place when I was younger, but have never actually seen them in the wild, in a park."

She took a sip and seemed to think about her answer. "Their season here is short, but the most likely wild place to see them is Weaselhead Flats at the west end of the reservoir."

"I know that area. I used to ride my bike down there, but I never saw hummingbirds." Had they been around me and I'd missed them?

"You have to hike off the main trail quite a bit, then be patient. Unlike bigger birds, they're quite susceptible to temperature changes. I've sat for ten hours, three days running, just for a peek at them, and been disappointed."

"How about owls, then? Dr. Ella said that this one" I tapped the envelope on the table, "was right next to the parking lot, and that's unusual."

"It was unusual at the time, but now the pair are a common sight. I guess they liked the area and decided to stick around. I usually have to hunt out the owls. The one big exception is the two Great Horned owls in Fish Creek Park."

"Really? Which part?" Have I been living down the street from Great Horned Owls and didn't even know it? Hummingbirds when I biked, owls when I hiked... I guess I've been a special kind of oblivious.

"A bit of a walk from the Sundance parking lot." She pulled out her phone, entered a code that she shielded with her hand, opened Photos, tapped an image, and held it up for me to see. "Two big owlets from last spring."

Holy shit, they were gorgeous! Big, fluffy, creamy brown beauties with big yellow eyes and deadly iron-grey talons. "Wow!"

"Exactly. You just need to know where to look."

"And you know?"

"Within the city, yes. I know all the parks pretty well, especially Fish Creek. After the big flood in 2013, though, some parks closed and some I had to learn all over again because some of the species relocated to adapt to the changed landscape. The Bird Sanctuary was hit quite hard."

"You explore the parks? You're not afraid of the Geocache Butcher?"

She got quiet and broke eye contact. After a moment she gave me an odd answer. "The killer only uses the parks as a dumping ground, not for hunting. All of the victims were picked up and killed somewhere else before being left in the park."

How the hell did she know this? "Oh. OK."

"The birds have led police to two of the remains, specifically the magpies and crows, but they were closer to Canyon Meadows than where the Great Horneds are."

He's not near my house, then... Change of subject. Quick! "What other species are at my end?" I might have to spend more time hiking the neighbourhood.

"Osprey, Swainson's Hawks, and Bald Eagles are the biggest raptors. Herons in the ponds, a dozen or more duck varieties, white pelicans, various swans during migration, and all sorts of songbirds and woodpeckers." She searched through her photos and held up one of a little black, white, and red-capped woodpecker sitting on a hand! "Downey woodpecker—very friendly."

"Oh my God!" It was so *cool*! "This is in Fish Creek Park?"

"Yup. You're welcome to come with me next time I go. The owls and woodpeckers are easy to find at this time of the year."

"Really? I can come?"

"Why not? Have you got a camera?"

"Just an early digital point-and-shoot." It was an old piece of shit.

"Ah. A PhD camera."

"No, it's quite simple. Any idiot can use it."

She smiled. "No, Ph.D. stands for 'Push Here, Dummy'."

Really? That's perfect! "Oh, it's definitely a push-here for *this* dummy."

"If you want, I'll bring my spare. It's a PhD but with a great zoom. If you have a spare SD Card, you can pop it in, take some shots, and then pop it out when you're done. Nice and simple."

"I'm sure I have one. Thank you." I guess if I'm going to wander into a killer's 'drop zone', at least I'll be going with someone who knows the park. She also moves like someone who can handle herself if trouble crops up, unlike the former cellist sitting opposite her whose sister taught her to duck and hide rather than hit back. Besides, the Butcher isn't likely to be there in daylight, and we can hardly go bird watching at night. I needed to get out into the fresh air more than I do now. V-Dog had always been good for making sure I got out. "That sounds great. Other than my physio appointment tomorrow—" I held up my claw. "My schedule is wide open."

That cast off some of the cloud that seemed to have settled over Charlie with talk of the Butcher. "Great. How's Wednesday? It's supposed to be sunny and warmer."

Sunny and warm? I could use that. I was freaking done with winter. "Perfect."

She nodded at my claw. "What happened?"

"An accident." I decided to keep it as simple as I could. "Nerve damage."

"Ah." Just the one-note reply. Either she was respecting my reticence or she had just asked out of politeness and decided that it wasn't worth prying more information out of me. Either way, we both let it drop and sipped our drinks.

I liked Charlie. She had a soft manner that belied her height and suspected strength, but she kept her cards close to her chest. In fact, she may not have asked more about my injury to avoid answering questions about herself. Questions about birds and cameras, though, seemed to be fair game, so that's what I went with. "What's the rarest bird you've ever photographed?"

"The Northern Pygmy Owl was the most unusual *sighting*. In parts of B.C., he's not uncommon, but here in Alberta, it'd been ten years since there'd been any confirmed sightings. Now they're back. Every time I photograph a species for the first time is exciting. Sometimes it's not even a rare find, it's just a first for me. Last summer it was a pair of Black-Crowned Night Herons."

Night herons? "I've never heard of them."

"They're smaller than Great Blues, which are common enough in Calgary, and I wouldn't have seen this pair if I hadn't glanced over the highway guardrail and down into a drainage pond. Just fifty yards from the highway." She showed me a picture on her phone of a short-necked, stocky bird fading from a dark grey back to a pale belly with a long, straight beak and a black crown like a bad comb-over.

"How odd." He looked like a long-nosed, hunched-over butler from an old movie.

"His mate flew off as I was approaching, but this one stuck around for a few minutes. He was a long way off, so the shot isn't as sharp as I'd like."

She was being super-critical. "I think it's great."

"Thank you." She flashed her half-smile. "But the longer I do this and the more shots I take, the pickier I get. The owls—they're perfect. Crisp, focused, lit just right. *This* is a good record but not one I'd write home about."

Ah, yes. "I understand. I am—*was*—a musician." I flinched. "Some of my performances were applauded loudly, but they weren't ones I'd want recorded. Others I wish I *did* have on disk. On those occasions the music transcended the musician, and maybe even the composer." Oh shit, my *music*. I tried not to look like I'd just punched myself in the gut.

"You *do* understand." She put her phone face down to attend to her Frappuccino. She didn't ask about my music and I sure as hell didn't volunteer anything. I, too, drank.

We both went quiet, savouring the sweetness of the drinks while watching the traffic in the lobby traipse past, to and from the front desk or the front doors. We looked just about anywhere but at each other. It was like a first date, trying to conversationally find a common ground without coming across as a complete doofus, except that I'm not gay and I wasn't getting that vibe from Charlie. Considering our common connection with Dr. Ella, I suspected that we were *both* shattered individuals just trying not to look like we were. Well, we both liked birds, so that would have to be enough of a foundation for our acquaintance to progress. At this point, I didn't know who the hell *I* was going to be, going forward, and I sure didn't want to subject a near stranger to the confusion.

My phone did a mute, vibrating dance on the table, bumping me out of my haze. A message box appeared on the screen. I couldn't help but grin. It was Reggie, wondering how the session with Dr. Ella went. I'm not one to ignore the person in front of me to respond to a non-emergency, so I put the phone back down.

"Sorry about that." I wanted to tell her that it was a text from a dear, dear friend who was worried about me, and casually checking up on me, but I didn't. I didn't share any details at all. Was I getting paranoid, or just extremely protective of my world, having lost so much of it? I have no clue. Maybe telling her would lead to 'Why is he checking up?' and then whatever friendship we might be starting here could change tempo and pitch and become something it didn't need to be, yet. I didn't need her pity, I had enough of my own.

Chapter Eleven

"It's OK. I have to get to an appointment across town in Bowness. So, Wednesday?" Charlie looked like she'd cry if I said no. OK, so we *both* needed to reach out.

"Wednesday it is. What time?"

She had a lovely shy smile. "Is eight too early? We want to catch the morning light." She wrote something on her napkin and slid it across to me.

"Eight is good." On the napkin was a phone number.

"Text me your address and I'll pick you up. I'm guessing you're not driving, yet." She pointed at my claw.

"Not yet. Soon, maybe." Or never. Even if I could physically control a car, I'm not sure how long it would be before I could do it emotionally. I still had flashes of that other car slamming into me. In my mind, the other driver was a leering, suicidal, killer clown, but Dr. Ella said that was my mind's way of keeping me from putting a face on a man who was about to die, no matter *whose* fault it was.

"Then I'll pick you up. That works well because you live close to the park."

I must have flinched or winced or something because she quickly backpedalled.

"Or we can drive down to Frank Lake if you want to stay away from city parks. There's a boardwalk and a huge blind and *thousands* of birds."

"Owls or hummingbirds?"

"No. Mostly waterfowl and shore birds, or are you OK with Fish Creek?"

Of course, I was. It would be daylight. I just wouldn't tell the boys. They'd probably get all freaked out. "Sure. No problem."

"Then we'll go find the Great Horned owls. It needs to be a bit warmer for hummingbirds, so another week or two. The second week of May is always a safe bet."

"Owls sound like a good start," but hummingbirds were definitely on the list.

"Perfect. Wednesday at eight."

"Eight." I smiled, she smiled, and then she was gone, leaving me with my still-cold, caramel-loaded drink, and the owl photo yearning to be hung on the wall over my desk. I had a couple of empty frames in the basement, so I didn't even need to go shopping. Instead, I leaned back and sipped my drink, kind of excited to see owls in person and hang out with someone who didn't know anything about me or my recent past. Unless she owned a gold mini-van with tinted windows. I texted Reggie that all was good and I was going home shortly.

o0o

The train ride south was uneventful until we were leaving the second-to-last stop. I was peacefully reading the latest novel by local author, G. W. Renshaw, on on my phone, when a little electric wave of nausea rippled through my gut and I nearly threw up all over the two chatting girls in front of me. I gritted my teeth, gripped the bar topping the teens' seat, and made it one more stop to my bus connection. After a couple of slow, deep breaths, the nausea slipped away. Dr. Ella warned me that this would happen if I messed with my meds, and apparently, she was right. Again.

Over at the bus loop, I had a choice between a packed bus that would take me three blocks from home, or a nearly empty one that would mean a six-block walk. I just wasn't up for crowds or standing, so opted for the empty bus that would drop me next to the neighbourhood convenience store. Now that the urge to puke had passed, I needed sugar and a lottery ticket. Christ Almighty, I could use a lottery win right about now.

When my too-expensive QuickPick ticket was tucked safely in my wallet and a Mars bar was half tucked away into my soul via my belly, I had to choose between a twelve-minute walk alongside busy streets, or an eight-minute scuttle down back roads, laneways, and interconnected paths. I was ready for a nap and wanted nothing more than to click my heels and be home, but my phone rang. The ID said that it was an Unknown Caller, again, but before I could swipe to answer it, it stopped. Could someone track my phone to find me? Shit. The long way home it was.

Truth be told, the extra four minutes of fresh air did wonders for me, so that by the time I checked my mail in the community boxes near the house, I had a bit more energy. Of course, between the Frappuccino and the Mars bar, I also had enough sugar in my system that I was sure I could leap a tall curb in a single stumble.

Once I was back in the dim and empty house, with the door locked behind me, I shed my outerwear and went down into the basement in search of a frame for my new roommate. I picked a nice, thick wooden frame that had once held a photo of James and me dressed as super-spies for a theme party a few years ago. Soon, the already matted owl, whom I'd named Deepak, for the peace he brought me, was framed, and hanging above my desk, next to the shelf with V-Dog's little urn. It may sound stupid, but between the two of them, I now felt truly watched over and protected.

While the computer was booting up, I went and made myself a strong ginger tea, to fend off further pukey moments. It was time to get shit done. First, though, I was curious about replies to my eRomance notes. Reggie and Karl had kept me too busy for the notes to even cross my mind, but the healing feeling from my session with the doctor, as well as connecting with Charlie, gave me a boost of courage. The tea was steeped to perfection three beats after the computer opened up the eRomance home page. I entered my log-in info and sipped while I waited.

There were eleven replies, but nothing from Niko, the abandoning asshole. I flipped through them slowly. It's easy to dismiss people who use online dating services, but I was starting to realize that they weren't all geeky, bespectacled, overweight horndogs any more than I was a bon-bon-munching cat lady who loved paisley and reality TV. I vowed to give each of the men a fair read.

The first one, from *KyleSmile33*, made me want to run straight to the bottle of mead in the fridge. "HEY JULES! THANKS FOR THE NOTE! I TOTALLY DIG YOUR LOOK AND THINK I'M IN LOVE!"

Beyond getting my name wrong—that could have been auto-correct's mistake—all those caps were a warning sign I couldn't ignore. Oh, and the use of the L-word. His photo showed him in some dimly lit Polynesian-themed bar with a perky co-ed under each arm, an umbrella drink in each hand, and half a dozen plastic Hawaiian leis around his neck. It was such a cliché that I had to click on his profile to see if it was a joke or if I had missed something during my vetting of these finalists when I first separated the wheat from the crap.

Kyle's profile pic showed a heavier, bearded version of the party animal with the co-eds, and he was dressed in a University of Alberta hoodie, sitting on a sea wall with a little Boston terrier on his lap. I remembered this photo. It made me smile and reach out to him. So, who was the real *KyleSmile33*? I checked the captions of the two photos. Hoodie Kyle was from a trip to Oregon three years ago, and party Kyle... was taken during March Break of this year. I guessed that through diet and exercise, *KyleSmile33* had given himself an extreme makeover and was now loving every minute of his "new you" lifestyle. I deleted the message and took a *long* sip of tea. Congratulations, Kyle, but the new you isn't for the now me, and probably never would have been. No one knows better than me that people change, but Kyle didn't need a crippled stick-in-the-mud cramping his party style, and I couldn't stand the creepy, choky feeling of a plastic lei around my neck. Call me odd.

TerryChef32 had sent a simple, polite note with a nice, two-sentence summary of his quiet life. Him, I left in the queue, for further consideration later.

GinoGinoX had a smile, a tan, and long, dark wavy hair that wouldn't look out of place on the cover of an airport kiosk romance novel. His reply was sweet and gentle and almost too good to be true. He went back in the queue, at least for now.

I had to get some work done, so I gave each of the remaining nine notes a cursory once-over. *JackOTrades*, queue. *EricPEng*, queue. *LucioOh*, queue. *Jazzman2N* was a musician and a dog lover, but the bong in the background of the photo turned me off. My days of smoking dope and face-planting into a bowl of Doritos were long gone. My memories of the first month of freshman year were hazier than those of my accident. Sorry, dude. Into the bin, you go.

ConductorG and *KwanTumFlex* both stayed in the queue, but *PierreTheFiddler* was released quickly into the wild. Call me picky, but his reply to my note was so full of grammatical and spelling errors that I couldn't even finish reading it. Then I remembered the movie "Sleepless in Seattle" and how the young son, Jonah, tried to find a wife for his widowed father, played by Tom Hanks. That's what Pierre's note read like—one written by a fifth-grader. I went into the Trash file and retrieved his note. I told myself it was just out of curiosity, but the nervous, lopsided smile in his profile pic told me that there was more to his story. He went back into the queue.

Once again, like the bitch I am, I composed a simple skeleton reply to the letters, mentioning the spring weather, the Calgary Flames, and the new Meryl Streep film I was looking forward to. I then tweaked the skeleton to fit each suitor and sent the ten notes off. They all seemed like nice guys, on par with Niko, so maybe there was a gem in this rough group. I'm not sure I was serious about the whole thing, but doing this was a step forward, not a tumble back, and *that* was vital.

When that was all done, so was the tea. I rinsed the cup and filled it with tap water before starting in on the actual work I was contracted to do. I got maybe fifteen minutes into a tedious edit of a safety procedures manual when I started to nod off. I considered topping up my tank with coffee but instead curled up under the blanket on the couch. The sugar rush was done and the inevitable follow-up crash rolled over me and pulled me under, dragging me down into a nightmare that would have scared the shit out of Freddy Kruger.

One second, I was pulling the blanket up to my chin and letting my heavy lids slide down into place, and the next I was driving down a blizzardy country road with huge, hand-sized snowflakes flying at me like stars at light speed in the Millennium Falcon. Muse's wipers slapped away like a metronome on cocaine—leftrightleftrightleftright. Star-flakes whipped at me, each a blinding point in the headlights just before smacking into the windshield and being executed by the coked-out wipers with neither pomp nor circumstance.

V-Dog whimpered beside me, then frantically scrambled onto my lap, as freaked out as I was. He cried like it was the end of days and in a little corner of my dreaming mind I somehow knew that it *was* the end, in so many more ways than one.

The slippery road curved to the right, so I gripped the steering wheel tighter and urged Muse to follow that curve, and that's when I discovered that my left hand was missing and all I had in its place were two stainless steel hooks forming pinchers that couldn't grip the wheel. My right hand held on like a vice grip, doing all the work. At the very moment my grip began to slip and V-Dog jumped back to the passenger seat and then down onto the floor to cower, the reflective yellow diamonds marking the curve straightened out and I recovered back onto the runway-straight road.

The radio suddenly turned on and blasted Rimsky-Korsikov's manic *Flight of the Bumblebee.* "FUCKING HELL!" was all I managed to shout before the road started weaving back and forth, the reflective diamonds curving right, then left, then right, being my only warnings, because now the snow was so heavy that I couldn't see anything but flakes and mere glimpses of the bright yellow markers.

When we were kids, Dad would turn the headlights off in a snowstorm and we could see better because a trace of moonlight showed just enough of the road for him to follow it. Desperate, I now reached for the headlight switch on the left side of the steering column, but I still only had the shiny steel hooks to grip the switch and turn the headlights off. I gave it a try and the fucking hooks jerked and *pulled* on the armature, kicking on the goddamned high beams!

I went from flying blind in a crazed star field to blasting straight through the heart of the high-beam sun. I screamed so loudly I thought my throat had ruptured. Then, amid the scrambling with my damned hook to turn the fucking high beams off, two spots of light appeared in my left mirror, coming up fast. Just as the car drew even with Muse, he slammed into us. I jerked the wheel to the right, but the whole entire world slowed, from a bumblebee's flight down to the slow, measured chime of London's Big Ben. The entire world except me... I moved at normal speed.

No matter how hard I cranked on the wheel, though, there was no effect on the trajectory into Hell that Muse was on. V-Dog appeared back up on the passenger seat beside me, his dark eyes sad and lost. My claw slipped in its vain attempt to pull harder on the wheel, and when I finally looked left at the attacking vehicle, the snow had stopped and the other driver, made up as the evil, yellow-toothed clown, Pennywise from "IT", was staring at me.

He was mid maniacal laugh, with one white-gloved hand on the steering wheel of his old, blue Grand Am while the other hand held up his cellphone for me to see the text he was typing. I didn't think the universe could move any slower without actually stopping completely, but it did. Frame by frame, the impending sideswipe of death and destruction advanced.

My heart screamed out for my precious V-Dog and I turned to look at him, nearly motionless, eyes wide and filled with terror. I tried to reach out for him, to pull him close, cradle him safely with my own body, willing to die so he could live, but my arm was now handcuffed to the steering wheel. I pulled and jerked on the cuffs, frantic, but it was useless. I looked back at the Clown of Death, and he rammed us again. Back to V-Dog, then back to Pennywise, to V, to the clown, to V...

I have no idea how long this horror went on because, at the moment of the second impact, Muse spun slowly and inevitably away from the Grand Am and down into the ditch. As the roaring bass crunch of metal-punching-metal deafened me and the windshield shattered into a million little blades, I woke the fuck up. I woke up screaming and thrashing and wrapped in flying, suffocating, metal-glass-and-plastic death. I woke up...tangled in the blanket on the couch, feeling like my heart had been torn straight down and out through my stomach.

Rolling to my side, I puked, all over the rug. And puked and puked and puked until I was empty both physically and emotionally. I clumsily wiped my vomit-dripping chin with my sleeve and wanted to die—felt like I *had* died. I shut my eyes as if I could block out the image of V-Dog's pleading eyes, and fell back to sleep remembering something Dr. Ella had said about vivid nightmares and random withdrawal from the meds. No, shit, Doc.

o0o

The Sleep Symphony's second movement was night-terror-free, but since I hadn't changed my clothes after the first movement, I was still sweat-wet an hour later when my bladder decided that it needed to be syphoned. I dragged my ass off the couch, taking the damp Afghan with me, careful not to step in my drying vomit. Despite the extra effort and distance, I clomped up the stairs to the main bathroom.

By the time I was sure my reservoir was well drained of sugary coffee and tea, I was awake enough for a much-needed shower. When I finally crawled between the sheets twenty minutes later it felt so good that I rolled straight into the third sleep movement and, as far as I can remember, coasted straight on through to the coda without another nightmare.

o0o

It was dark outside when I finally peeked out from under the covers. The red, two-inch-high numbers of the clock radio on the tallboy dresser said it was 9:15. Damn. I *must* have been tired.

Already my head was grasping at the wisps of remembered horrors of that earlier nightmare. I shook it off as best I could, grabbed my robe, slipped on a pair of woolly socks, and aimed my well-rested ass down to the kitchen for food. The house was too damned quiet, so I risked the radio, for company. It was jazz time again, so I heated, cracked, whisked, dipped, and fried with a hint of a bounce in my woolly-sock shuffle. I wasn't quite dancing like that old guy on YouTube who recorded himself bopping to whatever beat in his kitchen while he cooked and gave his cat high-fives, but I smiled and wiggled it, just a little bit.

I was ravenous. I like to clean as I go in the kitchen, but my puked-empty belly begged me to just sit the hell down and eat. I ate at my desk, gently pushing the computer to one side to make room for the plate of goody goodness. The egg-soaked French toast was tender enough to fork-cut, but I was determined to train my claw to be useful, so I knife-and-forked it. I dropped the fork only once before figuring out the best grip, and after that, every mouthful felt like a Goddamned victory. Physio tomorrow was going to be a piece of cake. OK, maybe not, but I was ready to give it another shot.

Savouring each of those forking victories, I took my time, concentrating on not just keeping the food on the utensil but keeping the utensil held tight in my pincers. By the time the last piece was in my mouth, my left thumb and first finger ached. The good news was that my middle finger had deigned to weakly join the party. Three out of five digits—I could sort of live with that, for now.

I stuck the dirty dish and flatware in the dishwasher then grabbed the dish with the egg shells, and popped open the garbage can to dump it all in. Damn! The can was full. Keeping my foot on the pedal, I dumped the shells in, put the dish on the island, and then hauled the full bag up and out of the can by its collar. I tied it shut with the built-red plastic loops, then plunked it by the back door. The door always stuck, so I leaned on it with my shoulder and twisted the knob with my good hand, slamming the deadbolt back with a sharp metallic thump. When I opened the storm door it set off the motion-sensor security lamp, flooding the entire twenty-by-thirty yard in painfully crisp white LED light. The back gate was wide open!

Chapter Twelve

What the hell? I jammed my feet into my boots and charged out into the yard, hefting the full bag of garbage like a weapon. I tossed the bag in the bin just inside the gate, slammed the gate shut, ensuring that the latch clicked, and then charged back up to the house. Once my boots were off, I slapped on the regular back deck lights. I didn't want to take a chance that someone could move slowly enough to not set off the motion sensor. Then I sock-skated my way to the front door to check *that* lock. Who the hell had been in my fucking yard?

I clomped back upstairs, more angry than scared. We had a problem with bottle pickers combing through our recycling bins in our back lanes. They usually came and went in almost complete silence, so we didn't care, but every so often an intoxicated picker would just dump the blue recycling bins over and pick the returnable bottles out of the mess on the gravel lane. Twice, after summer long weekends, neighbours had caught pickers on their back decks, looking for bags of bottles from big parties.

Even though we weren't on the far side of a long weekend, some aggressive bottle picker had probably just paid a fruitless visit to my back deck. Of course, it might have been the Geocache Butcher, but since I didn't have any real proof it was him, locking my doors and closing my blinds was going to have to be enough. So why did I sit in the desk chair in my dark spare room, staring out the window at my empty yard, the laneway, and the neighbour's yard? I even wrapped myself in the duvet off the Murphy bed, and slid the window open so I could hear footsteps, should someone be sneaking about.

After twenty minutes of watching eight of the neighbouring households return home, walk their dogs, or step out onto their decks for a smoke or a toke, I was cold and tired, and convinced that the bottle picker had come and gone hours or days before and I simply hadn't noticed the open gate. I went to bed, setting my phone's wake-up alarm for eight, with a text reminder to check the gate before trundling off to physio.

oOo

I popped up, wide awake at seven, a full hour before the alarm. It was a dreamless, restful sleep, so I nudged the computer awake, too, to get some work done. Before it was alert and ready, though, a throbbing started up behind my eyes and I wanted to throw up. That's when I remembered the puke puddle from last night, next to the couch. Damn. I really should have cleaned that up before passing out. But first I threw on my coat and boots and ducked out to check the back gate. I looked around, but couldn't see any sign that anyone had been in my yard. Back inside, I put some bread in the toaster, started the electric kettle, and knocked back a small glass of juice to give me strength to deal with the puke.

Karl and Reggie had obviously found the paper towel when they cleaned up my dishwasher fiasco because there was a fresh roll in the upright holder on the counter. I grabbed a couple of old plastic grocery bags from under the sink, a wide serving spoon, and the paper towel. I only hoped that the rug could be saved.

The sight of the vomit—mounded, splashed, and dried—made me gag and nearly hurl again. The toaster popped at that very moment, so I left my cleaning tools on the couch and went back for the toast and tea. I hated cold toast more than I hated cleaning up puke.

While the tea steeped, I took my time nibbling and sipping, knowing full well that as much as I didn't want to attack the mess on the rug, there was no one else to do it. Truth be told, cleaning up the puke wasn't all that tough. I just imagined it as V-Dog vomit, and I'd certainly cleaned up enough of his crab-grass-caused regurgitations over the years. The toast done, I filled a pot with hot water and softened the crustiness with a damp cloth, making it easier to scrape and dab up. It was unpleasant, but it was what it was. The can of spray-on-vacuum-off carpet cleaner was still nearly full, but the directions said to not leave it on for longer than an hour, so it had to wait until after physio. I hardly wanted to clean off the puke only to find I'd bleached the rug.

Instead, I gave the computer my attention for forty minutes, accepting two new jobs and putting the polish on one big one. I was out the door ten minutes before the bus was due to arrive at the stop a five-minute walk away.

Hussein at physio was more patient than I was. He worked and worked on my hand, strengthening the good fingers when it became obvious that the two little ones would never again do more than flop around. The only slightly floppy middle finger seemed to be improving and I promised him I would keep at it. And I would, if for no other reason than it would still be useful at the computer keyboard as I increased my editing and writing work.

As a reward for seeing a little blue sky in my future, I took myself for lunch at the local sushi place and gorged out. I avoided anything with Pacific salmon because I'm a freak about the radiation levels in post-Fukushima-leak Pacific seafood, but there were still plenty of other options. After sushi, I wandered through Walmart and picked up a few odds and ends like moisturizer and cocoa butter for my scars. To keep them supple, Hussein said.

From Wal-Mart I drifted into Best Buy, just to see what new tech was on the shelves, and lastly, I decided to stroll through Michael's craft store. I didn't feel coordinated enough yet to do crafts, but I love the smell of the place, especially in the potpourri and candle aisle. Just as I reached for the automated entry door, I caught the reflection of a gold minivan cruising slowly past, behind me. I spun around so fast that I wobbled. Shaking off the disorientation, I tried to spot the van again, but the big lot was nearly full and he'd vanished behind one of the hundred or so big pick-up trucks and SUVs so prevalent in this oil-and-gas town of conspicuous consumption. Bastard. He was here somewhere. I could *feel* him.

I wanted to charge around the entire parking lot, searching for him, to call him out and force him to tell me what he'd done with Elteen, but I wasn't *that* stupid, yet. Because if I was wrong, I'd look like a complete idiot and Mom would be right about me. I could hear her voice in my head and began to believe I'd imagined the van, so I told myself I was being paranoid and entered the craft store, letting the scents of candles, potpourri, and art supplies distract me, give me something *real* to latch on to. Why in hell would anyone stalk me? I was no one.

I wandered the aisles slowly, although eventually, I had to go home. Since I wasn't buying anything, the store staff gave up trying to help me and just took up watching me out of the corner of their eye whenever they spotted me. Or I was still being paranoid. Either way, it was time to get back behind the barred and locked doors of my sanctuary.

o0o

As soon as I got in the door, I sprayed the pukey rug with cleaner and set about prepping food. Karl and Reggie had bought me all the ingredients for a slow cooker stew, so once it was simmering on an eight-hour countdown, I convinced the computer that it was a perfect time to get some shit done. I was tempted to log into eRomance, but resisted, now that work was fun again. I enjoyed editing, revising, and generally making sense of manuals. There was a pride to be found in making something complicated into something comprehensible and useful, much like interpreting composer's dots and lines into soul-lifting songs of angels. My favourite editing projects were safety manuals because a good safety manual can save lives. Also, I got to watch videos of staged emergencies to assist in my 'translation', and sometimes those videos were unintentionally hilarious. Anything was better than worrying about being too worried. The city was brimming with worry and fear and hate and anger, and my adding to it would only keep my work from getting done, not catch the Butcher.

I took a break to finish cleaning the rug, then another just before six to heat some soup and freshen my coffee while listening to the news on CBC Radio at the top of the hour. There was a riot somewhere, a bombing somewhere else, a trade summit in Asia just winding up, and yet another bit of WTF news from the U.S. I was more than happy when the short newsbreak was done and the music started up again.

I put in a good day of work, feeling stronger than I had in weeks, and even a bit hopeful. If young cello-playing internet sensation Tad Lietz could bow with his foot, and finger with his right hand, maybe I could relearn it all. I poured myself a nice solid rum and Coke and sat down at the island with my soup and saltines. Halfway through the soup, and ten or so crackers into the sleeve, the doorbell rang, scaring the living fuck out of me. I dropped the soup-loaded spoon, splashing the gooey chicken-noodle-cracker mix in my lap, and frantically slipped off the stool, swiping at the mess, trying to keep it from burning my lap.

The doorbell hammered again, twice. I reached for a tea towel to dab at the mess. Thinking that the damned Girl Guide or whoever at the door had better have a merit badge in stain removal and crotch burns. I stomped to the door, threw the bolt, and yanked the big door open, ready to eviscerate whoever had screwed with my meal.

"Mom?" What the *hell*?

Mom hated to be kept waiting, especially by her youngest daughter, so she opened the storm door, looked me up and down with blatant disapproval, and marched right into my house, pushing me aside to do so. She didn't say a word, which was how she usually lit the gaslight under my soul. She always let my imagination run through everything I might possibly have done wrong so that by the time words oozed out of her disapproving slash of a mouth, I was a mess, wracked with guilt. Except that I had nothing to be guilty about this time.

That didn't stop her from trying, though. "Jubilee Jayne." She leaned in and tried to smell my breath. *I* tried not to breathe. "Have you been drinking?"

"I've had half of one drink."

She took her coat off, deliberately making sure it didn't touch my furniture or me, and then she hung it in the closet. "And you've soiled yourself. I knew I was needed here."

"It's chicken soup. I was..."

"Where is it?"

"Where is *what*?" I had no idea what she wanted, but I was glad she was alone. She couldn't interrogate me and search my house at the same time. At least not easily.

"Your crack bong or whatever you're using for your drug hits. You're such a mess that you must be back on the drugs. I worry about you, Jubilee Jayne."

"*Crack bong?*" I made the mistake of laughing, but really, she was too absurd to not find funny.

"Your sister says you've been getting high." She started walking around the main floor, looking for something she probably had no idea what it looked like, yet too finicky to touch anything to pick it up. My house was clean, so her visual scouring for contraband was short-lived.

"I'm *on* medication, Mom, not *doing* drugs." Although until recently I was technically abusing my meds, it was still none of her damned business.

She stopped in the kitchen and turned around, folding her arms over her tall, slender frame. "And you've accused her of stealing your alcohol when all she was doing was trying to you from drowning yourself in misery."

As much as I wanted to shut her down like I did with Joyce, this was *Mom*. Her tongue was sweeter, smarter, and sharper than Joyce's and I was powerless against her death by a thousand cuts. Instead of 'get out of my house, you bitch!' I just said, for no good reason I can think of, "Someone has been watching me."

"Oh, Jubilee Jayne. Come, sit." She led me to the couch, her arm around my shoulder, unaware of my stunned expression. What was she up to?

"Jujube, I did some research and this medication they've prescribed for you causes *hallucinations*. You can't trust anything you see or hear. Add to that all the alcohol you consume, and I'm surprised you can stand upright."

Say what? "Mom, I didn't hallucinate the open gate, and someone has been following me."

"You probably opened the gate to take out your garbage and recycling, forgot to close it, and then forgot that you even opened it in the first place."

"That's not what happened, Mom." Or was it?

"Are you taking drugs?"

"Yes." Although I'd slowed their intake to a trickle.

"Are you still drinking? Rum and Cokes? Whiskey? Wine?"

"Some."

"Do you have any gaps in your memory?"

"No. None."

"So, now you remember what happened on the highway?"

The accident? Only the nightmare version. "Not exactly."

"So, you *do* have gaps. Are you feeling nauseous? Having headaches or shaky hands?"

"Yes." So? Where was she leading this damned conversation?

"That's your head injury, combined with the drugs and alcohol. Are you back smoking pot or snorting cocaine?"

Coke? What the...? "I haven't smoked pot in years, Mom, and I've never done coke in my life."

"Joyce says otherwise. When she was here last week—when you insulted and abused her—she could smell marijuana."

"Not in the house. The kids next door are chronics. It's why I never open the kitchen window." Joyce was so full of shit!

"Then you don't deny the cocaine?"

"I just *did*. Never. No coke. Not even freshman year."

"Well, if you say so, dear. Maybe Joyce got it wrong."

What Juicy got wrong was which one of us was doing coke at that party, and since I promised her I'd *never* tell, this is how she repaid me. "She did, Mom. She got it *very* wrong."

"Maybe so, but I'm still worried about these things you're imagining. Let me fix us some tea. Why don't you go get cleaned up and put on something nice, like that dress we got you for your birthday."

She was right that I needed to get cleaned up, but that a dress, though? And she was worried *I* was on drugs? Biting my tongue, as usual, I went upstairs, gave my face a leisurely wash, scrubbed my teeth, and brushed my hair before changing into tights and a big sweater. I may be powerless against Mom's presence, but I could still stand up for myself in the little ways. Besides, that dress was an insulting bag; the kind of gift you give when you want to insult someone by saying they're not good enough for something stylish or pretty. The kind of gift my family had repeatedly shoved my way for more years than was healthy to count.

The tea was ready and waiting on the counter when I finally wandered back downstairs. Mom sat on a stool at the island, sipping hers. As I sock-shuffled past her I could smell the rye emanating from her cup. It warmed my twisted heart to know that the woman who gave me shit for being a drunk and an addict was still carrying her own secret little stash. She used to have a purse with a secret flask pocket, but nowadays I think she was using a hollowed-out copy of "Atlas Shrugged". I shudder to think that she probably read and enjoyed Ayn Rand's propaganda shit.

"Well, that's a bit of an improvement. Better to dress like a twelve-year-old than a mental patient, I suppose."

"Or a twelve-year-old mental patient," you miserable cow.

"You're always quick with the jokes to hide the truth, Jubilee." She took a sip, probably giving me a chance for joking or denial, but I sipped, too. Silent. "We're worried about you."

Bullshit, they were.

"You pushed James away until all you had was that wonderful dog and your lovely symphony, and now you don't even have those. Even though I'm your mother, they wouldn't show me the police report, but Joyce wonders if maybe you had been drinking when you slammed into that other car and killed the driver. I mean, what sober person goes off to meet some stranger from the internet?"

I sat, stunned. I truly had nothing to say. No argument I could give her would carry any weight because I didn't remember enough of the day. I sipped tea, hoping she didn't notice my white knuckles on the cup. Was I drunk that day? No! I *never* drink and drive. I remember being nervous about meeting Niko. I remember V-Dog being excited about the car ride. I remember...nothing else clearly, for certain. I've had so many different nightmares about that day that I can't separate truth from dream. Was Mom *right*? Or was she gaslighting me again, making me think I was wrong, that she was the one who knew the truth, the whole truth, and nothing but the truth?

"And now you won't come to my birthday. Well, seeing you like this, I think that might be best. Maybe a few more months with your psychologist are in order before you start coming to family functions again. It would hardly be good for you to sit moping in a corner popping pills and doing shots like the world is ending. Take some time, Jubilee. Get healthy. Let Joyce and I help. Or even your father. You always preferred him to me. Maybe you two could take a drive to Banff for some fresh air."

Um, did Mom just let me off the hook from family functions? That was a dream come true, except that I was pretty sure she'd spend the entire time telling everyone who would listen about how hard she was trying to help her snowflake-fragile little girl, but was being fought the whole way. So sad, poor Jubilee Jayne.

"Just let your father do the driving."

My head spun, less like vertigo and more like a one-two hit with a heavy feather pillow—less pain and more stunned disorientation. Mom was an expert. She could pummel me down without leaving a bruise.

I needed a drink, but not in front of her, so I sipped my tea and tried to stay steady. I remained quiet, hoping she would take the hint and just leave me alone. Maybe the accident made me a physical cripple but Mom got all the credit for me being a psycha-plegic. I mean really, there's no way I could have been drinking before heading out to meet Niko. *No way.* Was there? Dammit. I stared at my mug, mute.

At some point, Mom must have realized that her work here was done and I was down for the count, because she slipped off her stool, rinsed her cup of all evidence, and left. No goodbye, no hug, no kiss on the cheek that caring parents do on television when their children are upset. She pretty much shit in my cornflakes and walked out, leaving the air thick with doubt, as usual.

I knew I wasn't crazy, but I was pretty sure I could hear my warm rum and coke calling my name. After I bolted the front door behind her, I drank, knowing that whatever had happened in the past, I sure as hell wasn't driving anywhere tonight. I took my drink over to the couch and sipped, but no matter how hard I squeezed my eyes shut and concentrated, I couldn't remember whether I'd had a drink to fortify myself *before* meeting Niko. I remember being nervous as shit, changing outfits twice, and starting to text him three times to cancel—and I remember taking V-Dog across to the park to pee before we left, but no yay or nay on the booze.

Again, could she be right? I was spending so much time in a haze now that it sort of made sense. Do I drink because of the accident, or was the accident because I'd been drinking? Fuck fuck fuckety fuck.

This time I drank to forget not remembering, which was as good a reason as any. Let me be clear here. Even after James lit out for the Vancouver Island I didn't drink much, especially at home. The wine in my 'cellar' had been for social events like symphony potlucks and birthday parties. The hard stuff was for the occasional chill-down after a long concert tour. The bottle of rum in my fridge was nearly six months old. V-Dog had kept me too active to be continuously buzzed like most of my family. I grew up with alcoholics, so I'm consciously aware of my addiction risks, but damn-it-all, could Mom be right about the day of the accident?

I dozed off on the couch around eight with Sandra Bullock's *The Lost City* playing and woke up fuzzy and feeling more than a little blech, with the Roku screensaver dancing on the screen. I checked my phone and was surprised to see that it was only eleven. I reached for the warm but tolerable remains of my drink and remembered that Charlie was picking me up in nine hours.

There was no way I was going to be in any shape to birdwatch at that damned hour, so I sent off a text asking if we could postpone it, that I wasn't feeling well and needed sleep. I hoped she would get my note before she left in the morning.

Before I even finished swallowing my next sip, my phone chimed at me. Charlie's note was simple. "How about we go out in the afternoon, instead? About three?"

I started to type that another day would be better, but I remembered the look on her face when I said 'yes' in the first place. Besides, an afternoon in the park would be good for *both* of us. I deleted the started text and just sent "Thx. 3 is perfect." She replied a moment later with a smiley face.

I pushed up from the couch, took my glass to the sink and dumped out the last little bit. Maybe I didn't remember the day of the accident, but I couldn't let my mother keep crushing my soul, even if she was right. I took a double dose of vitamin B to quell the quickening tempo of the doubts starting up again, then got my ass off to bed... but not before checking all the doors and windows. Someone was watching me, I was sure of it. I wasn't crazy, dammit.

Chapter Thirteen

I f I wasn't crazy, then my nightmares must belong to someone who was. I tripped right back into that damned snowstorm accident hell again and woke up screaming and soaked
and exhausted. I got up, shuffled to the bathroom, threw water
in my face, dragged myself back to bed, and fell back to sleep almost immediately. I dreamed again, this time of owls watching
me, sitting in trees, on eaves, and even driving a bus, but they
only watched. They blinked and stared and turned their heads
on those freaky pivot necks, following me every which way I
moved, like silent judges who knew my crimes, even if I didn't.

I was a bit wobbly on my feet as I made up my veggie-loaded
omelette. I was tempted to pop a happy pill but held off out of
sheer stubbornness. Screwed-up thoughts still bounced around
in my head, so another dose of Vit B and my previously neglected Omega 3s went into me before I pulled the stool up
to the island and forked back my omelette-on-toast. Mom's
suggestion that I'd been driving drunk was still niggling at me,
like her bony poking finger, over and over. I knew there was
no way, but Mom had turned up the gaslight just enough to
introduce serious doubt, which, of course, was her superpower.
She played emotions like I once played Mozart and Chopin.

Making and eating breakfast forced me to slow down, which was a good thing, a thing I needed. I also needed a bath—a long, slow, men-never-understand-this-kind-of-bath bath.

The tub of hot love embraced me, seduced me, and heated up my core so high that when I was done, I slipped back into my jammies, donned my winter gear, and went out to my reading gazebo in the backyard. It was just a little three-sided hut with a bench, a table, and an Adirondack chair on the gravel bed—a place out of the wind and rain, but it was outside in the cool, fresh air.

I undid my jacket to let the heat out and planted myself in the chair, setting the timer on my phone for an hour, just to be safe. If I fell asleep, I didn't want to freeze to death and be found weeks later. I was still radiating heat like a bread oven, so I pulled the hood back and took my mitts off. The heat was slow to dissipate, but I could feel my body cooling off. My mind still stumbled in dissonance after my time with Mom, but she wasn't here right now, so I pushed back a bit and got myself some mental distance. I needed restful adagio, not schizo scherzo.

Karl was right when he said my family was toxic, but I've known this for years. The problem wasn't the soul-draining sludge they called 'love' and 'caring', but rather *my* inability to break free of them. How do you just cut off family and walk away? Do I treat them like an abusive former lover or a bullying boss who screwed me over so I quit but now I can't find another job? If I still had Gavroche and could draw his songs out with the bow, then there were cities where I could find a home with an ensemble of some sort. But there was no Gavroche and no songs, just the shackles of my family in a city where a serial killer hunted women like a hawk hunts sparrows.

I pulled my hood up and closed my eyes. My cousin Susan once told me that she dealt with the shit in her life by visualizing each problem, bundling it up, putting it into the basket of an imaginary hot air balloon, then letting it go, to float up away from her. One problem, one balloon. One at a time. So, I tried it. I envisioned Mom and Joyce as tiny little dolls. I imagined picking each of them by the collars and placing them in a festively decorated little balloon like the one in The Wizard of Oz.

Of course, they wouldn't stay as inert dolls and just *had* to come to life to shake their fists at me and scream, but because it was *my* imagination, I pictured them as mute. With one hand I pulled the slipknot from the string anchoring the balloon to a hook in the ground, and up, up and away they went. I imagined that there was no gazebo roof over my head, so they rose quickly because I wanted to be quit of them as soon as possible, and mini-Joyce shook her fist and mute-screamed the entire time. When she was nearly out of sight, a mere speck of a bitch in the sky, I smiled up at her and flipped her the bird. It felt great.

That's the last thing I remember before the alarm woke me from the nap my body decided I needed. I was cold and stiff, but not so cold that I regretted falling asleep. It took a moment to get oriented and coordinated, but I got it together and went back inside. Since my parka was a little heavy for hiking and birding in late April, I hung it back in the closet and tucked my big boots beneath it, on the rack. I still had about three hours before Charlie picked me up, so lots of time for a little work, and a little rum.

Yeah, I know. But this was the *good* kind of rum   a celebratory one. I'd opened a new door in my 'relationship' with my family and had walked clean on through to the other side, and *that* called for a fucking celebration. I stayed in my jammies, woke up the computer, and dug into one of the smaller editing jobs in the queue.

o0o

At 2:55 I was bundled up and waiting with a rum-laced, dark-chocolate-mint cocoa in my to-go mug. Two 16-gig SD cards were tucked into my pocket, ready for whatever bird action we would find. The idea of holding a camera steady with my claw had me a little wound up, but I'd deal with it when it happened. I sipped the cocoa, a bit tired of rum. I fumbled my phone out of my pocket and started a list of items to restock now that Joyce was verboten in my domicile. There needed to be Irish Cream of some sort, Uncle Nearest 1856 bourbon, and maybe an Ice Wine, to accompany the occasional self-indulgent dessert.

A car door slammed outside so I got up and opened the front door just as Charlie arrived at the stoop. She was all Xena-smile in khaki and leather, again straight out of the 'Tall & Lanky' section of the L. L. Bean catalogue.

"Hi. I just heard from a friend that the owlets are active today and there are a couple of snow geese hanging around before continuing their migration north."

Owls and snow geese? "Lead the way, Annie Leibovitz!"

She got the reference and her smile expanded. "Hardly, but thanks." Instead of an old gold Dodge Caravan, she drove a nice dark green Subaru Forester that she was very proud of, based on its showroom-spotless condition, inside and out. Unless of course she was like me and cleaned it this morning because she knew she was going to have company. The little plastic surfboard air freshener hanging from the mirror was a nice touch, speaking of dreams of somewhere else.

"How are you feeling?" It was nice of her to ask.

"Better, thanks." A sip of the cocoa made it even better still. "I had an unexpected visitor last evening, and she got me a little wound up." A little?

"I don't even answer my door if someone hasn't given me a warning that they're coming over. I like my little cave. Always have."

"I wouldn't have answered either, but my mother is one persistent bi—, *woman,* and would have rung the bell all night long or called the fire department to break down the door."

"Family...the people in our lives that we don't get to choose. My parents died years ago, so it's not a problem. I talk to my brother, but only occasionally."

Not talking to or hearing from Joyce would be wonderful. "My sister and parents are very much alive and *very* much here in town. I'm not quite at the point of changing my phone number, but I did take back my spare key last week."

She laughed. "I'll bet *that* felt great."

"Damn straight it did!"

"You have to exercise the power you have, and work slowly to take back as much as you can."

She sounded like she was speaking from experience, not just spouting Instagram platitudes. "It's tough to find a balance between retaking your power and trusting others to help you," I added. Reggie and Karl were my complete trust circle right now. Even Dr. Ella had a way to go before it felt like she was being more than a professional hired to do a job. She was brilliant at that job, and I know she cared, but I still don't know if she would be completely on my side if things got fucked up.

"I don't trust," she admitted. "It's easier. I chat, I listen, but I rarely open up. No one gets in, except maybe Dr. Ella. I even closed my Facebook account. My friends try to set me up on dates, just to get me out of the house, but I can't. I even tried a dating website, but they're nothing but liars and lies."

She glanced over at me as she guided her car into the park parking lot. There was something odd in her expression like she was waiting for me to take a hint that I just wasn't getting. Just as I was thinking I could trust her and had maybe found someone I could open up to, my instincts hit a sour note and I decided to keep playing it safe. "My Facebook account is still open, but I haven't posted anything in a while. I used to tweet and blog, but not so much anymore. Each day, same refrain, just in a different key."

We parked, but instead of getting out of the car, Charlie reached behind me. I don't know why, but I bristled, tense, and reached for the door handle, ready to run. She pulled a small black camera bag out of the back seat and handed it to me. I relaxed. Holy shit, I was wound up!

"Here's my little Nikon." I took the camera out of the bag. "Your memory card goes in *here*." She pointed to the battery compartment, "and this is the power button. I've got it set on Sports Mode, so it will shoot as fast as it can. Here's the zoom, and this is the shutter release. Press it halfway down to focus, all of the way to take the picture. Pretty much the same as any digital camera, though a little more complicated than a phone."

"Easy peasy. Thank you." I popped open the battery compartment, inserted one of my SD cards, and checked the display to make sure everything was ready to go. The camera was built like a bigger SLR but was self-contained and small enough to be used by someone with just one hand and a claw.

"I have the spare batteries in my pocket, so you don't need to carry the bag. All ready?"

I pushed aside the stupid niggling feeling and took a breath. "Ready. Let's go hunt some owls." I was psyched, and the zoom on the camera looked *long*, so I hoped for some great photos, provided the owls were home. We got out of the car and Charlie fetched her *much* bigger camera and a tripod out of the back seat. She also took out a drab-olive, multi-pocketed photographer's vest, and once she had it on, with the camera hanging from her neck and the tripod over her shoulder, she looked like a combat photographer in Afghanistan or some other war zone. Tall, broad, and suited up, she gave off a solid don't-screw-with-me vibe. Lara Croft with a camera. I was completely jealous.

She locked the car with a beep of the remote and smiled. I wanted to like her, but there was a lost hollowness in her eyes that worried me. I smiled back, masking my worry with excitement, and followed her down the trail.

And that's when it hit me. We were marching into Fish Creek Provincial Park, where the Butcher geocached body parts. I hadn't been here since before the left hand of his first victim was found. *Now* I wished I had a gun instead of a camera. What I *did* have, though, was my strength-giving cocoa forte. I took a half-dozen good solid sips to bolster my courage. The double kick of chocolate and rum bolstered me from the toes on up.

We walked slowly, Charlie pointing out big, dark, woodpecker holes hammered out of course bark and soft meat of tall trees, the yards-wide areas of flattened grass where deer bedded down recently, and a fifteen-foot-tall stump where a Canada goose peeked up over the rim.

"Canada geese nest in trees?" I had no idea. It was so bizarre that I had to get a picture. Charlie waited patiently while I figured out the camera and took a three-shot burst.

"They do, in a hollow stump, when they can. I suspect that it keeps them safer from some of the predators, and it's easier to defend. Sometimes they move into the man-made osprey roosts before the ospreys have migrated back, and the park staff try to shoo them out before they lay any eggs. The ospreys are raptors, but they're not stupid. There aren't a lot of birds that will take on a Canada goose. Their forewing is strong enough to break your arm, and the bill on the end of that long neck strikes like a cobra. I've been chased more than once."

"Me, too, but only because I wouldn't give up my sandwich at Prince's Island Park." The big bastards ruined James' and my second date. Then again, maybe I should thank them because we fled back to his apartment where we ended up shagging like mink on his worn-out bachelor couch until neither of us had the strength to walk. So, mixed feelings about Canadian geese.

For the first time since I was a kid, I paid *real* attention to the woods. There was the high, nasal *ank ank* that Charlie said was a red-breasted nuthatch, the staccato hammering of a woodpecker quickly spotted in the distance and confirmed to be a yellow-bellied sap-sucker, then the various chirps and tweets of the dozens of black-capped chickadees around us.

Charlie stopped on the trail. "Get the camera ready, Jubilee, and aim it at my hand when I raise it." She took her left glove off as she spoke.

What? I did as she said, and within seconds of her opening her hand up and away from her, there was a chickadee on it. I was so shocked that I almost dropped the camera. I did manage one frantic photo before the little cutie was gone. "Oh my God!"

"I know! If I'd had seeds in my hand there would be two or three of them, or even a woodpecker, like that picture I showed you, but it's illegal to feed the animals in the park. Of course, if I just put my hand out to stretch my fingers and a bird happens to land on it, who can blame me for taking a picture before she flies away?"

I smiled. "I like how you think." Letting the camera hang around my neck, I held out my right hand, high and open. Charlie lifted her camera and was ready. The chickadees nattered at us from the branches around us, and one or two darted past my head, but none landed.

Charlie lowered her camera. "They're smart. We fooled them once, but won't fool them a second time without food. Want to go find some owls?"

"Of course!"

It turned out that we didn't have much farther to go, and when we arrived at the clearing there were already two seriously serious photographers there with cornet-sized cameras and lenses pointed up at a barren tree at the edge of the clearing. They smiled and nodded and Charlie waved hello, but everyone remained respectfully silent except for the snaps of our footsteps on the twigs, needles, and leaves of the forest floor.

Figuring that their cameras were pointed at something interesting, I followed their line of sight but didn't see anything except the tree. Then the tree moved and I let out a soft 'wow'. Sitting on a thick branch, close to the trunk and blending in almost perfectly, was something big and grey. I took the camera out of standby mode and pointed it at the greyness. Zooming in increments, I tried to zero in on it. After a couple of wobbly tries, I got it on the view screen and kept zooming in.

Holy shit! It was a Great Horned owl! He was looking right at me! He was *huge*, eighteen inches tall, at least. I pressed the shutter button down and hoped I was holding the camera steady enough. Beside me, I could hear Charlie's big Canon snapping four or five frames a second. I risked a peek over at her and she was using her tripod like a monopod, the legs still together, not spread out, yet. The grin on her face told me everything I needed to know—Charlie was in her element. I went back to snapping my photos. They looked damned good on the little screen during that brief preview after each shot, so I kept going.

I got so caught up in it that I forgot my claw and just snapped away. It was a huge memory card so I kept going until one of the other photographers gasped and turned her attention to a twenty-foot-tall stump to our right. She pointed, smiled, and quick-as-a-wink spun her camera around and was shooting away like a mad woman. The second one joined in and after a moment, so did Charlie. I couldn't see what they were looking at until Charlie leaned in and pointed up at a big opening a yard from the top of the stump.

Eyes peeked up over the rim and blinked. I had the camera up and zoomed in as fast as I could. A baby owl! What a rush! I wondered why Papa Owl was so calm, but so far away. Then Mama Owl rose into view next to the owlet and I understood. Papa was calm because he was completely confident in Mama's ability to defend their baby. A third head popped up! *Twins!* Mama glared at all of us, then chirped something that sounded a lot like a reprimand. All three heads dropped down out of sight.

A glossy, long-tailed, black-and-white magpie skirted around the outside of the clearing, swooping amidst the trees, but he stayed away from the stump and the open sky, probably well aware of the Great Horned Papa nearby and knowing damn well how dangerous the clearing was. That's when I noticed how the few other birds kept their distance. The sparrows and chickadees were around us, but just a bit removed. It made perfect sense. Why risk *being* lunch just to *get* lunch? I sipped my cocoa forte and turned back to the tall stump.

Another photographer sauntered down the trail, and joined us, nodding a greeting. Dressed in walking shoes, jeans, and a lightweight spring coat, he hardly looked like a bird watcher prepared to sit or stand patiently for hours, but his camera was similar enough to the one on Charlie's tripod that I knew he was serious about photography.

His eyes were shielded by imitation Ray-Bans and his dark green baseball cap cast his bearded face in shadow, but there was something familiar about him. By the way he cast sideways glances at me, I got the impression he was trying to place where he knew me as well.

There was sudden motion in the stump nest and we all lifted our cameras, ready. The owlets both rose into view behind Mama, so I snapped away, just as the others did. Something was off, though. Something was just not right. Or I was a little drunk. Without lowering the camera, I turned quickly to look at the secretive newcomer and caught him with his camera pointed at Charlie and me, not at the nest.

"What the hell?!" Charlie and the others turned. "You want a picture of my ass, you ask, douchebag. You don't just stand behind me and snap away while I'm distracted." If the camera in my hand wasn't a loaner, I probably would have swung it at his head. Who the fuck did he think he was, anyway?

He didn't argue or protest. He just lowered his camera, muttered an apology and left. He was probably one of those assholes who rode escalators just to take up-skirt photos.

Charlie took a step closer to me. "You OK?"

"He was taking pictures of me taking pictures. How screwed up is *that*?" I lifted my travel mug out of my big pocket and took a couple of good stiff drinks, trying to ignore my shaking hands. The cocoa felt great all the way down, but it didn't suppress my nausea. Was someone following me? Or was he just some random asshole who thought I had a nice ass?

"Do you know him?"

"I don't know. He looks like someone I saw on the weekend, or maybe it was on the train yesterday." Was he the man on 17th Avenue in the bomber jacket? No, he couldn't be. This creep had a beard, Bomber Jacket didn't. A man could shave a beard off in minutes, but I'd never yet met one who could grow it full and furry in three days. I shook it off but wondered if he drove a gold minivan. Would the Butcher be stupid enough to walk right up behind us in broad daylight? With trembling hands, I chugged back the rest of the cocoa, less eager for the chocolate than the alcohol.

"He's gone, Jubilee. Off toward the boat launch, east of here."

Charlie's voice barely registered. My pulse pounded in my ears. My breaths were shallow and fast and no matter how hard I tried to slow down and breathe in through my mouth and out through my nose, I couldn't change the tempo. Or was it in through my nose and out through my mouth? A dangerous feeling was growing in my stomach like a super-hot ghost pepper had been dropped straight down inside me. It was hot lava, it was cold fear, it was wrenching acid, it was—I wobbled.

Chapter Fourteen

"Jubilee! *What's wrong?*" Big hands grabbed my shoulders, and although my gut churned, my hands shook, and my head swam, the grip on my shoulders steadied me. I needed out of this place! I needed to be safely inside with the doors locked and bolted and barricaded and welded shut. I needed to be Butcher-free, I needed Vivaldidog, I needed Elteen, I needed to be held and told I was safe... "I need to go home. I'm sorry."

Oddly enough, Charlie's expression wasn't one of hurt or confusion. She nodded slowly, knowingly. "Done. Let's get out of here." She motioned me to go ahead of her.

"No. You go first, Charlie. I'll stay close, but I probably couldn't remember the way back right now." I was seriously screwed up, and the cocoa forte wasn't helping at all. She led the way and although I stumbled on my first steps, I steadied and mostly kept up to her long strides.

Without stopping to tease chickadees or gawk at geese in trees, the walk didn't take long at all. Charlie must have had a pretty good understanding of what I was going through because she didn't say a word, just got us to the car and out of there. I managed a simple "Thank you," as we exited the park. She took me straight home, although I'd sort of hoped she would take a meandering route, to keep anyone from following us. Then again, if someone was stalking me, he probably already knew where I lived.

She turned around in my cul-de-sac and pulled up right in front of the house. "Will you be OK? I'll stay and watch you go in and lock the door behind you. Unless you want me to come in and make sure it's safe before I leave."

Make sure it's safe? The *inside* of my home? I managed a weak "No thanks. I'm fine. I'm sorry about this." But I *did* want her to come in, so *she* could be safe, too.

To her credit, she didn't touch me, a relative stranger having a meltdown, she simply nodded. "You have nothing to apologize for, Jubilee. He's an asshole. Now, if you need anything, please call. I'll help any way I can." She left it at that.

I nodded back. Quickly, I popped my memory card out of the camera, fumbling a bit to hold the device with my claw. Then the camera went into the bag and the SD card into my pocket. As I opened the Subaru's door, I found my voice again. "Thank you, Charlie. I'm sorry." I fled back into my refuge, throwing the bolt behind me, then freezing in place. Did I hear a scrape of a boot on hardwood? The rattle of a doorknob? Or maybe it was heavy footfall on the carpet upstairs.

Fuck fuck *fuck*! I couldn't live like this! Coat and boots still on, I stomped into the kitchen, grabbed the dirty Henkel carving knife from the sink, then boldly, methodically, *angrily*, searched my home from top to bottom and front to back—every nook and shadow. When I was damn well sure I was alone, I poured myself a stiff drink and settled on the couch, the knife placed on the wooden TV table in front of me.

The top half of the tumbler emptied quickly but I slowed down a bit for the bottom half, feeling the stress either drain slowly away or get so numbed down that it was muted by the tangle in my head. By the time I was down to no more than a splash in the bottom of the glass, I wasn't sure I needed another. I was chill and calm and fuzzy around the edges. I drifted off.

Thankfully, my sleep was dreamless, though it was interrupted once or twice by the phone ringing. None of them were Elteen's ringtone. Eventually, I shook off the Sandman's grip to get up and go to the bathroom, and the phone beeped at me, so I fetched it and read the message. Karl and Reggie. I fired back a quick note to reassure them that all was good and that I'd call them around ten in the morning. There was no way I wanted them rushing over at this insane hour, especially since I was pretty sure I was finally going to be OK. My emotional fever had finally broken, and to prove it, I decided to stop drinking. Immediately. And to get my ass upstairs and into my bed. So, the doors were bolted and the Geocache Butcher was nowhere in sight. Of course, if he was any good at stalking, I wouldn't see him until it was too late. In an OCD moment, I double-checked the door bolts and window locks; then I scrubbed and brushed my face, hair, and teeth, set the alarm for nine, and climbed into bed. The Sandman must have been hiding just out of sight around the corner because sleep came quickly.

o0o

Except for a hint of a headache, I woke up reasonably well-rested. I showered, then, after checking that the back gate was still latched and no one was lurking in my yard, I took the time to fill my belly with solid goodness with a barbequed steak and a side of eggs. Every single bite was a charge to my battery and another brick in the wall between me and another meltdown. I didn't plan to leave the house, but since Dr. Ella had recommended getting up and getting dressed every day, even to work at home, I was happy to change out of my pyjamas.

Happy? Sure, I knew brief moments of happiness, but I wanted more—deserved more—than a bunch of happy moments strung together with shit and meltdowns, and looking over my shoulder for some geocaching asshole. I needed to make a list, a place to start, things to do to drag my crippled, whiny, sorry, sad ass out of the hell I'd built for myself. I used to be a huge list-maker and they helped me get organized and get done what needed doing, but James started mocking my lists, so I made fewer and fewer until I was down to only two—groceries, and things to pack for concert tours.

I opened my phone's list-making app and thumb-typed my way back into the old comfortable pattern.

Chapter Fifteen

As per item two on my new list, I called Reggie to check-in. Once I was sure that *he* was sure I was OK, I hung up and called Charlie to apologize again for cutting yesterday short.

"Would you like to come to the gun range with me?" What? I had no idea how to respond to that question, but she seemed to understand. "I was introduced to shooting-as-therapy last year and now I teach classes at the Calgary Target Training Centre. The point isn't to turn you into a killer but to help you regain your confidence. Martial arts like karate and Tae Kwan Do do the same thing. We strive to give participants back a sense of control over the world around them."

"Guns, eh?" It could be interesting.

"It's not for everyone."

"They don't bother me." Music had been my shield, but with that gone I needed something to give me back some power, or confidence, or whatever. Hell, even as a hobby it would help because drinking and weeping and panic attacks are hardly shareable past-times. "Just say when. Can I get there by transit?"

"You can. Or I can pick you up. How's tomorrow? The range is pretty quiet before noon on Fridays. I'll text you the address and you can decide whether you'll take transit or want a ride." I could hear the smile in her voice. I had to start trusting people sometime, and a gun range would be the definitive litmus test. At least if the

Butcher showed up, I'd be armed. "Tomorrow is great. I think it'll be fun."

"I *know* it will. I just have one favour to ask, Jubilee.

"Sure. Go ahead."

"No 'special' cocoa, please."

No cocoa? What? Oh. "Of course not, Charlie. One of the leaves I've turned over since last night was a liquid one. I'm going to have a go at sobriety."

"I think that's a wonderful idea. I've been sober for two years now. If you can't handle it alone and you eventually need a sponsor, I'll be happy to help."

"Thank you." AA? Please God don't let me be *that* far gone. I'm not my family.

We finished up with Charlie repeating her promise to forward me the address and me wishing her a nice day, which always sounds lame coming out of my mouth but I appreciate it when it's said to me, so I hoped the feeling was mutual.

Determined to make permanent changes and not just road bumps to be forgotten not long after I've left them behind in my emotional mirror, I retrieved the bottle of rum from the fridge and poured it down the sink. The intense, sugary, slightly medicinal smell of Jamaica's best as it spread out like an amber soul around the bottom of the stainless-steel sink nearly convinced me that one more drink would be OK, just to give the rum a fond farewell. *Nearly.* I clutched the edge of the countertop with my claw and kept pouring. My good hand and the bottle shook a little, but nevertheless, I persisted. After that went the remains of the mead and the one bottle of merlot. I ran the hot water into the sink to dilute and expedite the purging, and maybe remove the temptation to lick the sink of residue.

Thanks to Joyce, that was all that was left of my formerly extensive cellar. Thank God the boys didn't take me to the liquor store when we picked up groceries. I hated to waste money, but it *all* had to go. I rinsed the empty bottles, dropped them into the recycling bin, and made myself a nice Lavazza Italian roast from one of the bags in the freezer. It was going to be a long day and I needed to start it with a delicious kick. I took the steaming mug to my desk, and popped the SD card loaded with yesterday's photos into the card reader plugged into the computer to see if they were any good. My expectations were low, given that I had been supporting the camera with a floppy-fingered claw and not a tripod.

Once Photoshop was open, I scrolled through the images much larger than the camera's little three-inch screen. I was right. They were blurry as shit, but as I scrolled through from the beginning, I noticed that they got clearer and clearer until finally there was a perfectly focused image of the owlets.

"Wow." I remembered that shot, too, because I had just changed my grip on the camera and it felt better in my hands. I scrolled through the remaining photos. Most of them sucked, but there were a couple of gems that might look good in small frames on my wall. Not bad for a first day out. As minor as the success was, it was something positive, and encouraging.

I went online and did a little research, checking out reviews of various digital cameras. I quickly narrowed the choices to three—two Nikons and a Canon, based on their features and their prices. I wasn't quite ready to sink a small fortune into a big camera but a few hundred dollars was do-able. I printed off the sheet with the specs for all three and took it over to the couch, along with my coffee. My headache was still present and accounted for, but it was slipping back to a slow, soft beat I could ignore with a little effort.

The three cameras all looked great, but I ended up picking the one with the biggest sensor, the longest zoom, and pre-set modes that included moon photos and bird-watching. It looked a lot like Charlie's little one, and judging by the model number, it was probably the updated version. Five minutes later I'd ordered it from Amazon, along with a bag and a light but sturdy tripod.

Booze: gone. Camera: invested in. Emotions: Still screwed up, but with a little closure I could see a faint light at the end of a tunnel. Or maybe it was a train coming. With Elteen still missing, and V-Dog still gone, sometimes it's hard to tell the difference. I fired off a text to Reggie.

Are either of you gentlemen available on Saturday to crash a party? If I was going to take my life back, then crashing Mom's birthday party might just be the best terrible idea of the week. Reggie didn't take long to text back to me that he was available because Karl was in Vancouver until Sunday afternoon. We texted back and forth until we had all of the details set, including the gift I was going to bring that he would pick up. I wanted to bring something sinister like rotten meat to reflect what having them as a family had done to me, but Reggie, bless his heart, suggested rather strongly that I take the high road and show them all what class *is*. It was Mom's sixtieth, and she loved roses, so Reggie put forth the idea that an arrangement of silk roses would be more appropriate.

It was a much nicer gesture than I owed her, that's for sure. I argued for cut roses so they could die like my love for them, but Reggie nixed that idea, too, saying it would be better if she had a daily reminder. Mom would be torn between keeping something perfect for her tastes and tossing out a reminder that I didn't play their game anymore.

Now I had a camera kit and some fancy schmancy silk arrangement to pay for, which meant I needed to move my ass from the couch back to the desk and earn my keep. I woke the laptop with a tap on the touchpad on my way past into the kitchen, and by the time I had another mug of java and retrieved a couple of decadent cookies from the freezer, the laptop was ready to earn my keep.

I spent three hours slogging through my work—slogging not because the work was tedious, but because I was still a little tremolo around the edges and unable to completely banish the headache. At the three-hour mark, the gurgling of my stomach dropped a not-so-subtle hint in my lap that I was hungry, again.

If I was serious about recovery, eating regularly and properly was going to be necessary. I went with a sandwich and soup, doing minor strengthening flexibility exercises with my claw while eating with my good hand. There was a shitload of work to be done, but I had nowhere else I had to be, so slow and easy it was. By the time the last spoonful of canned Campbell's was slurped up, the headache was finally gone and more resolve had waltzed into its place.

The dishes went into the dishwasher, slowly and carefully. I stretched the kinks out of my back, clicked on the eRomance bookmark, and finally sat back down to continue the 21st Century courtship ritual. There was still nothing from Niko, but I found that I didn't give a shit anymore. Every single one of the other men had sent a reply of one sort or another, but only *TerryChef32* appeared to have read and understood my note. He seemed very sweet, but I was quickly losing my taste for net-dating. I closed the browser without answering any of the notes, but I also didn't delete any of them, so no doors were closed, yet.

The contracted manuals weren't going to write or edit them-selves, so work easily overruled my 'need to breed'. I checked my phone for the text from Charlie and quickly found the gun range address online. I texted her that I'd meet her there at ten, then I dug in deep with the computer and lost myself again in the job at hand and claw.

o0o

The sun gave up and set not long before I called it quits for the day. I was finally dragged out of my work groove by a photo text from Reggie of a nice silk arrangement he'd picked up for Mom at a shop around the corner from their condo. I sent him a quick thank-you-love-you note, tossed a bowl of my slow-cooker stew in the microwave, and started up Netflix. Thoughts of seeing my family all at once got my gut churning a little, but the stew would mute the rest of the churning. I thought of popping a Happy pill, but fought the temptation and soldiered on, instead opting for vitamin B. I couldn't condemn my family for their substance issues if I was leaning heavily on one or another myself.

I lasted fifteen minutes into a crappy remake of *The Saint* before I gave up and put myself to bed for the night.

oOo

I was up at seven, reread and fine-tuned some of my late-night edits, showered, ate, checked my list for the day and calendar reminders on my phone, then ventured out into the warming-up-fast day, where the peonies in the bed under my bay window were starting to wake up and shake off the last of the cold weather. As I walked to the bus stop, I looked around for any sign of the geocaching prick's van, but apparently, he wasn't in my 'hood today. The more I thought about it, the more certain I was that he was the asshole at the park on Wednesday and I should tell the detective. It's too bad that with all those cameras none of us had taken a picture of him. I sent Detective Marlin a text just saying that we may have met the Butcher in the park. I'm sure he'd read me the riot act when he saw that we'd gone into the lion's den just to take pictures of birds, but what was done was done.

Feeling cocky and ready to take on the world now that I believed I could survive in it—even without V-Dog or my music—I stuck my earbuds in and hit shuffle on my only playlist. After a beat, my head filled with Bach's Orchestral Suite #1 in C, and although my heart ached, I forged ahead. "Fuck it," I said out loud, not caring who might hear the crazy neighbourhood cripple talking to herself.

Detective Marlin called me back not long after the bus reached the train station. "Ms. Krawetz, if you were my daughter, you'd be grounded."

"I'm sorry. But it was broad daylight and I was with someone I trusted. We were with others, too."

"Were these others armed, and trained to deal with a psychopath?"

Good question. "To be honest, I have no idea. We were all just taking pictures of the owls."

"Why do you think this man is the Geocache Butcher?"

"Well, he fit the profile, and he wasn't taking pictures of the owls, he was taking pictures of me."

"That's it? Can you describe him, please?"

I told him everything I could remember about his height, weight, facial features, colouring, and clothing. "And he looked familiar, like I've seen him on the train and then on the street following me downtown on Saturday, although he didn't have a beard then." Holy shit was I sounding stupid.

"Did you speak with him?"

"On Saturday, no. In the park, yes. I gave him shit for taking pictures of us and he mumbled an apology and walked away."

"OK. Did this man appear to have any weapons, a hiker's GPS, or even his phone out with a geocaching app on it?"

"Um, no. He also didn't have a bag big enough for a head."

"I didn't think he would. We now believe that he's not just using geocaching as a way to taunt the police and the media but that he's part of the actual geocaching community. You said that the photo of you and your goddaughter was taken while you were doing a geocaching course?"

"Yes. With the online club Elteen belongs to. They have a team."

"The Knightly Girls of Cache-a-lot."

"That's them. There are seven or eight of them."

"Seven. You got me thinking, so I did some digging. The two Butcher victims to date—Tess and Gemma—were both members of the group. They're from B.C., and Saskatchewan, respectively, which is why we initially had trouble connecting them; and they use aliases online, which slowed us down even more. It wasn't until you showed me that picture and explained where it was taken that we started to see the geocaching as something more than the killer's signature. It's possible that the reporter found that connection and was following that lead. He's written a few articles on geocaching for various magazines."

"But I'm not a member of the group. I don't even have the geocache app on my phone."

"But for some reason he had your name written down with your goddaughter's. If the Butcher has targeted you, he'll find a way to take you. Please don't unnecessary risks."

"Of course."

"We also suspect he has an accomplice, due to the physical distance between the abductions, yet how close they were in time. They disappeared within twenty-four hours of each other, so he's either the most efficient killer I've ever encountered, or he has help. Even if you know what he looks like, it might be someone else who takes you, or at least is keeping track of you for when he wants to make his move."

"I'll be careful. Thank you, Detective." I'm pretty sure he didn't believe me.

So Bearded Jerk may or may not be the Butcher, but he could also be the killer's sidekick. Fucking great.

o0o

The bus stopped two doors down from the gun range and Charlie was leaning against her Subaru, reading something on her phone. She looked up, saw me, scrambled to put her phone away, and gave me a big smile. The smile was so sudden that I couldn't tell if it was genuine, but her eyes had that sparkle I was coming to recognize, so my best guess was that the smile was honest.

"I forgot to ask if you've ever fired a gun before."

Not a real one. "Only in video games. I had a bow and arrow set when I was a kid, but archery is hardly the same."

She led the way into the range. "In the hands of a hunter, a bow is just as deadly, but you're right, it's not the same."

As she opened the inner door, I could hear bangs and pops that I must have been masked by street sounds while we were outside. Gunfire! Cool! Maybe not so cool if it was in an urban street setting, but here, with targets and security and stuff, it *was*. After my conversation with the detective, I was ready to learn it all, get a permit, buy a Magnum or whatever, and go Butcher hunting.

I know it's weird, but in video games I always treated guns like an instrument and the games like a symphony, finding the rhythm and seeing the manoeuvres as notes progressing. I had no idea if real guns were the same, but as Charlie led us through the gun-themed gift shop filled with everything from coffee mugs with revolver handles to those realistic-looking 'toys' that fired soft white pellets, I was looking forward to experiencing the feel of steel in my hand and claw. I didn't want to live in fear like some delicate snowflake.

We arrived at check-in and the three men behind the counter were all 'packing heat' on their belts, right next to their cellphones.

It was surreal. Not wanting to stare like a rookie, I looked down at the counter instead and discovered that it was a display case *full* of guns, each one labelled for tourists like me.

The labels meant very little to me, though I was sure I was looking down at one from a James Bond movie and a huge one that looked like what Clint Eastwood would have been comfortable hefting.

Charlie asked for my driver's license, I was handed a release form to fill out, and five minutes later we were standing side-by-side between partitions on the range wearing industrial-strength ear protectors and safety glasses. In Charlie's hands the Beretta we were starting with looked like a toy, but when she handed it to me it looked plenty big enough in my slender hand and claw. I felt the heft of the steel, the seriousness of the tool in my hand, and the nature of what I was doing settled over me.

This little tool served only one purpose—to end life. Sure, it could be used to intimidate and add an air of security, but in the end, pulling the trigger announced that Death was in the house. Yes, I was only going to 'pop off a few rounds' at a paper target, but if one of the five of us currently on the range wanted to turn the weapon on themselves or one of the other four, there were no safety features in place other than common sense and the watchful eye of the range master on the stool in the corner.

Charlie took the weapon out of my hand, pointed out the safety switch, which position was ON and which was OFF, how to release the magazine, load it with only five rounds, replace it, and then line up the front and rear sights. Part of my brain wondered how much could I trust this stranger who seemed to have her share of secrets—including some odd connection to the city's parks—that I couldn't quite figure out.

The stray thoughts vanished in a puff of gun smoke when Charlie calmly lifted the weapon, pointed it at the target, and pulled the trigger five times quickly. Even with the ear covers on, it was loud, but somehow not as loud as I'd expected. Damn you, Hollywood, for getting my hopes up. Charlie placed the gun on the rubber mat in front of us and smiled at me. This lady was my kind of crazy.

I didn't wait for her to give me permission. I picked up the Beretta, popped out the magazine and reloaded it while she brought in her target, replaced it with a fresh one, and sent it back out about ten yards. It was just concentric circles on paper, but when she nodded the go-ahead, I pointed and squeezed once. The gun kicked in my hand with a roar.

HOLY FUCK! I have no idea why, but it sounded so much louder when *I* pulled the trigger. What a rush! I squinted at the target, but it was still virgin fresh. I must have frowned because Charlie said. "It's OK. Try again. Line up the sights, take a breath and hold it, then squeeze. Absorb the recoil, resight, and fire again. All four times. Let's see how you do."

'Empty the mag'. Isn't that what they say? I lined up the stubby little sights, breathed, held it, squeezed, and BOOM! Smile, re-peat. Four times. A hole appeared in the bottom right corner of the target after the third shot and a second hole appeared halfway from there to the bulls-eye. Wow and *wow*! I hate to admit it, but I *loved* this! I didn't need to tell Charlie, though, because she could see my shit-eating grin.

She nudged the box of ammo to me. "Go again. Reload, fire. This time after each shot, re-evaluate where you hit and adjust your aim to compensate. Does that make sense?"

Perfectly! "If I'm low and right, nudge it up and left." I reloaded.

"Exactly. Now, how's your left hand?"

"It hurts a bit, but I'm OK."

"Good. You seem to have found a grip that works. Five more, when you're ready."

I was ready. The third went right through the bulls-eye, but I was so excited that I fired off the next two, bang-bang, and neither hit the paper.

"Nicely done, Jubilee!"

"Except for the last two."

"To hell with the last two. Half of my students don't hit the target in the first ten shots and at least one in five has to be reminded to keep her eyes open." She reeled in the hole-punctuated circles and sent out a big, man-sized silhouette target.

"Ten more rounds, in two slow sets, aim for his chest—the centre mass."

I looked out at the target, then at the gun, and finally at her.

"It's OK Jubilee. It's still just paper."

"Just paper." Then I imagined it was the Butcher and he was armed with a saw. I reloaded, fired five, reloaded, and fired the second five, not rushing, barely breathing, tuning out the other shots in the range around me. A nice, easy tempo. I could hear it in my head. A beat to acquire, two beats to breathe, a beat to squeeze and recover from the recoil. A simple 4/4. I adjusted my aim a little each time and kept up the rhythm. When I was all done, Charlie reeled in the target.

My aim was all over the place, but three were in the centre and nine were accounted for. "I missed one."

"Hardly. Look closer." She touched her finger to the hole over what could be the heart. It looked odd, wider than the others. "Two slugs, one hole. You're a natural."

"Or lucky." Which was the more likely explanation.

"Well, *that*, too." She looked down at my claw. "I think your hand has had enough pistol work for one day. How about we try a few rounds with the M-4 assault rifle and call it a day?"

Assault rifle? "With a silencer?"

She laughed as she picked up the pistol, ejected the clip, and made sure both it and the gun were empty. "No. Those are only legal for police and military. The M-4 Carbine is more like the M-16 that you've seen in movies about the Vietnam War and is often the replacement for the M-16 in many infantries, or so I've been told."

Chapter Sixteen

I f the Beretta made me feel like 007, then ten minutes with the M-4 made me feel like G.I. Freaking Jane or Milla Jovovich's Alice in the Resident Evil movies and games. To say that something was empowering about firing a gun and hitting a target would be as gross an understatement as saying performing Mozart for Queen Elizabeth was 'a bit of a rush'. I've now done *both*, and although they can hardly compare, at least I know there's a damn good chance I'll be firing a gun again, soon. I picked up a range brochure on my way out, after thanking the staff profusely. They probably thought I was high, judging by the stupid smile on my face as I paid the bill, but maybe they were used to seeing noobs react the way I did. I can't imagine *anyone* not having a completely guttural, orgasmic rush "discharging" a weapon.

"So, Jubilee how are you doing?"

I knew she knew, but I think she needed some confirmation that she'd done something good. This was a woman who'd done some serious screwing up in her life, I think. "Thank you, Charlie. It was great. I feel..." What was the word?

"Invincible?" She unlocked the car remotely as we arrived and got in. She handed me my rolled-up targets.

"Exactly! And high."

"Adrenalin. Me, too, every time. It'll fade after a few hours, but the feeling that you are now in control of your life again will stay a lot longer."

"Good, because that's what I've been wanting for a while." And I was. She'd given me back a bit of what I needed and I owed her. "Can I buy you lunch?"

"Um, sure." She checked her watch. "I guess it's that time of the day."

"Pick a place, my treat. I'm so starved that I'm open to anything."

o0o

'Anything' turned out to be the best damned Vietnamese sub I'd ever had, found in a little take-out/dine-in place just off the city's main north-south road, Macleod Trail. We were pretty quiet while we ate, but once we started in on tea, I couldn't stop asking about the range and the classes they offered, membership benefits, and the types of weapons they had. And I now knew that they were 'weapons', not 'guns'. It was a small distinction, but one showing the difference between a civilian and a shooter. 'Firearm' was also acceptable, because that's what they were.

We were having such a good conversation that I only put up token resistance when Charlie offered to drive me home. I hated to take her out of her way. I wasn't quite ready to invite her in, which she seemed more than OK with. At least I didn't catch any hints of her sad-clown look when I climbed out of the car.

"Thank you, Charlie! Can we do it again, soon?"

"Sure. No! *Hummingbirds!* That's what it was I wanted to tell you. The hummingbirds are back at Weaselhead Flats and I was going to go out on Sunday, if you want to come. They're calling for rain tomorrow, but mostly sun for Sunday."

"Hummingbirds? I'm in!" That would be great!

"This early in the season, they like midday, when it's warmer, so I'll pick you up around eleven. Riding transit will take you all day, especially on Sunday."

"Eleven is good. I won't have my new camera, yet, so if I could borrow yours again, that would be great. Please."

"Of course. Eleven."

"Eleven." I closed the car door, and scanned the area for the van or the Butcher or his sidekick hiding in the playground with a burlap bag for my head, then I was up my walk and into the house with a kick of confidence. Guns and hummingbirds—the week was getting better. Of course, crashing Mom's party tomorrow with Reggie could end the week on either a high note or a flat one so low that I would feel it thrum in my soul for weeks. I was determined to *aim* for the high note, but be prepared, mentally and emotionally, to watch my family play a new low. Better safe than sorry with those tone-deaf drunks.

Not wanting to freak out any houseguests I might *ever* entertain, I took the bullet-punched targets down to the basement and taped them up on the concrete dividing wall, out of sight, behind the stairs. I stepped back and again admired my marksmanship. They announced that 'Yes, I am a badass', albeit a shy one, and God forbid my mother ever see them.

Back upstairs I was slammed with exhaustion, like someone had cut my strings with a hedge clipper and I needed a professional-level nap. I stayed upright only long enough to brush my teeth and take my hair out of its ponytail.

I woke up when I woke up and just went back to work. My claw hurt like hell, so I took a break every twenty minutes or so to do some of the stretching and strengthening Hussein had assigned me. A couple of painkillers and some heat rub helped, too.

Calling it quits just before eleven, I dragged my bone-weary ass to the kitchen for food, then returned to the big hugging couch with my sustenance and logged onto Prime. I was *way* behind on my bingeing. Part of my brain felt like I was slacking off when I plunked myself down in front of the widescreen, but since music had been my release after work, I had to adopt another way to de-stress. Until my new camera arrived next week, Netflix, Prime, and Disney it was. Thankfully, James didn't change the password after he left, although I'll have to get my own account at *some* point.

I watched an episode of *this*, then a couple of episodes of *that*, and then realized that the second episode I watched of *that* was a complete blur in my memory because I kept dozing off. Time for bed. I yearned for a big glass of Chilean shiraz or a simple South African cabernet but settled for spearmint toothpaste gargle-and-spit. Despite my nap, I was asleep seconds after I secured the immobilizing brace on my left hand.

o0o

My sleep was messed up. I wasn't quite as ready to confront my family as I thought I was, because I dreamt I was six inches tall, running around the house I grew up in and my parents still lived in. In the nightmare I made my way to the stairs to climb up them like a Sherpa on Everest while giant Joyce chased after me wearing floor-slapping scuba flippers, trying to step on me while Mom threw dirty shot glasses at me every time I passed her in the kitchen. Dad just laughed a sitcom laugh track and hit himself on the head over and over again with a wine bottle that refused to break.

I woke up three times in the night, but every time I tripped back into sleep I fell face-first into the same nightmare like it wouldn't let me out until it was finished with me. By the time the sun came up at six, I was a wreck. I was also sure that going to the party was a *really bad* goddamned idea.

o0o

To start the day I put a load of laundry in, clumsily hand-washed all of the dirty dishes, scrubbed all of the kitchen countertops, emptied the toaster's crumb tray, wiped down the inside of the microwave, checked the expiry dates on all of the shit in the fridge, scrubbed both toilets, sterilized my toothbrush in the microwave, wiped off the few errant fingerprints on the doors and frames, fluffed my pillows, made a list of spices I was running low of, and arranged my shoes and boots in the front closet, left on the left, right on the right, and toes to the back wall. *Then* I nudged the computer awake and climbed up into my desk chair to get some *real* work done.

I got halfway through a long edit when I must have nodded off. Yeah, I know. How could I nap when I was so stressed out? I think it was my body's safety mechanism kicking in, a failsafe to make sure I had the energy to deal with the Krawetz Family Circus & Bloodbath tonight. The stupid thing is that I could back out without getting any grief about it because they didn't even know we were coming. In fact, they were specifically expecting me to *not* put in an appearance, which is, of course, exactly why I was so determined to drop in and screw with their expectations.

I shook off the snooze, stared at the dark, sleeping laptop screen, and decided that any further work done today would need to be redone tomorrow anyway, so a long soak in the tub would be a *much* better way to fill some of the hours before Reggie swung by to get me. A brine of Epsom salts and vanilla, lit by tea-lights, and smoked by Lebanon cedar incense would be the adagio-slow wash away of all that ailed me, recharging my battery and strengthening my emotional shields just enough. Those little bath details were important. They kept my focus away from the things I couldn't control.

oOo

By draining cold water and adding more hot as time passed, I managed to nurse that therapeutic soak for a full hour. When I finally levered my clean, wrinkly Epsomy-vanilla-flavoured self out of the tub, I had only enough strength to wrap myself in the fluffy robe, set the alarm on my phone for ninety minutes before Reg was due to arrive, and then fall face-first onto the bed.

Sleep was instantaneous and deep, and if I dreamed, I didn't remember a thing when I woke up to the just-irritating-enough-to-get-my-attention alarm. I snoozed it twice, maybe three times, so when I finally felt human enough to roll over and climb out of bed, I had an hour to get ready. The hour should have been more than enough—I'm hardly high-maintenance with the need for flawless make-up—but I'd slept on wet hair and now it was a scary mess.

Fixing *that* took a large mug of raw black coffee and thirty minutes with every heating, drying, and curling tool in my arsenal. I didn't need perfection, I just needed to get rid of the crazy-daughter-with-crazy-hair look I'm sure they always expected from me. As I worked away at the sparrow's nest on my head, I thought about what the hell I was going to wear. Days ago, I'd narrowed the choices down to four—all variations on the LBD, the Little Black Dress.

If there was one thing I had in the closet, it was variations of the LBD, from Symphony days. I even had two tailored boy's tuxedos, which, by the way, are much more comfortable than tuxes made for women. But tonight, was about more than comfort. I was aiming for mature but feminine, fun but not slutty, conservative but not matronly. By the time my hair was re-tamed, I'd decided on my lovely black peplum lace dress with midnight black pointed-toe slide heels. It wasn't an expensive ensemble by any means, but it was a little flirty, a little conservative, and a lot of fun.

The thing about being a classical musician in a professional ensemble is that black is *de rigeur* for performing and socializing, so I had *far* too many choices. Even though I'd decided on the lace doesn't mean I shouldn't try on a few other possibilities, which was a mistake. The lace number was still leading the voting, but I had three other dresses and even one of the tuxedos laid out on the bed when the doorbell rang.

I jogged downstairs and after a quick peek out the window to confirm that it wasn't a geocaching crazy, I threw the bolt and let Reggie in.

"I'm early, Sweetie. Sorry. Traffic was better than I expected."

I threw a hug around him and in that long 4/4 embrace so much of my stress was crushed into submission that I let out a sob of relief.

"Are you OK, Jubidoo?" He held me at arm's length and looked at me sternly.

"I am *now*. But I need your help."

"*Anything.*"

"I can't decide what to wear."

He laughed. "Oh shit. I thought it was something simple and manly like opening a jar or reaching a high shelf."

"Not this time. This is my family. I need armour." I let him unlace and slip his shoes off and led the way upstairs to the bedroom, hurried footsteps muffled by the thick carpet.

He took one look at the choices I'd laid out on the bed and gasped. "No wonder you're having trouble, Little One. These are all *gorgeous*." He ran his fingertips over the material of each as if he could glean a decision through touch alone. "Not the tux. Too deliciously boyish and something they will all pounce on immediately, especially with *me* on your arm." He looked at me and raised an eyebrow. "I forgot to ask. Do you need me to butch it up a bit for this evening? Channel my best Daniel Craig?"

I had no doubt whatsoever that Reggie could pull off a hard-as-nails super spy impression in his tailored blue blazer, grey slacks, trimmed beard, and button-down white silk shirt, but that's not what I wanted. "Oh hell no. Be *yourself* one hundred percent. There'll be more than enough role-playing amongst these drunks tonight. Let's just aim to be sincerely ourselves and anyone who doesn't like it can go screw themselves."

"Excellent! I'd do it for *you*, but I spent almost thirty years pretending to be someone other than myself, so I'm happy to be me." He did a little curtsy and blew me a kiss.

I howled! "I'll pay you fifty dollars to do that tonight when I introduce you to my mother."

"Save your money, Sweetie. I'll do it for *free*. You can even record it, so we can show Karl later."

"Deal!"

"Now slip that lacy beauty on and let's go scandalize your *familius gaslightus*."

He left me to get dressed and I did so, quickly, now that the decision was made. When I finally looked at the finished ensemble in the mirror, I knew we were right. The black lace overlay with the cute peplum detail and the capped sleeves said exactly what I wanted it to. It was something my mother would *never* buy for me, but it fit me comfortably without being either a sack or second skin.

My make-up was simple, adding just a hint of colour to my winter-indoor-life pale skin. When I arrived downstairs, Reggie had my long, black wool coat ready and waiting.

"Shall we storm the castle, princess?"

I couldn't help but laugh. "I suppose so, my brave knight."

He huffed. "You've known me *how* long, and you think I'm a *knight*? Honey, I'm a queen and nothing but!"

"God damned right you are, Majesty!"

o0o

Ten minutes into our what-have-you-been-doing-since-I-saw-you-last conversation, Reggie interrupted me with a squeal.

"I forgot to tell you. We got a letter from Madan."

"Your *madam*?"

"Not madam. *Madan.* He's our foster son in India. I'm sure we told you about him. We've sponsored him through Plan Canada for about ten years."

Really? "Don't forget that I have memory gaps. You may have told me, but the memory of that conversation has flitted off, along with a few others, I think. I don't know what I can't remember, or I can't remember what I've forgotten."

"You have big memory gaps?"

"I didn't *think* I did, but there's stuff about the accident that I just can't pull up."

"That's to be expected. Severe trauma does that."

"That's what Dr. Ella said, but to be honest, I have *zero* reliable recollection one way or another. Mom says I must have been drunk. It's next to impossible that I'd been drinking—I was nervous—but *next to impossible* isn't the same as *impossible.*"

"*Yes*, it is. I know you and although you enjoy a drink or three when you're out and about with us, you've always been adamant about not drinking and driving, even after James abandoned you. *Never*. Your mother is just messing with your head. You sure as hell aren't your sister. The other driver was texting, *he* sideswiped you, *he* ruined your life." Reggie growled and I almost laughed.

"That's my mother's skill, sewing seeds of doubt."

"Well, that ends tonight. No one puts Jubidoo in the corner."

"I love you for the thought, but tonight I fight my own battle. I'm a stressed mess, but I'm ready."

"Excellent. But I'm here if you need me. So, what's the plan? Eat the food, dance on the table, vanish into the night?"

I wish. "I don't think it'll be that easy. It'll be more cocktail party than a sit-down dinner. When Mom plays hostess, she prefers to flit from guest to guest than try to convince my father to drunk-carve a beast while she doles out undercooked sweet potatoes. It's less about the food and more about her accepting the adulation."

"Wow. Sounds like we should be wearing body-cams and recording the fun."

"That would keep them from denying any silliness that happens, but this isn't about taking them to task or holding them responsible, it's about me taking back the power I've let them suck from me over the years. We go in, give the gift, mingle *politely...*"

"Will the food be safe to eat? The Wicked Witch of the North-East won't try to poison us?"

Ha ha! "Hardly! The food will be catered. She's usually bloody cheap, but not when it's about *her*. Also, we're arriving early enough that they'll be *relatively* sober."

"Pun intended?"

"Very *much* so." We turned the corner onto their street and Reg checked the address I'd had him input in the GPS.

"Almost there. Ready?"

"I'd be readier if I was carrying pepper spray."

"In the glove box."

"*What?*" No way! I reached for the glove compartment latch but Reggie laughed and I stopped.

"Joking."

"Too bad. Could have been hilarious."

Parking spots on the poplar-lined street were limited, so we ended up driving past the house and parking half a block away. I would have preferred to be closer, to expedite our getaway if this turned into the fiasco my churning gut suggested it would be, but no such luck. At least I wasn't alone and travelling by transit—it's tough to make a dramatic exit when you have to wait by yourself at a bus stop.

"How about we leave our coats in the car, just in case we need to make a running exit?"

"Good plan." Great minds think alike.

Mom and Dad still live in the same house I grew up in, and in fact, Mom grew up in it, too. The street was lined with massive poplars, but our big front yard had a beautiful blue spruce I'd named 'Bruce' when Dad, Joyce, and I planted it thirty years ago. It was taller than the house, now, and wide enough to hide the sitting room windows from the street. Decorating it at Christmas had been the highlight of a usually painful season of adults and alcohol, but after Dad's heart attack, Mom agreed to hire a service to string the lights. Dad just wanted to leave them up, and like most of their differences of opinion, Dad's opinion didn't make the least bit of difference.

As much as I was making an appearance at the party as a show of strength, I wasn't above messing with my family in petty little ways. "Stand here and hold up the gift to your chin, with a huge smile."

I positioned Reggie in front of the door's peephole, then rang the bell and ducked behind him. The bell's note was an e-flat and it had always grated on my nerves since I was the only one in the family who had a sense of pitch. From my hiding spot behind Reggie, I heard the deadbolt thrown open, so everyone they were expecting must already be inside. A shot deadbolt was an old family habit I'd inherited.

"Can I help you, sir?" It was Joyce.

Chapter Seventeen

I peeked out from behind Reggie. "Surprise, big sister! Couldn't miss Mom's party, now could I?"

"Jubilee? But..."

I slipped past her and into the house of my childhood, leading a still-smiling Reggie. There was no pile of shoes by the door, so I just wiped mine off and made the introductions. "Reggie, this is Joyce. Joyce, this is Reggie, my dear friend, and the chauffeur-de-jour."

Reg chuckled, tucked the gift box under one arm, and extended his hand. "A pleasure to finally meet you."

Joyce, caught completely off guard by our arrival, reflexively shook his hand and then shuffled aside so he could fully enter the foyer. By the time she closed and bolted the door behind us, she managed to find her voice again, though just a single soft, sotto voce, word. "Mom..."

Holy shit. "Joyce, it's not like I've risen from the dead." I held my hands out for the gift box, which Reggie handed over with a wicked little smile. He was enjoying himself as much as I was, I'm sure. Without a moment's hesitation, I turned and marched down the hall to the kitchen/dining area where Mom did most of her entertaining.

"Happy birthday, Mommy Dearest." I nearly shouted, to be heard over the conversations I could hear as I approached, but as I stepped into sight, the conversations cut off as abruptly as if a conductor had cut the air with a baton. I matched my volume to the silence just in time to not look any sillier than I already did, crashing the party.

To her credit, Mom managed an almost sincere smile as she stepped out of the crowd of maybe a dozen people, and, judging by a few guilty and some very curious expressions, I just might have been a recent topic of conversation in the room. I was hardly surprised. I flipped her a big smile.

"Jubilee how *lovely* to see you!" She reached out as if coming in for a totally uncharacteristic hug, so I handed her the boxed gift and blew her a couple of long-distance European cheek kisses. She faltered in her step and her smile slipped away. Confusion reigned for the briefest of blinks, and then she recovered, just as Reggie stepped up behind me.

"Happy birthday, Mrs. Krawetz." With my back to him, I couldn't see what Reggie did, but judging by the sing-song tone of his voice and my mother's jaw-dropped expression, he must have winked and curtsied, or blew her a kiss; and, of course, we forgot to record it. But he did it as promised and I loved him all the more for it.

"Mother, this is my friend, Reggie. You met his husband, Karl, at the symphony fundraiser last year." At the word 'husband', eyes around the room widened and I was almost certain I could hear sphincters snapping shut tight around sticks stuck in deep.

The silence was as wonderful as any concertino I'd ever heard. It was a truly delicious full measure of shock and awe, and then it was shattered like four deep timpani drum beats by my Uncle Howard, one of the few drunks in the family who was honest about his liquid hobby and still managed to combine a little kindness with his slurring bluntness.

"Jubilee! We were just talking about you!" Yeah, no *shit*.
"Well, not exactly about you but about your neighbourhood,
down in Fish Creek Park."

Oh shit. Butcher talk. Oh well. Better that they were talking
about something in the news than one of my mother's demor-
alizing assessments of my life, such as it is. I glanced over at
her and she'd already swapped the unopened gift for a drink.
Probably Joyce's doing, being Mom's little bitch and all.

Uncle Howie didn't bother to get up from the low chair his
scrawny ass was parked in, but rather the occupants of the room
moved left or right to give him a clear line of sight to me. I
laughed and walked the gauntlet to lean in and give him a quick
hug. I got along OK with most of the people in the room, not
counting my immediate family, so I relaxed when he hugged me
back and kissed me on the cheek.

"Thinking of doing some hiking in the park, Uncle Howie?"

"Ha! Not a f... not a chance, missy." He almost dropped an
f-bomb at Mom's party but caught himself. He was rarely sober
enough to fear anyone or anything, but he was scared shitless
of his older brother's wife. Family rumour had it that he'd
once slapped my mother's ass at a pool party back before I was
born, and she had spun and hit him in the head with the wine
bottle she'd been sneaking from the host's poolside bar. The
bottle had shattered, and Uncle Howie had crumpled, bleed-
ing, and unconscious, straight into the pool. He was rescued
and patched up quickly, and my mother's don't-fuck-with-me
reputation was cast in stone and forever burned into the memories of even people who weren't present. Aunt Lydia once
whispered to me that Mom's reputation wasn't built so much
on the assault and near drowning, but on the fact that she
didn't even blink, and *never* showed any remorse whatsoever
for nearly killing her idiot brother-in-law.

"No, Jubilee. We were talking about that Butcher and all the bodies he's hanging up around the parks."

"He's not hanging them up, Uncle Howie, he's hidden the hands, feet, and heads of three women. Geocaching them, in fact."

My mother's oldest friend, Doreen, chimed in. "No, I'm sure it was five bodies, and he rapes them then stuffs their panties in their mouths. Or does he rape them *after* he stuffs the panties in?"

"Or maybe he rapes them after he slices and dices them," Joyce suggested.

Mother joined the fray if only to reprimand a daughter in front of company, as usual. "That is a disgusting thought, Joyce."

"And he removes their faces..." Carole the neighbour slurred.

Holy shit, these drunks were worse than teenage girls! I looked around at them and they were all nodding in agreement and starting to look seriously rabid. All I could think about was the victims, and missing Elteen.

"But they're all just prostitutes, so really..."

"Good girls gone bad. No chance of redemption."

"Lost causes."

"Sluts."

I snapped. "Where do you fucking idiots get your information? He murdered these women and left their *body parts* hidden in the different parks as part of some sick game. My goddaughter is *missing* and may be a victim, so, enough of your crap about sluts or prostitutes, or lost causes. Elteen—my goddaughter and friend and Reggie's *niece*! —is a sweetheart, and so were the three victims."

"Oh, no, Jubilee you're wrong. I read it on NewsBuzz or some such."

"And I saw an article on that thing that used to be Twitter, or a link to one."

"Jubilee Jayne is right." I turned at the unexpected support, and it was from Mom! "She would know. The Butcher has been stalking her, hasn't he, Jubilee?" She believes me, now? What the hell? "Jubilee found her back gate open, so it *must* have been the Butcher. The most famous serial killer in the province's history just *must* be stalking the broken musician from the suburbs, after abducting her dear goddaughter who could never have just run away."

The goddamned bitch! It's as if she'd orchestrated the entire conversation in order to kick out what little foundation I had left. I was speechless.

Then my queen-in-shining armour stepped into the middle of the killing pack and took my good hand. "Jubilee *is* right. Two sets of hands, feet, and heads, and a third hand. Three beautiful women. Three *daughters* were killed and defiled. My *niece* is not a slut or a lost cause. She did not run away. She's *missing.*"

A mute was shoved into the conversation's ass and it got quiet, fast. I squeezed Reggie's hand.

Uncle Howie broke in, speaking softly, sort of respectfully. "She's one of the six missing women?"

Reggie spoke slowly and succinctly as if to make sure every one of the idiots he found himself surrounded by understood him. "My niece, Elteen, is one of fifteen women currently missing in Alberta, not counting children and teens. She just turned twenty. A couple of weeks ago she suddenly stopped returning everyone's calls." His voice trailed off at the end. His pain was heartbreaking.

Enough was enough. Screw them all. I led him out of the room by the hand. I led him to the front door, where he unbolted it with his free hand and we left. We didn't flee, we didn't scream in rage or frustration, we walked and we cried.

We arrived at the car, got in, still silent, then Reg wiped away his tears with a tissue from a box on the back seat and handed me one.

"Want to go to a real party, Jube?"

"Hells yes."

"One caveat, though. It's not an official symphony party, but it *is* at Shauna's.

"Our violinist?" I thought about it for a few beats and Reggie gave me the time. Shauna was one of my favourite symphony members, but was I ready to socialize with anyone from the group other than Karl? I flexed my claw. I was irreparably broken, and destroyed as a musician, but I couldn't hide away forever. If I could face the uncaring, callous assholes and bitches at my mother's birthday drunkfest, then as hard as it would be, Shauna's would be a piece of cake in comparison.

"Yes. It's time."

"You're sure it's OK?"

His concern was sweet, but I had to face up to my new reality. This was a good next step. "Yes. You'll be there if I melt down, won't you?"

"Of course. But you're not going to melt down. And if you *do*, who cares? You'll be surrounded by friends in a place of absolute safety."

"Unlike my family?"

He pulled away from the curb. "Unlike...yeah. *Wow*. What a bunch. Was that typical?"

"No. That was *tame*. If Mother hadn't had company, the three sharks would have circled for hours, nipping pieces out of my confidence, out of my soul, forcing me to leave or, when I still lived at home, retreat to my room and my music."

"At least you weren't locked under the stairs." He laughed, half-heartedly.

"Harry had his magic, and I had my music. I wonder what he would have done if he'd lost his magic? Would he be a wreck like me?"

"Probably, and it would have been a much shorter series of books. Besides, you're doing great. Hardly the Wreck of the Ella Fitzgerald."

"Ella was no wreck."

"Not at all. Married three times and was shy when she wasn't making music, but no wreck. I was trying to do musical cuteness, like Karl does."

"Ah." It *was* cute. "I *am* a wreck, though. Maybe not as bad as I was a week ago, but if I'd been at that family roast alone, I'd be curled up on the floor shaking while they took potshots at me and posted updates on Instagram."

"*That* group on Instagram? Not bloody likely. Anyhow, Shauna has turned her loft into a speakeasy for the night, so we're heading back in time to the Roaring Twenties—flappers, whiskey, and Gatsby quotes.

Booze. Uh oh. "I quit drinking, Reg."

"I know, but we'll swing by a grocery store and pick up some alcohol-free beer. All the taste, none of the hangover, and perfect for this particular party."

oOo

With a six-pack of cans in hand, Reggie rang the buzzer for Shauna's East Village loft. Six beats later, just as he was reaching up to press it again, Shauna's voice—backed by a loud Charleston—blared out of the tinny speaker.

"Hola Sheiks and Shebas, the Speakeasy is open!"

"Hey Doll-face! It's Reggie and some moll I found wandering the street, looking for a whoopee."

"Come on up, Reggie-oh!" The door lock buzzed and in we went.

Shauna was standing in the second-floor hallway when we stepped off the elevator and I could tell she'd had a few drinks because we were halfway to her before she finally recognized me. I smiled and shoved my claw deeper into my jacket pocket. I was both terrified and relieved to see her.

"JUBILEE?! JU-BIH-FUCKING-*LEE*?!" She was done up in a low-cut, sleeveless, sparkly black flapper dress and pointy-toe heels with her trademark spider-web motif nylons. She looked dangerously delightful. I've always been amazed at how well some women can run in high heels, and Shauna was such a pro that she sprinted down the corridor, picked me up and spun me around. She was my height, but symphony/city life hadn't leeched away any of the farm girl she was at heart.

After the third spin, she wobbled on her heels, came to a slow stop, and put me down. She didn't let me go, though, and planted a big, wet kiss right on my cheek. Or the kiss was dry and the wet was from our abundance of tears. Oh God, I missed her and the other symphony rats.

When we finally released the hug, she stepped back and poked a hard finger into my left shoulder. "You little fuck! You haven't called!" A lot of the symphony members cursed like sailors away from the pit, but if anyone had a bigger trash mouth than me, it would have to be dimple-cheeked, bright-eyed, always laughing, Shauna Lee.

I held up my claw and muttered, "I wasn't ready." I still wasn't ready, but I was here now.

She stared at my crippled paw for a moment, then gently took it in her hands, raised it to her lips, and kissed it lightly. "I don't blame you. This is heartbreaking." Releasing my hand, she smiled warmly. "But you're among family now, so it's time to party!"

I couldn't help but bark out a cynical laugh. "How about we leave family out of this."

"Whatever you say, Jubidoo!" She took Reggie and me by the hands and led us into her loft. "Hey, daddies and dames, look who Fly Boy Reggie dragged in!"

Chapter Eighteen

There were maybe fifteen people I could see and at Shauna's pronouncement, every head pivoted around to see. I knew about half of them. For the second time tonight, a room shut the hell up when I walked in, but because of the smiles and joyous gasps, for the first time in a long time, I felt welcome in a group.

o0o

I'd love to say we spent all night just laughing and dancing and forgetting tragedies personal and otherwise, but that would be a pile of shit. Oh, we *did* laugh and dance, but only after Shauna dragged me and our seven fellow CSO rats up to the loft's huge bedroom where we piled onto her king bed. I told them what little I'd been told about the accident, and the aftermath I'd been dealing with. Always near the surface, the tears came, and I was hugged and loved by the people who understood me best. Reggie wandered up and the big group hug made room for him. We mourned V-Dog, we mourned my music, we mourned the other driver, and after I told them about the stalker probably being The Butcher, we mourned the three women the fucker had taken from the world and Shauna led us in a prayer for Elteen's safe return.

When we were all cried out, we ladies took turns in the bathroom repairing our demolished make-up, the men took turns splashing a little cold water on our faces, and then we all joined the others downstairs. I let everyone else go down the stairs first, needing a little extra time to find the energy to party. Waiting with me, Shauna linked her arm in mine and we descended the open stairs one deliberate step at a time. I could feel the beat of the music infuse me with hope. We reached the little landing and paused dramatically. The party exploded in a standing, dancing ovation. We lifted our chins and both said, at the same time, "We're ready for our close-ups, Mr. DeMille."

Shauna leaned in and whispered, "Fuck the tears, let's dance!" So we did. We danced, we ate, and we brought that speakeasy to roaring life.

Sometime after midnight, I was out on the tiny balcony over-looking the lights of downtown and catching my breath, when Reggie joined me.

"Welcome back, Jubidoo."

"Thanks, Big Guy. It feels great. I wish Karl could have been here."

"I've been posting pictures on Instagram, so I'm sure he wishes he was here, too. Next time."

"Definitely." As good a time as I was having, I was spent. "Do you mind if we sneak out?"

"I hardly think they'll let us *sneak* out, but I was wondering how long you'd last, especially after your mother's debacle."

"I needed this in order to recover from Mom's, but since I'm going hunting for hummingbirds with Charlie tomorrow, I need some sleep."

"Oh yes, the hummingbirds. Then let's get you home, missy."

o0o

Leaving the party was easier said than done, of course. There were hugs, kisses, more tears, and heart-felt promises to go for coffee or pasta or shooters. There were reassurances that I was loved and missed and was not to hesitate to call, for *any* reason. As we waved to Shauna in the hallway when the elevator arrived, I made a deep, silent wish that I could bottle all of that love and energy and take it home with me so I could tap into it whenever the world overwhelmed me, which was too damned often lately.

Reggie and I didn't say much on the drive home, just hummed along with whatever the Top 40 radio was playing. It had been an evening of shits and giggles, with plenty of both, and I knew *I* didn't have the energy to chat. I was just happy to bask in the loving afterglow from Shauna's party and have Reggie as my wingman. Tomorrow would be a day of fresh air, exercise, and hunting hummingbirds.

The expected light rain was finally falling by the time Reggie walked me to my door and sent me inside with a hug and his usual kiss on the top of my head. I hoped the weather wouldn't affect tomorrow's hunt, but as I made my way to bed feeling pretty damned good about life in general, I wasn't going to worry about hummingbirds. I set my alarm for eight and swan-dived into the deep end of sleep.

o0o

For people who find sleep elusive and tenuous, being awakened in the middle of the solid REM embrace of somnambulant safety can be a disaster. For me, being awakened by a phone buzzing with an incoming text is grounds for a nuclear meltdown. I have no idea how that soft 'bing' and brief buzz managed to shatter my dream of lounging on a beach, but it did, smashing a scintillating hedonistic Hawaiian moment into a thousand shards of anger.

My heart pounding, I rolled over, got tangled in the damn sheets, screamed in frustration as I kicked and punched and twisted out of the sheet trap, then I snatched the phone up so angrily that I pulled it right off the charging cord.

"From Mom? At three-oh-seven in the fucking morning?!" I was so awake that it was now too damned late to ignore it.

Well well well, Jubilee. Was it your intention to ruin my special birthday, you and your foul-mouthed fruity friend? Wow. *It is quite obvious now that your accident did more damage than the doctors first suspected. Everyone here agrees that we need to step in and get you professional help away from offensive friends and distractions like imaginary stalkers. We will be at your and James's house Wednesday evening at seven.*

Wednesday at seven? That sounded like an excuse to go to a movie, or out for pizza, or *anywhere but home.* They were right about me needing professional help, but I needed the kind that would get me *away* from my family, not make me 'fit better' with those mutants. I knew that Mom was drunk-texting, but even so, she managed to make me feel like I was responsible for any failure of her party to be the event of the year for her circle of co-conspirators. They were going to step in? Like *hell* they were. I'm pretty damned sure they had no legal grounds since they weren't even beneficiaries of my insurance policies. They *might* still be listed as emergency contacts with Dr. Ella as well as my family doctor, but that was easily fixed before Wednesday.

The nerve of them. The fuck fuck fucking nerve! I hesitated a moment but finally popped a make-me-happy-dammit pill, squirted some liquid vitamin B down my throat, and rolled back over. Screw her. Screw them all. I may be a broken, divorced cripple, but I'm *not* crazy and I sure as hell aren't ready for involuntary institutionalization. This was a battle they weren't going to win. I was done being their whipping girl and they were about to find out that I may have lost V-Dog, but I still had teeth and claws of my own.

I jammed my face into the pillow and screamed until I ran out of breath, then I rolled over, impatient for the sleep I'd been ripped out of and was even willing to face the inevitable nightmare, which would have been a sight better than my soul-sucking reality. After half an hour or so of tossing and turning, and generally cursing my family both singly and as a collective, I decided to get out of bed and do some cleaning, or cooking, or ...

I woke up half in and half out of the covers, clutching V-Dog's blanket as if I'd fallen asleep while trying to get out of bed, which is probably what happened. I saw that it was six-twelve, pulled the covers over me, and tripped back down the rabbit hole to Happyland.

I dreamt a little of this and a little of that, but nothing resembling the horrific nightmares that had been screwing with my REM for the last month.

At one point I got up to the bathroom, half asleep, then stumbled back to bed, hoping that I'd actually made it to the toilet before relieving myself, rather than just dreaming I had. How screwed up is that? I was such a mess that it was a possibility that I'd pissed the bed. Wouldn't Mom love to find out I'd done something like that? She'd have me locked up permanently for fake-stalker-induced incontinence.

I woke again with the alarm, showered off the night sweats, stripped the bed, and then dragged the sheets and my other dirty stuff down to the laundry room.

Although I was wobbly, sleep-deprived, and still a little wound up from Mom's text, I bypassed the pill bottle and went straight for the kettle. Determined to be methodical and proactive rather than emotional and reactive, I knew I needed food. There was quick, commercial crap in the freezer, but—I checked the clock—I had plenty of time and all the supplies I needed for a *good* breakfast.

Breakfast took fifteen minutes to make and forty to eat. Some of the slowness was because of my fumbly claw, but most of the blame went to my need to concentrate on each bite, chew, and savour each mouthful, and not rush at all. Slowly, deliberately. Feel the sticky, taste the sweet, smell the greasy, savour the cold, cherish the hot. A little of this, a little of that.

I used to do this a lot, every weekend, with James across the table from me and V-Dog lying on my feet. Then it was just V-Dog for company. It had probably been a month since I'd just supped properly, willingly. No Netflix, no computer, no Cosmo on my iPad—just sup. It wasn't Brahms or Liszt, but it gave me some breathing room, an emotional hot tub soak, a temporary embrace of peace and quiet. I supped, I breathed, I reached for a bland, borderless place of limitless Zen expansion. In other words, I relaxed my ass off.

o0o

By the time Charlie pulled up out front, I'd checked eRomance-dot-whatever for more messages—and ignored them again—printed off a satellite image of the Weaselhead Flats where we were going today, put the two SD cards back in my pocket, thrown the washed sheets into the dryer, checked that the back gate was closed and latched, and snuggled my ass into the deck chair on the front stoop.

"Happy Sunday, Jubilee."

"Hey, Charlie. Happy Bird Day."

"It's not my—oh." She chuckled. "Nice one."

"So, hummingbirds?" I was psyched. I still didn't have my own camera, but the thought of seeing wild hummers made *me* hum.

"Hopefully. It's early in the season but they have been spotted." She looked down at my feet. "Good. You're wearing sturdy boots. It's a bit of a hike to their nesting area."

"Perfect! I could use some exercise." I needed more than a three-block walk to the bus stop. V-Dog and I would go for hours, exploring the pathways in and around the neighbourhood, but I hadn't walked any further than necessary since the accident. Just out of politeness, I asked, "How has your weekend been, so far?"

She hesitated, and I could practically *hear* the gears in her head turning as she decided what she should and shouldn't say. I don't know how many friends Charlie had, but our conversations so far led me to think that it wasn't many; and if she couldn't tell me everything then... Then *nothing* was OK, too. It wasn't a problem. She had a right to her privacy. She was shy and we'd only known each other a couple weeks.

"It's been good, thanks, Jubilee. Quiet. Just the way I like it."

"Me, too." I wasn't going to push her.

"Yours has been quiet? Weren't you thinking of dropping by your mother's birthday party?" She drove on.

Right. I'd mentioned that. "We did. It was exactly what I expected and all of what I hoped, which is to say that my family were all the complete assholes I expected and I got through it in one piece, as I'd hoped. Thanks to my friend, Reggie."

"I'm sorry to hear that they lived down to your expectations."

"I didn't expect them to change overnight, but they'd had enough to drink that they started in on the stupid even before we even got there. They were throwing around their misread, misinterpreted alternative facts about the Geocache Butcher, and I wanted to scream at their idiocy." I smiled. "Actually, I did raise my voice and may have called one or two or all of them idiots."

"The Geocache Butcher?"

"One and the same. They were saying crap about hanging bodies and panties and rape and—nothing at all like the news. It felt like an old Trump press conference with fabrication on tap."

"Hanging? Hardly. A handsaw was used to decapitate the victims, so why hang them? Besides, each of the remains was cached, in a container of some type."

How the hell did she know this? "That's still hideous, maybe even more so because it would take more time and deliberation than a chainsaw. But *why*?"

"Why? I would think power, anger, pure unadulterated hatred."

"Seriously messed up."

"Yes, but efficient and organized. Each body part was pretty well hidden." It sounded like she admired him. "Then he emailed the geocache data for a foot to one of the victim's friends, giving clues where to find them. Including today's." Her voice cracked while dropping that bomb, then she went silent.

"What?" Another one?

"Yes."

"They're sure it's the Butcher?" Say 'no'. Please say 'no'!

"Everything is identical except for the location."

"She wasn't in a park?"

"She was, but this time in the Bird Sanctuary." She went quiet.

"Charlie, tell me. It's OK." Shit.

"The woman was—" We turned into a strip mall parking lot so suddenly that I let out a little yelp. Charlie parked...and broke down.

Holy shit! I had no idea what to do! If it were Karl and Reggie or Shauna, I'd hug them and just let them cry it out like they did with me, but I didn't know Charlie all that well. Hell, I had brief moments when her knowledge of the killings made me wonder if *she* was the Butcher, but if she was, then this breakdown was Tony-Award worthy. I compromised. I squeezed her forearm briefly with my claw.

She sniffled and wiped her tears and nose with a tissue she dug out of the Subaru's center console. "Sorry about that. The first piece quickly led to the other four and once they had her head, they identified her as a missing single mother of twins."

Oh God, no!

I had no words to describe my pained disgust. I was so repulsed that someone had done this.

"They've positively identified the victim?" I was terrified of the answer.

"Yes. Her sister, who received the first geocache coordinates, reported her missing five weeks ago. The twins were with their father when she disappeared.

We both stared out the windshield for a handful of beats, then I asked her, "Don't you wish you could just take an M-4, hunt his ass down, and empty the magazine into his centre mass?"

"Every damned day."

"Yeah, me too."

"I guess we should get moving. Unless you want to skip the hummingbirds and just go for coffee."

I was sick with the thought that two children had lost their mother in such a horrific way, but I was also beyond relieved that it wasn't Elteen. "I think the hike and fresh air will be good for me, thanks."

"Me, too."

She got us back out on the road quickly and quietly, giving me enough time to ponder the moment and make a decision.

"Charlie, that creep in the park with the camera—do you think he might be the Butcher? Like I said at the range, I think I'm being followed or watched or even stalked, and I feel like I've seen him before. Am I sounding crazy?" I nearly told her about my conversation with Detective Marlin and my connection to the missing reporter, but I held back, still.

"Crazy? Well, yes and no. No, you don't sound crazy for suspecting someone is following you. There's no shortage of freaks out there. But thinking that the Butcher would risk being seen in broad daylight in his dumping ground... *that* sounds crazy."

"Oh." I'd thought I was on to something. I guess my description wasn't going to do the detective much good.

"I don't mean crazy/insane, just crazy/wrong. We're dealing with a skilled, meticulous, twisted bastard who probably does wander the streets of Calgary gloating in his secret identity, but like I said before, the jerk we saw didn't give off that kind of confidence."

"I guess not." How did she know this shit? "That's a relief, I guess. Then who the hell is following me?"

"Just because I don't think that man in the park was the Butcher, doesn't mean that the Butcher isn't the one following you."

"Someone I spoke with thought that the Butcher might not be working alone."

Charlie went mute for a few bars too long. Could she be—

"So, he could have been the accomplice. We need to keep our eyes open, Jubilee. You said he drives a van?"

"A gold minivan with tinted windows."

"Of course, now we'll see gold minivans *everywhere*. So, a Caucasian male, beard, dark hair, age thirty to forty-five, six-foot-one, a hundred and seventy pounds."

Wow! "Exactly! How did you...?"

"I remember people, especially ones who do something freaky like take pictures of my friends."

As we exited Glenmore Trail down into Lakeside, approaching the Flats, I realized we needed something cheery to talk about or I was going to snap. "Change of subject! My research tells me that there are two areas where hummingbirds are found in this area."

Charlie let out a relieved sigh. I think she was as keen on a change of tempo as I was. "The sightings so far this season have all been on the north bank of the river, right next to the Tsuu T'ina First Nation, so I thought we'd try there, first. Either route will be muddy after last night's rain, but not flooded, like last year. If we don't have any luck there, we'll try the south shore. Either way, there are plenty of other birds, including phoebes, nuthatches, a cliff swallow colony, hawks, mergansers...we'll have plenty to keep us shooting."

"What's a phoebe?"

"A little flycatcher. Tubby, quick, friendly, but not as common as chickadees or sparrows. Her call sounds like this." She made a shrill chirping call.

"I'll keep an ear open for it, and an eye open for freaky stalkers."

"Once we get down by the river, we'll be off the busy path and it'll be easy to spot anyone following us."

"Perfect." We pulled into the big evergreen-surrounded parking lot and had to drive all around it to find a small spot tucked in the back. I drew in a long slow breath. I used to bring V-Dog here all the time when he was a puppy and we lived closer. Today, though, I just had to watch for hummingbirds, phoebes, and the Butcher—more than enough to keep my mind off a certain choco-poodle.

We gathered up our gear, Charlie handed me her spare camera and we were off. There were still enough dark clouds to be a threat, but the day was warming quickly and the remnants of last night's puddles were evaporating quickly. We were on a plateau above a wide river valley and with so few trees here up top on the fields, the sky was immense. Cyclists, families with strollers, runners, and inline skaters cruised past in both directions. After a minute of walking in silence, Charlie led us to a bench on the south edge of the plateau, overlooking the flats. The ground dropped away gradually, with a narrow dirt trail winding its way down into the scrub and aspens.

Charlie pointed to the south, at two bridges in the distance, one green steel-and-concrete, the other a smaller wooden one, a little further on. "We're going down there, but turning off onto a little side trail before we get to the river, then we'll follow it for about a half a kilometre."

She pointed west toward a trail we couldn't see from there, but my gaze strayed up and out of the valley, to the Rocky Mountains, a hundred kilometres away. Some of the higher peaks still had a dusting of late-season snow and suddenly I yearned to be there, away from the city's noise and people and dust and serial killers... but there were no hummingbirds in Banff, so the Weaselhead Flats it was today.

"Shall we?" She nodded back toward the paved trail as wide as a single road.

Hummingbirds would be good. The hike would be good. "Let's go hunting!" She laughed, and off we went.

Chapter Nineteen

A s soon as we cleared the playing fields and the road-wide path started down into the valley, the forest crowded the ditches on either side. I watched for hummingbirds or owls or phoebes or *any* bird I'd never seen before, but between watching where I walked on the gradual downslope and having to look back over my shoulder every time a cyclist rang their bell to warn of their impending passing, I didn't have any attention to spare. To not block the path, Charlie walked a couple of steps ahead of me, periodically stopping in place to snap a photo of something or someone she found interesting.

I watched her, fascinated at how relaxed she became when she was using her camera. I still had no idea who she really was, though. She could handle a gun, knew the city's parks, and was a whole lot familiar with the work of the Geocache Butcher. Sometimes she looked like she wanted to talk about him, and sometimes I got the impression that the killings were at the heart of whatever had hurt her. She had such energy and power, but seemed off-balance half the time, like a musician playing a different time signature and key than everyone else in the ensemble.

The pathway was busy, but wide enough for everyone and sloped gently enough for determined parents to push strollers up. Of course, there were a surprising number of fitness freaks *running* up the hill, even pushing three-wheeled jogging strollers. Charlie looked fit enough to do that, but I'd been away from both yoga and my elliptical machine long enough that I got short of breath even *thinking* about running up the hill.

Just as the pathway snaked around to the east, levelled off, and straightened out toward the south, Charlie very quietly stepped into the trees on the west side, looking back to make sure I was following. Stepping softly, she stopped behind a wide tree and raised her camera. Expecting owls or woodpeckers, it took me two beats to see what she'd spotted—three whitetail deer. Very cool! I found a tree for cover and readied the camera.

Accustomed to people, I'm sure, the deer looked up in unison, seemed to deem us harmless, and went back to munching on spring greenery. Every so often the one facing me lifted her head and watched us, her jaw doing that funky circular grind-and-chew they do. I zoomed in the camera close enough for heads-only por-traits and snapped away. Over on my left, I could hear Charlie's big Canon softly rapid-firing. I zoomed out to get all three deer, then framed just two of them, and finally turned the camera to a vertical position and tried to get a couple of good shots with the deer in dapples of sunlight at the bottom of a tall frame. I think I got some pretty good pictures, but when I checked, I couldn't tell on the small screen in the sunlight.

Charlie must have seen me stop snapping and squint at the images because she lowered her camera and joined me. With her movement, the trio of ungulates drifted deeper into the woods. "There's always *something* to photograph down here," she com-mented.

"They're gorgeous. How did you know they were there?"

She led us back to the big pathway and we continued toward the river. "This is kind of their hang-out, but I haven't been able to get this close in a long time." As we walked, she told me about the time she followed them a long way into the woods but just couldn't get even one good picture. I realized then that whether photographing wild creatures or killing them, the same skills were necessary. When we were joking about 'hunting' owls and hummingbirds, we *were* hunting. An image flashed in my mind of a small box being opened to reveal a severed hand, and I realized that the Butcher was a hunter, too. "Wow!" I stopped, my breath short and ragged, my heart racing.

"What's wrong?"

"I just...I thought...the Geocache Butcher. He's a hunter like we are. He's following and watching women like we were watching the deer." Holy shit! My knees wobbled.

"Take a long, slow breath, Jubilee. It's OK." I took a breath. "Sure, he's hunting like we are, but *we* are recording and enjoying the life around us, while *he* is destroying it. There's nothing healthy about him. He needs more than therapy."

I took another deep breath, and Charlie kept reassuring me. I listened to her, concentrated not on her words, but on her tone, her cadence, and rhythm. I don't know if she realized she was doing it, but like Dr. Ella's, her voice was extremely hypnotic. With Charlie's projected calm, my shit slowly came together.

"He's a sick, twisted bastard who probably deserves a bullet between his eyes, Jubilee, but he's not here and *we* are. We can't let him control us, beat us down remotely, can we?"

She was right. "Hell no, let's go." I curled a weak smile at her and led the way.

"Do you know where we're going?"

"Not a clue."

She laughed kindly and stepped up beside me. "Almost there."

And we were. Fifty yards later she once again stepped off the pathway, this time stopping at a muddy puddle as big as my living room. "It doesn't look too bad," she reassured me. "Once we skirt this mud, we'll be on a mostly dry trail."

Off we went. Although I didn't slip and fall on my ass in eight inches of diarrhea-consistency mud, I did get a soaker when my right foot slipped and went in. It wasn't a big fumble, it's just that when I grabbed out for a thick branch with my left hand, it didn't get any kind of real grip. The 'grip' I got was no better than a loose-fingered slap. My boot got soaked and my useless knuckles got bark burn. Neither was a big deal, so I took a calming breath and sloshed on after Charlie.

The dirt trail was on a slope with knee-high scrub and medium-sized trees at first, then as it led further from the paved pathway, the trees thinned out and the slope got steeper, forcing us to slow down and walk single-file, lest we trip on a root while looking for the tell-tale flitter of winged activity, or listening for the hum of high-speed wings I'd heard in several YouTube videos while researching hummers.

Charlie stopped and pointed her camera at a flash of yellow in the trees fifteen or so feet away. "Warbler." She managed five or six quick photos, but by the time I powered up the little loaner, the warbler had flitted deeper into the trees and was gone. Frustrated, I decided to try and keep the camera powered up all the time, to be all 'Boy Scout prepared'.

We kept walking, my one boot squishing out a slow, wet beat, like a limping sponge. Every so often a chickadee or sparrow would venture close and perch on a branch with new buds long enough for me to raise the camera, but they were too quick for me. The day was warm, but a nice breeze along the wide river valley kept me cool.

A flash of black in the sky forward and above us caught my eye. A hawk. He was a long way off, but the silhouette was nice. I took a few shots, then hurried to catch up to my guide, who was walking and staring at the trees ahead of us, up the slope. I'd read that hummingbirds like to perch on top of dead trees or ones with at least dead top branches, but I couldn't see any of them in the direction Charlie was looking.

We walked a little further and she stepped off the narrow trail, between a waxy-leafed shrub and one with spiky needles. I didn't think a thinner trail was possible, but this skinny hint of dirt and grasses looked like nothing more than a game trail for mice. I have little feet, so I had very little trouble finding footing and keeping up with her as she worked her way around *this* bush, over *that* deadfall, through *those* little puddles. Eventually, she stopped and indicated a scrawny stand of tall trees with a sweep of her free hand.

"This is where I've spotted them before and where a friend saw them earlier in the week. It's still warming up, so fingers crossed." She pulled two plastic grocery bags out of her vest pocket and handed me one. "It can take a little while after we noisily arrive for them to come back. We can watch for them from these stumps." She spread her plastic bag out on a saw-cut stump about twelve inches across and sat down. "They'll still be wet after last night's rain."

There were five other stumps similar in height and diameter, so I chose one neither too close nor too far from hers. I didn't want to be rude, but I didn't want to be nearly on her lap, either. I repeated her trick with the plastic bag. I could feel the cold stump through the bag and my jeans, but my butt stayed dry, and that's what mattered most. I took my phone out, put it in Airplane Mode, and shrugged when Charlie raised a questioning eyebrow. "It's too peaceful out here to risk having my phone shatter the hush," I explained.

She nodded and smiled. "Mine's been off since we parked. Old habit."

We sat there, like two bumps on stumps, whispering about everything from the latest Star Wars movie to the different types of firearms she thought I might want to try next time at the range. I took the time to take off my soaked boot and sock, drain the boot of what little slop hadn't soaked in, and wring out the sock. When I was done, my hands were a mess, but wiping them on my jeans cleaned them up just fine. We talked about Subarus, Calgary neighbourhoods, and the latest word on the building of Calgary's Transit's Green Line LRT line. What we *didn't* talk about was either the Geocache Butcher or dysfunctional families. After about forty minutes, Charlie stood up, put her hands on her hips, arched backwards to stretch the kinks out, looked around, and huffed.

"Huh. Looks like we're out of luck here." She peeled her oh-so-expensive seat cover off the stump and stuffed it back into her pocket. "Sorry about this. Are you up for trying in the south meadows? The swallows and mergansers are on the way."

"Sure." The spring air was invigorating. "It's better than moping at home." And it was. I stood and stuffed my bag in my coat pocket. Charlie led us back downslope to the dirt trail, then back to the paved main pathway. Conversation en route was mostly Charlie pointing out where there had been damage done by the huge flood of 2013, and then us each revealing what we experienced during the disaster that overwhelmed the low-lying areas around the Bow and Elbow Rivers.

Despite the topic of personal experience, by the time we reached the steel and concrete bridge spanning the Elbow, I still knew very little about Charlie. I knew that during the flood she worked double shifts, but I didn't have a clue what she did for a living. I knew that her home had been clear of the flooded areas, and two blocks away her friends got a basement full of water, but I had no idea what part of the city she lived in, then or now. Bowness? Eau Claire? Inglewood? I did ask "What part of the city?" but she deflected the question with one about something I'd said a moment before. If she didn't want to tell me, that was fine, but her evasions were still odd.

Even before we stepped onto the big bridge, I could see dozens and dozens of swallows darting in and about the left side of the bridge, which I guess would make it the southeast side. The air was crazy with them, almost like a scene from a Hitchcock film, except that none of the ten or so people watching seemed to be in any danger of getting their eyes pecked out. As we approached, I could see that the swallows were zipping out, rarely far from the bridge, and then darting back beneath the bridge's overhang. I powered up the camera, but could only stare at first. Their midair agility was incredible! They never seemed to fly in anything resembling a straight line and were able to tuck, flip, spin, and catch bugs in midair without colliding with each other.

They were so damned fast that I got dizzy watching them from above, on the low-sided pedestrian bridge. All I could do was aim the camera at the heart of the beautiful blue-black and white maelstrom and push the shutter button. I snapped a few shots but had no idea what I was capturing. I lowered the camera and huffed my frustration.

"This way." Charlie finger-beckoned me as she finished crossing the bridge. She stepped off the path and made her way down onto the south bank of the river. What else could I do but follow her? I scrambled down the still-damp grass, nearly wiping out twice, but when I finally stood next to her and looked up where she was pointing her camera, I was flabbergasted. The swallow colony was a hundred or more round mud nests clinging tightly to the underside of the bridge's overhang, and the swallows darted in and out at incredible speeds, taking their catches home to feed their families, who poked their heads out and screamed for more.

I zoomed in and clicked off a dozen or so shots of the more active nests, simply hoping for something clear, then I let the camera hang around my neck and watched the acrobatic avian comings and goings. It was impossible to watch any one single bird, mostly because at these speeds they were all identical in appearance, so I sort of zoomed out my mind and tried to feel their energy. The sound was a cacophony of chirps, under-laid with the throbbing and splashing of the river only yards away. I tried to imagine Wagner's *Ride of the Valkyries* within the natural sounds, but the fit wasn't quite right. I shook my head and overlaid part of Paganini's *Violin Concerto Number 2 in B minor La Campanella* in my mind and it fit much better. The herky-jerky flight patterns of the swallows were like so many conductor's baton swipes and frenetic bow strokes of the strings section. I opened myself up to the visual concerto and let the twists and turns and dives and rolls and flips sweep me up. It was wondrous, and at first, my tears were only of joy.

Within the blur of their life, the swallows saw patterns, found rhythms, and understood the whys and wherefores of everything they did. Then it hit me. Within the blur of my own life, I couldn't see such things. Lately, my instincts were dulled by drugs, alcohol, grief, or shock... or all of it in concert. My joyful tears became ones of confusion. What was I to do? It was as if an entire philharmonic all dropped their instruments on the floor of the orchestra pit simultaneously, and I was expected to hear that harsh, insane discord and somehow find the Paganini of my life's music within it.

I closed my eyes, swiped the tears away with my sleeve, and took a deep breath. "Shit."

"Sorry. What did you say, Jubilee? I can barely hear you over the swallows and the river."

I forced a smile. "Just marvelling at the wonder of it all." Snapping a final few photos, I took a step back and lowered the camera to indicate that I was done and ready to move on, on all levels.

"I know. On some visits I just watch, hypnotized. They're so quick that I could take two hundred pictures and get *one* I'm satisfied with if I'm lucky." She led us back up the embankment to the pathway.

"I expect it's like that with the hummingbirds, too." Capturing their blur was going to be a helluva challenge.

"Not so much, no. The hummingbirds dart back and forth almost faster than you can see, but when they hover, only their wings move fast. They don't stay put for long, but unlike swallows, they do have moments when you can catch them in flight. The difference is like trying to photograph a jet fighter versus trying to photograph a helicopter."

"Then let the quest continue." I needed to get the hell away from the swallows before I imploded. Their energy was starting to suck mine right out of my pores.

The pathway soon branched off to the right and we took it, but Charlie stopped at a signpost. The top of the two posted signs was the 'No Bicycles' slash symbol, but the white one below it with red and black graphics was the one that stopped me short. Charlie didn't say a word, probably wanting me to read it on my own, so I did. One close look at the graphic and I just had to read it aloud.

"What the hell?" No way! "DANGER. Former National Defence Range. Military explosives and hazardous debris on this site may cause death or serious injury. Do not touch suspicious objects. Call 911!" The graphic was an exploding WWII bomb. I glared at Charlie but she was smiling so big she was almost laughing. "We're seriously going down here?"

Chapter Twenty

"The path is safe and I've *never* heard of anyone finding anything dangerous. Besides, a stalker would have to be a real idiot to skulk in these woods."

I got a mental flash of the Geocache Butcher stepping on a land mine and blowing himself the hell up. I couldn't help but laugh. I looked around at the dozen or so people on the main pathway behind us but didn't see my stalker. "We can only hope. Are there hummingbirds down that path? You think they'd be smart enough to stay away."

"Well, they can't read the sign, and nothing has gone boom down here in decades, so there's no reason for them to think there's any danger." Off we went down the trail, to a short, narrow wooden bridge.

"Is there? A risk, I mean."

"*I* don't think so, but if you're worried, we don't have to."

What the hell did I have to lose? My mediocre, screwed-up life? "No. I'm good. If the hummingbirds can handle it, so can I."

"Good." She smiled and started across the bridge.

Our boot steps echoed on the curved wooden expanse. Charlie stopped in the middle of the thirty-foot span over a little creek and pointed downstream at two ducks. "A pair of Barrow's Goldeneyes." She propped her elbows on the bridge rail for stability and started shooting. I followed her example and took advantage of the little camera's powerful zoom to get a close look at the pair, snapping as soon as I got them in focus. They were gorgeous. They were black and white with rounder heads than a mallard, and a white crescent on their faces, like a cheek highlight. They paddled around one bank of the creek, ducking down every so often, searching for food, I assumed. I snapped photos and smiled, pushing dark thoughts out of the way for a bit longer.

I focussed on the little things, like how the water beaded and rolled off the ducks' backs, how the bulrushes along the creek bank were a perfect place to hide a nest, how the trees leaned precipitously over the water as if at any moment they would release their rooted grip on the bank's soil and topple into the creek, to make a footbridge, to float away, or to become semi-submerged and change the flow of the water, and eventually the landscape, over time.

There was a black squirrel on the opposite bank, chattering away to itself. Or maybe even warning the ducks that two humans were spying on them. A flicker of grey to my left got my attention and Charlie whispered.

"Eastern Phoebe."

I turned in time to see it launch itself at a cloud of bugs, then dart back into the trees, out of sight. I had no chance at all to get even a blurry photo.

"He'll be back. Point the camera at the branch where we first spotted him, and keep your finger above the trigger, ready to push down."

I did as she suggested, but he didn't return. After waiting semi-patiently for a few minutes, Charlie shrugged and frowned. "Sorry. He usually does. They're cautious, so something may have spooked him." She started, so I took one last look for the Phoebe and then hustled to catch up with her. "Let's go check out the—"

She didn't get a chance to finish her sentence. Without even a single 'ding' of his bell, a cyclist blasted up behind us and onto the narrow bridge. There was barely room enough for two pedestrians to cross without touching, so he clipped me with his shoulder and knocked me into the railing. I only had enough time to yell "Asshole!" at him.

Somehow, though, Charlie had time to react. She sidestepped the prick and then he was unexpectedly airborne, up and over his handlebars as his bike got hung up on the bridge railing. I was so busy trying to stay upright and not drop Charlie's camera in the creek that I couldn't tell whether she punched him or just shoved him. He landed hard in the dirt beyond the bridge and his bike fell across the bridge, the front wheel bent between struts of the railing. Charlie marched right across the trail bike, her boots bending spokes and crushing his water bottle as she approached the logo-covered, lycra-wearing, forty-ish rider.

"You OK, buddy?" She didn't sound too concerned.

He tried to push himself to his knees, but one wrist gave out on him and by the way it bent, along with his agonized scream, it was pretty obviously broken. "You fucking bitch! You did that on purpose!" He managed to scramble to his feet, cradling his arm, the pain fighting with his rage for control of his face. But somewhere in his tiny mind was a smidgen of common sense, because he seemed to realize that Charlie was a good two inches taller than him and she not only wasn't backing down, she was smiling and holding her ground.

"On purpose? Hardly. *You startled me after you assaulted my friend while riding your bike on a restricted trail.*" She calmly pulled out her phone. "But let me call you an ambulance, and the Conservation Authority. I'm sure they'll be happy to assist you. They might even let you have your wheels back after you've paid the fines."

"You *bitch!*"

To her credit and my amazement, Charlie didn't hit him, but when I stepped up to join them, I could see her knuckles whiten as she clenched her phone. She took a breath.

Charlie kept her cool. "Or you can drag your ass and your bike back to the trail, call them yourself, and make up some story to tell the boys at the bar over watered-down Scotches tonight."

He wasn't done, yet, though. "I have a fucking race next weekend, and now I'm out." He lost his volume, but none of his threatening growl. Charlie took a step closer, but he stayed put. Barely.

"Look, *buddy,* your broken radius will heal in six to eight weeks, but the torn ACL in your left knee will need surgery and might never heal properly."

He glanced down at his knee. "What the fuck are you talking about? My knee is just f—" He got the hint just in time and shut his mouth. Pain was winning the battle with rage and common sense was starting to get its voice back. "Fucking bitches." He made a wide berth around us both and stomped onto the bridge to the wreck of his bike. We both turned, keeping an eye on him, wary of a surprise attack.

We didn't need to worry, though, because once he saw his bike, he was beaten. "My Stumpjumper... that's a five-hundred-dollar wheel." He grabbed the rear wheel with his good hand and yanked the whole thing out of the railing. Once it was free, he looked back at us. I was sure he was going to curse Charlie out again, but he kept quiet, hefted his bike onto his good shoulder with a little difficulty, and slumped off toward the main pathway.

"Are you OK, Jubilee?" She looked down at my right arm and I hadn't realized until then that I was holding my elbow with my claw.

"Thanks, just bumped my funny bone. Nothing serious." I knew the pain would pass, but wasn't quite sure what to say to someone who had just done to an asshole what I wished I had the skills and nerve to do. Then I noticed that her hands were shaking. "How about you?"

She forced a smile. "Fine, thanks. Just post-incident adrenalin shakes." She held up her hands. "I haven't stood up for myself like that in a long time."

"I gotta say that I'm glad he backed down. I'm not sure I could have handled seeing you kick his knee."

"*I'm* glad he did, too, because I think at that moment in time, I would have done it. Not now, but then, probably."

I gave her the biggest smile I had. "He would have deserved it. If it comes back at you in any way, legally, I'll back you up a hundred percent. He just 'had an accident'." I wiggled my bumped elbow and the last of the sharp tingling slipped away. "All good to go. You still up for more hummer hunting?"

"Oh, *hell* yes. This way." We followed a damp trail that ran parallel to the creek. Neither of us said much for a while. I don't know what was going through Charlie's mind, but *I* was trying to get my head around how fast she moved when she hit him, and how fearless she was in the face of his fury. The darkness in her eyes at that moment of resistance was disconcerting, though. I'd seen looks like that all too often on my sister's face just before she took a swing at me.

The walk to the meadows was much easier than the first trail along the slope, except that it started out pretty wet, with short boardwalks and some brief detours where the spring-high creek breached the shore. I couldn't help but look for bombs poking out of the puddles every time we stepped off the trail even a few feet. The scents of the spring forest were so much more intense down here, where things were damper. It was a rich, loamy essence; alive and vibrant, not dusty and dry like so much of the rest of Calgary.

Eventually, we turned away from the creek and out onto an almost unnaturally flat grassland. Tall evergreens crowded the edges of the open area, but few trees went higher than a couple dozen feet.

I looked for likely roosts for hummers and saw a few possibilities in sparse or dead treetops. A moment later, Charlie stopped and pointed up at the same decrepit pines.

"The one time I've seen them in this area, it was up there. Calliopes." She stepped off the pathway and I wanted to scream at her about unexploded bombs, but, unconcerned, she made her way through the tall grasses and shrubs. "Watch out for the burrs. They'll cling to you like..."

"Like perfumed soap salespeople in the mall?"

"Exactly. Cloying, irritating, and impossible to ditch."

We avoided the burrs, poking twigs, unexploded bombs, and green branches that excelled at face-slapping the unprepared. Charlie found us a log and we spread out our improvised plastic seat covers.

"How's your hand doing, Jubilee?"

I looked down at my claw, frankly surprised at how OK it *did* feel. "Better, thanks." I flexed the fingers I could. "I've been doing the exercises when I remember."

"Good."

The conversation petered off after that. Small talk about my claw wasn't too uplifting or even interesting. It took a few minutes, then the bolder chickadees and sparrows started to dart past, but when we didn't make an appropriate offering, they pulled back a bit to scold us from nearby saplings. Somewhere behind us, I could hear squirrels yacking, warning each other, flirting, or whatever they were saying. It was kind of relaxing, especially after the go-go-go of the swallows, and then the dipshit on the bike.

My mud-soaked boot had long ago warmed up, so the discomfort was easily ignored, and my elbow was no worse for wear now that the tingling had stopped. I had been so keen on seeing hummingbirds, but the white-tailed deer, the barn swallows, the Eastern Phoebe, and the Barrow's Goldeneyes were wonderful discoveries. I hoped at least a few of the photos turned out. I couldn't wait to get back out here with my new camera, which was due to arrive tomorrow.

There was movement at the top of one of the trees we spied on, but it didn't take a seasoned birder to see that it was a long-tailed magpie, and nothing even closely resembling a hummingbird.

Ten minutes later we looked at each other and laughed. Charlie threw her hands up in frustration. "Well, *this* has been a complete bust. Sorry."

"What? Not at all. Maybe no hummingbirds, but plenty of other stuff, including a limping Lycra tit, or twit, or whatever he was. Compared to *that* asshole's day, ours is a shining success. Besides, it's not like hummingbirds are here for one day only and then gone."

"True enough."

She sounded tired like the encounter with Fucknuts McBicycleshorts had taken a lot out of her. "But if you're done, so am I." I stood too quickly, wobbled a bit, and a yawn escaped quite without grace. "Oh shit. Sorry."

"Me, too. Done." She gathered up the plastic bags and started back to the main pathway. I took a final look up at the treetops, but nothing. Nada. The hummers had stood us up. Little pricks.

Back at the main bridge, the swallows had slowed their feeding frenzy quite a bit, but it was the sight of an ambulance taking up much of the pathway on the far bank that got our attention. Charlie looked sideways at me and snuck a smile as we sauntered toward them, part of the steady stream of walkers and runners. "Oops. My bad." She pulled a red Calgary Flames cap out of her vest pocket and tugged it down on her head, hiding her face without being completely obvious. I thought she was overreacting until I saw our cyclist friend sitting on the back step of the vehicle, pointing in our direction.

I couldn't hear what he said but wasn't going to take a chance, so I pulled the hood of my pullover up and on and tried to keep as many people between us and him as possible. I noticed that Charlie even hunched her shoulders a bit, to hide her height.

Within the watching and walking crowd, we snuck past while Bike Boy was distracted, but we needn't have worried because I heard him spinning his story to the pretty female medic.

"Yeah, a deer. Right out of the trees, like it was being chased by something bigger, like a wolf. Bowled me right over and busted the shit out of my custom Specialized bike. I was supposed to race next weekend, to raise money for kids' cancer..."

I was so thankful when we were out of range and I couldn't hear his lying bullshit anymore. I honestly wanted to turn around, go back and call him on it, but Charlie's long legs had moved her further past, and besides, I didn't want to get her into trouble. If I called him on his shit, we'd have to admit our part in his injuries. I hurried and caught up with her.

"At least he's getting some care." I figured we were far enough away to talk about it.

"It was a clean break. He'll heal."

"You could tell it was a clean break without examining it?" *That* was talent.

"Let's just say I've seen a few breaks." She smiled, but it held past pain of some sort. Had she broken a lot of bones, or did she do a lot of breaking? The first possibility was sad, the second, more than a little freaky.

We reached the bottom of the hill and it got steep quickly enough for me to just shut up and save my breath. I pulled my hood back and unzipped my pullover as the sun heated me up. Just as we reached the long straight stretch to the top, I heard a familiar laugh behind us. It instantly snapped me out of my plodding, one-foot-in-front-of-the-other trudge.

"Elteen!" I spun around and nearly fell into the gully beside the pathway. The sun was in my eyes, but there she was! "Elteen!" I took two leaping strides toward her but ground to a halt. The freaked-out expressions on the couple's faces pulled me up short, but once I got a better look, I could see that the young woman was too tall and a redhead rather than a blonde.

Oh shit. "Sorry. My mistake." I had nothing else to say, so I turned around, swiped at the tears leaking out from under my sunglasses, and walked back to Charlie, who had stopped but not followed me. Fuck.

"What's up?" Her tone was light and curious, unlike the condemnation my mother would have injected into her words.

"Just me being an idiot. I was zoned out and thought I heard my goddaughter. I scared the crap out of them."

"No doubt. You OK?"

A blanket of melancholy settled over me, but I didn't want to let on. I could handle it. I didn't want sympathy, which I'm sure is what I'd get. "All good, thanks."

"OK." She smiled, I smiled, and we finished the walk back up to her car. I have to say that as little as I knew about Charlie's life, I *did* know that she was extremely perceptive and sensitive, as she once again demonstrated by not pushing me to talk when I so obviously wasn't up for it.

The parking lot was packed and vehicles were slowly circling like hawks on a thermal, hoping to be in the right place at the right time when someone vacated their spot. We quickly loaded up and relinquished our patch of dirt, not caring whether the Corolla or the Mercedes got their nose into it first, laying claim to the trophy.

I wanted to do something to say 'thank you' to Charlie, plus I was in serious need of intravenous caffeine. "Can I buy you a coffee?" I slipped the memory card out of the loaner camera and stowed the camera in its bag. The card went back into the safety of my zippered pocket.

"Sure." She sounded happy I asked.

By the time we found a coffee joint, we were both yawning. Charlie's yawns may or may not have been a response to my own, but I still suggested we roll through the drive-thru.

"Sounds good." She joined the uncharacteristically short queue and in no time at all, we were sipping hot brews while she drove me home.

Part of me was still a little off balance by Charlie's knowledge of the Geocache Butcher, of broken limbs, and how she disabled the cyclist-asshole so easily, but I also really needed to trust her. I crossed my mental fingers and went for it. "Are you available for another shooting session on Wednesday? I may have to face my family that evening and I'm going to need all the confidence I can scrounge up." I'm not sure the range was the best solution, but I sure as fuck didn't want to be coked out on meds when *mi famiglia* came knocking on their self-appointed attempt at an intervention.

"I think so. Got another party to suffer through?"

"That's wishful thinking." I told her about Mom's text and the veiled threat to commit me. When I was done, she didn't say anything for a few long bars, but her white-knuckled, clenched hands on the steering wheel said all I needed to know. I let her have time to digest and contemplate whatever she was mulling over. We were almost at my house when she finally spoke.

"Tell Dr. Ella. If anyone can block something evil like that, *she* can."

I'd thought of that, too. "I'm seeing her tomorrow."

"Good. Of course, what you discuss with her is none of my business, but *this* is what she specializes in. She helped...a friend of mine with something similar."

"Thank you." A friend? Really? It was so cliché I had to fight my smile.

"If you simply need physical backup with your family, give me a call." We arrived at the house. "In the meantime, I'll see you at the range on Wednesday. I'll text you the time once I confirm the booking with the club."

"Wednesday. And thank you for today." It had been weird, but refreshing, too.

"My pleasure." I yawned, she yawned, and we both laughed. She waited until I was in the house before she drove off.

Chapter Twenty-One

I made it from the kitchen to the couch before sleep could no longer be denied, but I forced myself upstairs to bed. I covered myself in the comforter and down I went.

To call where my mind went 'dreaming' would be so insufficient as to be laughable. I tripped and fell id-first into a serious damned night terror, or living Hell. It was so deeply horrific that to write it out in detail would bring it back hard and fast and even now, with some temporal distance, I can't do it. But I can and should give you the gist of it because it all plays into what happened later.

It involved bloody body parts and the faces on the half-dozen or so heads were all women I knew—Charlie, Nola, Song, Dr. Ella, and Elteen. It involved a cello-only score that was a minor key version of a Paganini/Vivaldi mash-up. My extremities were all stumps, I was being chased by the eRomance.ca logo carrying a bloody butcher knife, and everywhere I stepped on my stump legs, I stepped on dead hummingbirds and chocolate poodles, crunching and squishing. And it was all in my house, everywhere I turned.

Just as the tacky green and yellow logo was smashing down the door to the bathroom I'd locked myself into, I woke up and lay there, gripping V-Dog's memory-crammed blanket.

"Shit!" I rolled off the bed, stumbled to the bathroom, bounced off both doorframes with my shoulders, yanked my pants down, and dropped onto the toilet. The blanket remained tightly clutched in my steely grip-and-a-half. I couldn't stop shaking. I was boiling, I was freezing, I was safe, I was in dire peril... I was well and truly *screwed up*.

The walls crept in and crowded me, leaning over and whispering words I couldn't quite decipher. My mind still latched onto the imagined corpses—both human and animal—filling the shadows with remnants of the horrors. I was sure the music continued, faint and just around the corner, mocking me while finished up, left the bathroom, and stood on the landing, still dressed from birding, including the one missing sock. I needed fresh air and I needed it in the worst way. I nearly tripped on the stairs in my rush to get downstairs and outside. I hit every light switch on my way past them, hoping real light would banish imagined shadows.

The front door bolt slipped in my good hand, but I got it open, my breaths were so staccato fast and shallow that I was dizzy. I couldn't tell reality from a nightmare, I needed air. I needed *out*. I whipped open the inner door just in time to see the gold minivan drive past, leaving the cul-de-sac.

"HEY!" I snatched up my collapsible umbrella on the table by the door and rushed after him, ready to beat his goddamned head in. One sock on, one foot bare, I leaped down my three steps, stumbled, went down on my knees, claw, and knuckles on the concrete walk, clambered to my feet, and limped across the neighbour's narrow, damp lawn in pursuit.

By the time I cleared the building and could see down the next short street, there was no sign of the van, just three pick-up trucks, an SUV, and a mini school bus, all parked and empty.

"God*dammit*!!" I screamed. I was ready to *end* him. Scraped up and pissed off, I hobbled home and slammed the door behind me. I was an idiot, charging out to take on a serial killer with a stupid-ass collapsible umbrella.

My mind was clear enough to know now that I was being stupid, but I was still sleep-fuzzy in some corners and on the edges. I wanted to call Charlie and go hunting this bastard, but I was clear enough to know that he was long gone and it was impractical. What I needed was air... or a drink. I needed to take get back on my meds and calm the hell down, but the stubborn survivor inside my fragile fucking shell screamed "NO DRUGS!"

I just couldn't sit still. I cleaned the scrapes on my claw and knuckles, applied Band-Aids with antiseptic cream, and then clomped around the house closing the blinds, sealing my home from watching assholes. If the bastard wanted to watch me, he was going to have to knock on my goddamned door and come inside. My injuries stung, but I couldn't let them stop me. I went back down to the kitchen, grabbed the big wooden Henkel block of knives, and went from room to room, planting one tool of death in each room where I could reach it if I needed to. I would have killed for a Glock with a full mag right then.

With the house armed and dangerous, I found my phone and sent Reggie and Karl a text.

The latest new victim is a single mother of two. Have you heard from our girl? Hugs to you both. Jube.

OK, so it wasn't much, but I'd just chased a serial killer with a Dollar Store umbrella and wasn't quite focused on texting an essay. A moment later Reggie replied with a text containing a link. No word. *The city has gone insane! Stay safe! Hugs! XO*

I had no idea what he was on about so I clicked the link, which took me to a local news report. Both anchors looked visibly upset behind their big desk. The woman looked directly at the camera, and so right at me. "This report contains graphic and disturbing images and video footage." The picture-in-picture insert changed from the station's logo to the interior of a transit bus. "A Transit Authority of Calgary driver was dragged out of his seat and brutal-

ly beaten by a group of teens accusing him of being the Geocache Butcher, who has been terrorizing the city for months
now.

"A witness said that the bus was parked at Dalhousie LRT
Station when one of a group of seven teens started vaping in
the back of the vehicle, blowing the scented vapour at the passengers around him. The bus driver—an eighteen-year transit
veteran—opened the back door of the bus with a switch by
his seat and ordered the offender off the bus. The youth swore
rather graphically at the driver, but continued vaping."

I knew exactly how that bus driver felt. No one was allowed
to discipline or punish the little shits, so they pretty much did
whatever they wanted. The report continued.

"At this point, the witness says the driver picked up his radio
handset and called for peace officers to come to deal with the
problem. Transit Authority has confirmed that this is the proper procedure. From within the group of teens one girl charged
to the front of the bus, confronting the driver in person despite
him being a tempered glass shield. She swore at him and told
him that he couldn't kick her boyfriend off the bus. The driver
told her that it was too late and that the officers were on their
way. Likely unaware that the three security cameras at the front
of the bus were recording their conversation, she then leaned to
the edge of the glass and whispered that she would just accuse
him of rape. The driver laughed, which the witness said set
the girl off into a rage. She turned back to her friends and
screamed "THIS GUY IS THE GEOCACHE BUTCHER! He
just threatened to cut my head off!"

The news anchor took a deep breath and a sip from her mug
to compose herself. "The situation escalated so quickly that the
witness barely got out of the way, but at some point, one of the
teens began recording it all with their phone. We warn you again

that this is disturbing footage. We have done our best to edit it for graphic language."

The inset image changed to a video and expanded to fill my phone's screen. The little vaping shits rushed the driver, shouting "Kill the Butcher!" and "Butcher the Butcher!" One idiot even yelled "Vaping is free speech, asshole!" as he charged down the bus aisle past the handful of stunned witnesses. There were a lot of expletive-censored beeps, but it was obvious what the mini-mob of suburban white brats were shouting. That's what they were, too. Nicely dressed, bored white brats with nothing to do on a Sunday but push back against authority because they knew they would get away with it.

Two teens half the size of the driver tore open the barrier, grabbed the driver by his sweater, and dragged him out of his seat while he begged them to stop. Fists flew from the kids until the driver went down and they started kicking him, still screaming about butchering the Butcher and laughing. One even asked the phone holder if he was getting it all. Just as I was about to stop it, the footage froze anchor came back on the screen.

"The forty-seven-year-old driver is in critical condition in a medically-induced coma due to the extent of the injuries to his head. What the assailant-made footage continues to show but we will not, is the teenage girl who instigated the attack stomping on the bus driver's head while he attempted to block her with his arm, crying out in obvious pain until she silenced him.

"Transit peace officers and Calgary Police arrived quickly and all six teens were arrested, but not before the video of the senseless and brutal attack was uploaded to TikTok, YouTube, and Instagram. We will be back after these messages with statements from a Transit spokesperson, the Mayor, and the Police Chief who cautions Calgarians against becoming vigilantes." The clip ended.

Now I needed air like it was, well, *air*, and the house was making my head all fuzzy and spinny. I needed *out*. And I needed food. Food that I didn't have to cook, out and away. Meat. And something fried. Reggie was right. The city was going insane and it made me sick.

Clean socks, coat, dry shoes, wallet, phone, plastic-sheathed paring knife in my coat pocket, and out the door. I was quick but cautious, sneaking out the back door, into the yard, and out into the laneway. I made doubly sure that I closed the back gate so that it latched. The coast was clear, so I pulled my hood up and followed the gravel back lane down two streets to emerge onto the sidewalk. I wanted to get to our little strip mall but was torn between following the roads where I would be visible both to the busy traffic and to the stalking Butcher, and the shortcut pathways through the centre of the community, away from traffic.

The community is designed around a circle, with a little ring road starting and ending at a thirty-foot-tall decorative windmill. Within the centre of the ring is a parkland/pathways system that meanders through all four quadrants of the area, behind houses with low chain-link fences. V-Dog and I would spend hours wandering the paths, past a variety of playgrounds, and even around our little man-made pond. One entry to the pathways is three blocks from the house, so that's where I went. There was one of the many exits two blocks from the little plaza with the grocery store, bank, a couple of pubs, and a few other restaurants. Plenty of eating options.

The warmer weather was coaxing people out of doors, and as I strolled along, trying desperately not to miss my little heart-dog, the occasional wave from a deck or patio reassured me that the Butcher wasn't going to be able to sneak up and snatch me without being seen. Besides, I had the sharp little paring knife in my coat pocket, so the bastard wasn't going to get me without a fight, either.

The pathway was busy and I blended in with the other afternoon wanderers, reaching the south end of the meandering park without being clubbed from behind and stuffed into a potato sack. The last two blocks to the shopping area were out of the park, past condos, a Mormon church, and a school. It was less populated by pedestrians, and vehicles like gold minivans could approach from any number of directions, so safety was not guaranteed. But I was famished, I was sort of armed, and I wasn't going to turn around now. Stopping by the tall, brown, steel, lidded, dog-crap garbage bin, I used it for half-assed cover and scoped out the approaching streets. The stink from the can was horrendous but I didn't move until I was sure the coast was clear of the Butcher or his accomplice's van. I strode across the street, looking much calmer than I felt.

My grip on that wimpy little paring knife tightened with every step I took, warily walking past shops until I was sure my fingerprints were impressed deep into the handle when I finally arrived at the first pub. My other choices were subs, coffee, pizza, Chinese, and Japanese, but they all had ground-to-ceiling windows and I just couldn't handle sitting in a goldfish bowl right then. This pub had a really good menu and a chef with more than an ounce of creativity, but just so long as I didn't sit on the patio, and kept my back to the wall, no one should be able to watch me without me knowing.

I smiled up the pair of smokers to one side of the entrance and entered the cool darkness of the establishment. As per the sign on a stand just inside the second door, I seated myself. I found a dark corner from where I could easily see the entrance but was partially hidden by the centrepiece bar. I had just enough time to pick up the menu and open it before the waitress swung past with a tray of draughts probably for the six rowdies sitting facing the largest of the screens featuring the end of a news update of the Butcher's latest victim, then back to the hockey playoffs.

"Hi Hon. Let me drop these off and I'll be right with you. Want a drink to start?"

I didn't realize how thirsty I was. "Ginger-ale, please. A *big* one."

"Done!" She scooted away, detouring back to the bar to order my drink, then off to the hockey fans. I opened the menu and went straight to the finger foods. My claw hurt like hell from my trip-and-scrape incident, so a knife and fork were out of the question. I just didn't have the damned energy to fight with my food. The burgers here were always great, but my taste buds wanted something I seldom made at home, so I opted for the Reuben. There was no way it would compete with a real Montreal deli Reuben, but today smoked meat, cabbage, and red wine Dijon called to me louder than ground sirloin. I closed the menu and laid it where the server could reach it, just as she swung by with the ginger ale.

"That was quick! A lady who knows what she wants. I'm Alicia, and I'm guessing you're hungry."

I couldn't help but smile back. "Famished, with two 'f's. The Reuben, with an extra pickle, extra Dijon, and fries on the side, please." Even as I said the words aloud, my stomach rumbled a low D in anticipation.

"Done. Any appetizer? The calamari today is great."

Rumble. "Sold." I reached for the ginger ale, trying to hide the drool I imagined was trailing out of the corner of my mouth.

"Good choice, Hon."

I sipped the bubbly soft drink and made a decision I was sure I would regret even as I said it. "And can I get a double Crown Royal to add to this, please?"

"Twin Crowns it is. Regular or maple?"

"Maple, please." Oh shit. What was I doing? This wasn't quitting, this was jumping back in with both feet.

"Coming right up," and she was gone before I could change my mind.

Movement in the pub entrance got my attention, but the silhouette was two people leaving, not one psycho entering. I took my phone out and thumb-printed it open just as Alicia silently deposited the rocks glass of maple-infused rye in front of me. I passed the phone to my claw and picked up the glass.

I had been doing so well since I fed the liquor to my kitchen drain, but the latest murder, Mom's threat, the asshole on the bike, mistaking that girl for Elteen, and the Butcher watching my home—my *refuge*—waiting to pounce, was too damned much. Besides, it was only two ounces. I could handle two ounces. It's not like I'd wandered to the liquor store across the parking lot and restocked my entire bar. I lifted the glass and swirled it around to let the whisky breathe a bit, then I took a long, needy sniff of the scent.

"Shiiiiiit..." I whispered. The rye was strong in this one. I sipped, letting the elixir slide over my lips and bite my tongue. "*Super* shiiiiit..." I took another sip, felt the second heat roll down my throat after the first and growled, just a little. It was almost blasphemous, but I poured the rest of the Crown into the ginger ale and stirred it with the straw. I wanted to make the two ounces last for the whole meal. As dumb as I was, at least I didn't have any meds in my system.

Another silhouette in the doorway bumped me out of my distraction. I grabbed the drinks menu and held it up so I could just see over the top.

With the daylight behind him, I could see that he was almost six-foot, medium build, and had short hair—which could easily describe the Butcher. He stopped just inside the pub's inner door and I could see by his profile that he was scanning the place, looking for someone. I lifted the menu higher and leaned back into the shadows, praying he couldn't see me.

His gaze swept over me and was gone, then he caught sight of the draught-drinkers, waved to them, and joined them. When he finally stepped into the light, I could see that not only was he black, but his short-cropped afro was snow white. He was sixty if he was a day.

Holy crap, I was a mess. I was jumping at everything. The calamari arrived at that very moment, Alicia popping up suddenly. I was so flustered I swore out loud. "Shit!"

"Sorry to startle you. I'll bring your sandwich out when you're done with the squid. OK?"

"Thanks." Damn. I felt stupid on all levels now. I grabbed the drink, discarded the straw, then gulped back enough to take the edge off, to settle myself down to keep me from screaming, weeping, or just face-planting in the battered squid and snarfing back the plate-full like a rabid wolverine.

The first mouthful was perfect. Tender, hot, moist, not rubbery, and not all-batter-no-squid. I needed to mellow out and slow down, so once again I used the food to get myself focussed. No rushing, no gorging—as starved as I was. I savoured each peppery, chewy, bite. I'm sure the kitchen was itching to get my sandwich out from under the heat lamp and on the table in front of me, but it was *my* meal dammit, and I would eat at a pace that did *me* good.

It was all bites, sips, and glances at the front door. It felt like forever, but the plate of calamari wasn't exactly overflowing, so I was probably done in no more than five minutes. Alicia must have been watching out of the corner of her eye, because as I wiped off the oil from the last bit, my sandwich and fries floated down in front of me and the crumby appetizer plate was whisked away.

"How was it, Hon? Tasty?"

It took me a beat to realize that she was talking to me. The whisky already seemed to be fuzzing my edges and I was staring off and away at the bright colours of the hockey jerseys on the big screen. I cast the zone-out off and looked up. "Perfect. Just what the doctor ordered."

She raised a questioning eyebrow as only the truly eyebrow-gifted can. "Good to hear. Enjoy the Reuben. How's the drink?"

The glass was half full. "All good. I'm a bit of a lightweight." I pulled the sandwich plate closer and plucked up a thick steak fry that teetered on the edge. "Thank you."

"Lemme know if you need anything," and she was gone, which was OK because the squid had barely scratched the surface of my famishedness, so I was ready to inhale the smoked meat right from between the thick slices of bread. With one eye on the front door trying to sort friend from foe as the place filled up, I one-handed the first half of the sandwich like a beast.

With the pincers of my claw, I snatched up the first of the two dill pickle wedges and chomped down. Green juice ran down my claw, onto my arm and down into my sleeve and I didn't give a damn. I ate like it was both my first meal and my last, the opening and closing movements of the Sandwich Concerto in the Key of Mmmm.

There was now so much traffic through the pub's doors that I gave up squinting at every freaking face and just put my head down and ate. The Butcher was a smart predator. He wouldn't try to take me in here, so when I left I'd just have to keep a fuzzy eye open for him, his sidekick, and their Van of Death. No problem.

I slowed down so much in my savouring of the repast that the ginger ale was refilled twice, and the tables all around me filled up. I ate, and even gave in and had the double crowns refilled once. Then I was *done*. After all that fried food, bread, and thick saliva-inducing meat, my taste buds yearned for their signature chocolate mousse to cleanse my palate, but my gut nixed the idea just as Alicia swung by for the dirty sandwich plate.

"Got room for dessert, Hon?"

"Good God, no. Not unless you want me to burst wide open right here at the table."

"Gotcha." She smiled wickedly, though. "Not even a wafer-thin mint?"

A Monty Python reference? Ha! With four shots of maple rye in me, I couldn't keep from replying with a husky-voiced, British-accented, "Fuck off. I'm full."

Alicia winked. "Well done, girl." She fished my bill out of her apron and placed it face down on the table in front of me. "I'll bring the machine. There's no hurry"

"Thanks."

True to her promise, she came by with the wireless credit card machine tout suite and I was settled up in no time, tipping generously. I made a *much*-needed trip to the bathroom, then was out in the parking lot and away from the growing oppressive pub noise. Between the hockey and the Butcher updates, the crowd was getting weird and a little off-key, for lack of a better term. Time to go.

As it always did in Calgary, especially during spring, it had cooled down considerably and the cold air was a welcome slap of mock alertness. I say 'mock' because I was as high as a fucking kite. The smokers had all gone in for the game so I was spared witnesses when I stumbled, banged off the big wooden planter box, tripped, and ended up on my already bruised knees on the damp sidewalk. Shit. I guess there were still a few remnants of meds in me somewhere, dancing with the four shots of whisky.

I reached up and grabbed the planter box. Graceful as an ox, I pulled myself upright and said a silent prayer of thanks that my humility was witness-free. Stuffing my hand and claw in my pockets. I shuffled off into the night.

Folks were out for post-dinner dog walks and family strolls and I managed to plaster an idiot's smile on my face and periodically mumble a semi-coherent 'evening' as I made my way back to the relative safety of the strip park. I thought I was doing a damned good job of not looking like a piss-drunk, dog-less cripple, but the odd eyebrow raised in my direction in passing suggested I looked and smelled as I screwed up as I felt.

I reached the big playground with the boot camp-style obstacle course but could go no further, at least for a few measures. My weebly-wobbly head needed me to sit. The usual mob of playground-swarming munchkins were gone home, tucked in tight, but three early-teen girls sat on the chain-and-canvas swings, chatting away. Much of the playground was spotted with puddles and the eight-foot-tall slide tower was surrounded by a rainwater moat, which was perfect for my needs. I'd be less likely to be considered creepy up there than on one of the benches near the swings.

Hardly giving a crap in my current condition, I waded straight into the puddle and sloshed my way to the ladder. I'm sure the water was cold and as deep as my ankles, but I could hardly feel the end of my nose, so knowing what my feet were going through was out of the freaking question. The claw slowed me down a bit, but I made it up without slipping or falling and disappeared into my new Turret of Sanctuary.

The industrial-strength plastic-and-steel roof had kept most of the rain out, so although my feet were soaked, the rest of me was able to curl up in a dry corner of the four-by-four space. Anyone watching would have seen a pretty sad case, hiding out in a playground, reeking of booze, with little pinpoints of mellowness for eyes.

I knew I was wasted, but I was also numb emotionally, and probably spiritually, so it was tough to give a shit. Once I pulled my hood back up and was tucked out of the wind, it really wasn't too bad up there. The teens on the swings chatted and laughed, but nothing too intrusive, so I tuned them out pretty easily. The sandwich, fries, and squid bits seemed to provide all the internal heat I needed.

Wondering why the boys hadn't called me, I pulled my phone out. As soon as I pressed the Home button, Karl's text message popped up on the screen. *We're at Jack and David's. Are you OK? Will call you when we get home.*

I'd missed their text. Dammit. I checked the time stamp. Shit. I'd been gorging myself in the pub, where it was too loud to hear the notification chime in my coat pocket. I turned up the volume and returned it to my pocket.

It was surprisingly peaceful here in the greenbelt heart of my suburban 'hood. The surrounding two- and three-storey houses dampened the noise of the nearby highways so the only sounds were the teens, the birds, and the wind.

o0o

I must have nodded off because I was suddenly cold as shit and not quite as fuzzy around the edges. I reached into my right pocket for my phone to check the time and my knuckles rubbed up against a mitten. *That's* what I needed—my mitts to keep my hands warm. I tugged them out of my pockets and fumbled a bit to get them on, but succeeded. My cold, numb claw was being an asshole but at least I wasn't wearing gloves or I'd be out here all night just trying to get them on.

An incoming text chimed and I swiped at it to open it up, but my mitten got in the way. I yanked it off and tapped the pop-up on the screen, just like I did just before the accident.

Oh no. No no no no...*no no no no no*....

I tossed my phone away from me like it was white-hot burning coal, but it was too late. The phone bounced off the opposite wall of the plastic castle and landed with a dull thump at my feet, but the vivid once-lost memory of that horrific night stuck to me like shit flung by a demon monkey.

No matter how hard I wished it was just a flash from a nightmare I didn't remember having, I was pretty damned sure it was my first clear memory of the actual crash. Remembering one little snippet of a clip of tugging my green leather glove off with my teeth now opened all the other floodgates of forgottenness from that Day One of my descent into Hell.

As the memories slammed into me, I realized just how screwed up and wrong my nightmares had been. In truth, the accident happened just after seven in the evening and it was light out, not dark. There had been a light snowfall melting on impact on damp roads, not a blizzard creating insanely hazardous conditions. The other car passed me all right, but he didn't sideswipe me intentionally, he had his head down texting as he passed and simply drifted hard into my front left corner.

I might have been able to break and swerve to safety, but I still had the phone in my right hand when I grabbed for the wheel and it kept me from getting a grip. I'd only wanted to send Niko a text to tell him I was running late, but instead, Muse was shoved toward the shoulder, caught the gravel, swerved, and flipped. *I* didn't make a sound, but Muse screeched the wail of a twisting metal soul, and V-Dog cried his plaintiff call of confusion. I grabbed for him, knowing only that even if I died, I had to protect him, but gravity flung him out of my reach and my head struck something hard enough to knock me out, though not before my sweet little heart-dog's final yelp of pain pierced my core.

At the top of the slide tower, I jammed my mitted claw in my mouth and screamed. And screamed and screamed and screamed. When I finally stopped screaming to catch my breath, I puked. No warning gag, no rising bile, just violent, terrified, projectile puke through the tower's plastic arch and out onto the slide. Whisky, squid, meds, smoked meat, memories... all up, as hard and direct as if my body were aborting my rotted soul. Cold, wet, and sobbing, I still managed to pass out, fall asleep, tumble into a black, spirit-crushing crevasse, or whatever the fuck happened to someone who lost consciousness from emotional shock.

oOo

My brain woke slowly, but my body didn't respond at all, at first. It was still dark out, I don't think I was hypothermic, and I still felt a bit booze fuzzy, so I didn't think I'd been out of it for too long. I unkinked my body, and as each joint unkinked, I wanted more and more to just die. The tears came again, not giving me a fucking break. *I had been texting, and I'd killed V-Dog. I* had. Not the other asshole, but the asshole driving Muse, pulling her glove off with her teeth, distracted long enough to react too late to avoid the texting dickhead in the other car. V-Dog was killed by the asshole-bitch that would look back at me from every mirror every day, for the rest of my goddamned life.

I wanted to die. I *deserved* to die, as much as the asshole in the other car had deserved to die. But I wasn't going to, yet. I couldn't shit on V-Dog's memory by ending my own life. It was a pain I had no right to end myself. It was *my* burden, and my penance was to look at his killer's face in every reflective surface I passed, forever.

Of course, I know that it was easier said than done, and I was going to need a *lot* of fucking help. Therapy, friends, and more therapy. I had seriously screwed up and was a long way from being out of the woods. Hell, I wasn't even out of the playground, yet, but that was something I *could* control.

I sure as hell wasn't going down the slide through the puke I knew to be waiting, so I retrieved my phone, shoved it in my pocket, backed out of the entrance and slowly worked my way down the ladder to the puddle. I sloshed my way over to a dry high point in the gravel and surveyed the playground. The girls were gone and most of the surrounding three-storey homes were dark. The greenbelt wasn't equipped with lights, but enough bled from various deck and yard lights on either side that I could see the path clearly enough to be sure of my squishy footing. The fact that I was making a habit of walking in sodden footwear ranked pretty low on my shit-giving scale, but I couldn't escape the squish-squirt accompaniment as I trudged along.

I might not have been hypothermic, but after a minute or two out of the shelter of the slide tower, I was ready to crawl back up and hope I'd survive until some poor nanny and kid found me in the morning. But the night was getting colder and I was ill-prepared for it. Hoodie hood up, mitts on, light jacket zipped up tight to my throat, I picked up the tempo from a slow lento dirge to a faster andantino waltz, hoping to generate enough heat to keep me moving and get me home.

Of course, the other reason to keep moving and stay in the dark was to stay out of sight of the Butcher. If he knew where I was, I'd be easy pickings for him and his sidekick right then, with no witnesses. If he knew where I was, though, he'd have taken me while I was a weeping, puking mess in the tower like some useless troll in a bad fairy tale good mothers don't read to their children. The thing about darkness is that unless he had night-vision goggles, he wasn't going to have a clue who I was until he was close enough that I could whip out the paring knife and core his Adam's apple, while wearing mittens, in squishy shoes. I'd have to jump up just to *reach* his Adam's apple. I sped up, sticking to shadows when yard lights glared, and sloshy-stumbling across streets when I couldn't stay in the park or use laneways.

Having puked up the wonderful meal, I was hungry again, but I also had less alcohol in my system now, so my edges were getting less and less jumbled. To keep my mind off of the shit it was dipped in, I made a mental list of my priorities as they now stood.

Food. Bath. Sleep. The Lads. Dr. Ella for confession time and to see if I could be patched up and made semi-functional again. *I* killed my dog. I destroyed my art, and I killed my dog. This wasn't going to be a quick fix. I *killed* V-Dog. Dr. Ella was going to have her hands full. I *murdered* my boy, my heart dog. I wanted to call and tell Karl and Reggie, but the shame was heavy. *My negligence took the life of my best friend.* I was supposed to protect him and keep him safe, and I did the complete opposite.

Monday was the doctor, Tuesday was Physio, I think, and Wednesday was supposed to be another morning at the range with Charlie, but I was sober enough to know *that* was a stupid idea, what with the emotional swamp I was mired in. I had ended my little boy and the temptation to so easily use the Berretta to end myself was too strong. No gun range.

I needed food. My head was thick with stupid thoughts. I pushed them aside. I needed a steaming soak. I needed sleep. Hours and hours of warm and dry sleep. And I needed to gut and skin the Butcher with my dollar-store paring knife for what he'd done to those women and what he was doing to me. I needed a Happy Pill. I needed sleep. I needed to walk up the steps in front of me now and go into my house. I'd left the house confused and needing fresh air and food and was returning as a murderous bitch who'd had her fill of fresh air but was once again in need of food, of course.

Even with my mitt on I was able to get the keys out and get the door open. But I couldn't go in. I reached in and slapped on the entry light, but I couldn't take that next step across the threshold. I couldn't. I just *couldn't*. The ache in my heart was insane. I stood there with soaked, numb feet, shivering, wondering if I could ever get over the sound of V-Dog's last cry for help as I lost control and crashed us.

I was dead certain the Butcher could sneak up on me and cut my head off on the threshold of what was once my sanctuary, and I wouldn't struggle, wouldn't even give out a whimper.

A car door slammed a few houses down and without so much as a glance over my shoulder, I leaped inside, slammed the door, and threw the bolt. My grip on the thumb-turn stayed steel-solid until I heard the storm door close with a padded metal thump, causing me to scream, jump back, trip over my own numb feet, and fall on my ass, again. I couldn't move. I didn't *dare*. My fuelled-up, fucked up imagination had the Butcher right there on my stoop, waiting to end me as penance for what I did to my beautiful pup.

Chapter Twenty-Two

T he four windows in my front door were merely five-inch squares in a row about six feet up. They were no good at all for a shorty like me to see who was outside, but I could see the light cast by the motion-sensor-equipped coach light. It was on a five-minute timer so I sat, frozen in place, barely breathing, waiting for the stoop to be plunged into darkness again. When it was, I sighed and swiped at my stupid tears with my sleeve.

Shit. I wanted to curl up right there, but my wet feet were finally just too damned uncomfortable. I struggled with the wet laces, then tugged and tugged and slipped and tugged until shoes and socks lay lifeless on the entry rug while my pink, wrinkly feet begged for dryness and warmth and comfort.

First things first. I gave up on fighting the tears and with shivery hands I dried my feet with the scarf hanging on the hook behind the door, then I hobbled upstairs to start the bath. That done, I clomped back downstairs at a granny's pace to nuke some soup. It took twenty minutes to fill the tub, so I set the phone's countdown timer for fifteen.

I ate, and then I soaked. I let the tears dribble down my cheeks as I saw reminders of V-Dog everywhere. It was bad before, but now knowing my real role in his death, it was a weight I wasn't sure I could carry.

I was in bed for maybe five minutes when the phone rang. It was nearly midnight and I picked the irritating device up, half afraid it was Mom, sensing my weakness and moving in for a killing stroke. It was Karl, so I answered. I put it on speaker, but I just couldn't find words.

"Jube? Jubilee? Are you there, Sweetie?" His voice cracked.

"Yeah."

"Oh, Honey. What's the world coming to that a woman-hating bastard can butcher the beauty right out of the world?"

Words eluded me, but a huge sob kicked off more tears. I was so far from 'OK' that I doubted I'd ever see it again. "Help... me."

"Jube" He must have turned to Reggie because his voice faded, though it sounded more urgent. "Reggie, go get Jubilee Now! I'll keep him on the phone!" He turned back to me. "Reg is coming, Jubidoo. Stay with me. What's happened?"

Reg was coming? I was torn between 'Thank God' and 'How can I face him?' Karl wanted me to talk. I *needed* to talk. Talking was cheap, and safer than actions. I didn't want action. "I remember the accident." Such a short statement full of so much pain of the past and fear for the future.

I could hear him huffing and puffing and doors opening and closing while he spoke. "Oh, Honey. *All* of it?"

"Enough."

"You can tell us all about it in person, but you have to keep talking to me now."

"OK." I had nothing to say. Small talk eluded me, but he seemed to sense that.

"Have you taken anything? Any pills?"

"No. They would help, but, I don't feel safe near the bottle. I had rye. Puked it up."

"Good boy. How about food?"

"Puked up a sandwich. Just ate soup." I was just so damned weary.

"Soup is good. Now, weren't you doing something special today with your friend Charlie?"

"Hummingbirds." The Butcher had an accomplice...

"That's right! The hummingbirds. How did that go? How many did you see?"

"None. Sweet fuck all." My brain jogged to one side and made a connection I'd been missing. The Butcher could be a man *or a woman*...

"Damn. Maybe next time. What else did you do? Did you get any work done?"

"Charlie is the Butcher." All of a sudden it made complete fucking sense.

"*What?!* That's ridiculous! The Butcher is a man."

Maybe not. "No sex assault."

"Only a man has that strength."

"She's big. Fit." It all started to make sense. Oh shit shit *shit*. I was finally starting to think straight, maybe.

"But still..."

"She knows the city's parks inside out."

"As do thousands of others, Jube."

"She knows details about the crimes not in the media."

"Really? How do you know they're true? *We* don't know what has been in the papers. She could be making it up, just to impress you."

"She's been toying with me, making me feel safe before springi ng.."

"But..." He still thought I was wrong, but *I* knew I wasn't and he was starting to question his own beliefs.

"She took out a big cyclist today with a single kick."

"She kicked a cyclist?!"

"After he banged into me and hurt my elbow."

"I guess he deserved it, then."

"She faced him down and threatened to cripple him."

"Good for her." Was he on her side?

"She loves guns."

"You do, too, now. Were any of the victims shot?"

"I don't know. Maybe. Not in the heads they found." It was her! It *had* to be! "Or she could be his accomplice. The detective thinks there could be one. She knows where I live and the killer's van drove past here this evening."

"Oh shit." *Now* he believed me. "When did you see her last?"

"This afternoon. We're supposed to go shooting again on Wednesday."

"Like hell, you are, Missy Miss. Now go make sure your doors are double locked and your blinds are closed. We're ten minutes away."

"You, too?"

"Of course. I was silly. It's a cellphone, so I can talk while Reggie drives."

"Good." I worked my way out of the sheets and blankets and slid off the bed. I closed the bedroom blinds, then went to check the ones in the music room. I only got as far as the bathroom because I suddenly needed to pee like a racehorse.

"Closing the blinds. Doors are already locked."

"Double check. Does she know where you keep the spare key? We put it back."

"No." Did she? "I mean, I don't think so." I finished up and flushed. A quick wash and dry of my hands and off to close more blinds. I left the lights off as I went room to room, just to keep her or him from seeing me.

"You need to move the spare, but not right now. Actually, we'll get your locks changed, because of her *and* your family. And we'll find an inexpensive security system slash service. Enough of this 'not feeling safe in your own home' bullshit."

"OK." He was right.

"Now pack a bag with at least a week's worth of clothes. We'll figure out later how long you want to stay, but there'll be no 'I have to go home for clean panties' excuses, again."

My heart warmed. "Yes, Dad."

"And bring your work with you, again. It's a healthier use of your time than fretting over a serial killing bitch."

"OK." I shuffled around the wall bed in my spare room and closed the blinds. "How was Vancouver?" I had to distract us both.

"What? Oh. We spent Saturday in the studio recording the tracks for the film, then celebrated at a party at the Fairmont downtown."

I made my way back downstairs. "Sounds like fun."

"It would have been better with you there, but I saw that you and my darling hubby had some fun of your own. Nola always throws the best loft parties."

"It was just what I needed after Mom's debacle." I closed the blinds in the kitchen and those on the back door leading to the deck. On my way past my desk in the alcove I saw the owl photo on the wall and froze. Knowing now what I did about Charlie, the image of the raptor staring, with one razor-taloned foot raised took on a much more insidious, sinister air. I leaned over the desk and lifted the frame off the hook with one hand.

"Are you still there, Jubilee? We just passed the windmill."

"Still here. Just doing some cleaning." I stuck the photo down between the desk and the wall. "I'm hanging up so I can go pack. Can you pick up the spare key on your way in, please?"

"Of course. Two minutes out. Go, pack."

"OK." I ended the call, stuck the phone in my pocket, and trotted back upstairs. Reggie and Karl were almost here, and that gave me a little hope. An extra boost of energy came from knowing I wasn't going to be staying in the house. That added up to a shade less guilt and a lot less fear.

While I was stuffing underwear and t-shirts into my weekend case, I heard the boys enter and bolt the door behind them. I also heard the soft honk of a car alarm being activated. I didn't stop packing. I needed to get out. Foot thumps came up the stairs and Reggie came in and gave me a huge hug, burying his face in my shoulder. He came to rescue me, but he was nearly at the end of his own rope. "Still no word about or from Elteen?"

He let me go and stepped back. "None. God, Jube, I'm so scared."

"Me, too. Let's get out of here."

"Let's go home."

So, we did, with a suitcase full of clothes, and a briefcase full of electronics and notes. We left a freezer full of anything that would go bad in the fridge in a week and could be safely frozen. Everything else stayed in the fridge. I had no idea when I would be back. It could be in two days or a week. First, we needed to point the police in Charlie's direction and pray that they could catch her, but I didn't even know her last name or address. I had her phone number, and that was it. Dr. Ella would have an address, but even if she gave it up, it might not be real. The Butcher had eluded capture for over a year, so she wasn't going to be so easy to catch now.

As we loaded into the car, I saw the time on the dash clock. "I have to be at Dr. Ella's in six hours."

"We'll get you to the shrink on time."

"I have to tell her that I killed V-Dog."

"*What?*" Reggie twisted around in his seat as Karl drove us out of my neighbourhood.

I told them everything, starting with Mom's text, then birding, the cyclist, the conversation with Detective Marlin and the connections to geocaching, the pub, my meltdown, my remembering, and my *crime*. When we eventually pulled into their parking spot, I felt like I'd lived the entire day a second time, but I had to be OK, at least long enough to get to Dr. Ella's tomorrow, so I sent the boys to bed and made myself at home in the guest room, again.

o0o

I'd love to say that I slept like a baby, but only if the baby was a demon stuck in Hell reliving the worst moment of her miserable life. Now that I remembered the truth of the accident, my night terror was free of the dark roads, the blizzard, and the laughing clown. That night dreamed and relived the whole messed-up reality again in ultra-slow motion, knowing full well what was coming and being completely helpless to avoid the end. I twisted and turned and kicked and fought it, but the inevitable impact, flip, and V-Dog's yelp of pain and confusion rushed at me so hard and slow that I ripped out a scream so loud it woke me.

When I jerked awake my mouth was open in the scream, but no sound escaped, which meant that I'd only screamed in my nightmare and didn't have to worry about the boys rushing in. I took a couple of long breaths. "Shit..." I whispered. I closed my eyes and rolled over on my side, fully expecting sleep to drag me back down as it usually did after a nightmare.

But sleep was as elusive as the truth had been for so long, so I risked a single Happy Pill. One would be OK. One was fine. One would just slow my spinning brain, so long as I didn't mix it with alcohol. No more alcohol. As I lay there staring at the ceiling of the not-mine bedroom, my thoughts flitted from Charlie to Elteen to my family to my crime to how bad it was going to get when everyone found out what I'd done. Eventually, Captain Happy put his arm around my shoulder and whispered in my ear.

"Calm down, Jube."

Mellowness reluctantly settled on me like a layer of fresh snow, so fragile that I was afraid to move for fear that it would shake off and melt away. An easy, deliberate breath in through the nose, out through my mouth. Thumbs and forefingers tapping out the slow, steady, calm tempo of *Wiegenlied: Guten Abend, gute Nacht, opus 49, number 4,* best known as Brahm's *Lullaby.*

I stared at a spot of light on the ceiling, reflected off some surface outside the condo and slipped in through a gap in the blinds. Breathe, tap, slow. Breathe, tap, slow...

The race in my mind soon geared down and I was able to add mental improvised notes to Brahm's beloved masterpiece. I shut my eyes and played it, lying on my back, imagining all of my fingers obeying every command as I teased personal nuances out of the instrument. How long this went on for, I have no idea, but I did calm down. Sleep still refused to even flirt with me, though, so eventually I got up, turned on the light, set up my laptop on the little desk, and dug into my never-ending workload. That was at 4:48 am. I worked for nearly two hours, though I didn't get much done.

My mind kept flashing memories of Elteen on *this* hike or *that* bike ride, and twisting at my reason was the idea that Charlie was involved in the murders. Now that I was sober and safe, the whole idea seemed so bizarre. She had such a fragile sweetness about her. But there was also a darkness lurking in her. She wasn't just private, she was downright secretive, and considering the time we'd spent together and the bonding we'd done, that was just...wrong. I mean, if I was a man and she'd been hurt by one, then I could understand her being gun-shy, so to speak, but if a short, broken, female, former musician had hurt her, why would she go out of her way to spend time with me?

She seemed to know more than was public about the murders, and she was fast enough and strong enough to overcome most women and many men I've ever met. She knew the parks inside and out. For all I knew, she had the geocaching app on her phone. When I started getting mentally wobbly and dozed off over the computer, I called it quits. At 6:45 I set the timer on my phone for forty-five minutes and lay down for a power nap. I was asleep before my head dented the pillow. My last dark, twisted, conscious thought was that my new friend had abducted my goddaughter.

The alarm woke me two minutes later, or at least that's how soon it felt. Eyes closed, snoring commenced, oops, get the hell up. My phone said it was 7:30, but my body and mind said it was insufficient-o'clock. Dear God, I needed a good night's sleep. If I'd had one in the last three weeks, at that moment I couldn't remember it. Better yet, I needed a *string* of good nights, to recharge my battery and get my head on straight.

There was a gentle tap at the door.

"Coffee's ready, Jubidoo."

"Thanks, Sweetie. On my way." I slipped on my socks, threw on a sweatshirt over my T-shirt, and went downstairs.

If I could have cancelled Dr. Ella and crawled back into bed, I would have, but I knew that realistically only Dr. Ella was going to be able to get my head around the pile of shit I'd accumulated in there. I could do all the online research I wanted on PTSD and whatever, but I wasn't yet stupid enough to think I didn't need a trained professional to guide me through the minefield. Then again, Dr. Ella *is* the one who introduced me to the Geocache Butcher, so maybe *my* best interests weren't *hers*.

"I need to bounce an idea off you two lovelies," I said as a 'good morning' when I walked into the kitchen and gave them each a hug.

"Bounce away." Karl handed me a big steaming mug. "What's up, Buttercup?"

"A conundrum. I have a *much*-needed appointment to see Dr. Ella this morning."

"We'll drive you."

"Thank you, but my concern isn't getting there, it's whether I should go at all." I sat at the breakfast bar, next to the toaster.

"But she's been such a big help in such a short time."

"She has, but she's also the one who introduced me to Charlie."

"Oh shit." Karl leaned back against the counter.

"Charlie is her patient, too, which makes me wonder how much the doctor knows about the Butcher's activities. Isn't she bound by the law to tell someone? Or is she protected and restricted by doctor-patient privilege?"

"Good question. We should Google it. I think she's protected from revealing information to law enforcement without a warrant, but I don't think it's the same as Catholic confession or lawyer-client privilege. If she knows, and introduced you two, then you might be at risk. If she doesn't know, then you *both* might be at risk.

"Damn."

"Do you want me to come with you?"

I seriously thought about accepting Karl's offer, but I also knew that Reggie's family was gathering at Elteen's parents' again, and right now Reggie needed Karl a lot more than I did. There's just *no way* kind, sweet, Dr. Ella could be in on Charlie's dark pastime. "No. I'll be OK. I'm sure I'll be safe." Reggie looked visibly relieved. He needed his husband at his side, but he wouldn't have denied me Karl's support.

"Have you told that detective? Or should we call 9-1-1?"

"I can't call 9-1-1 without any actual evidence, but I can send Detective Marlin a text. The thing is, I don't even know Charlie's last name. I'd better talk to Dr. Ella, first. If Charlie is the Butcher, then she needs to be taken off the streets before she takes another beautiful soul."

"Yes." Reggie quietly agreed.

"Definitely." Karl stood up and moved back toward the kitchen. "Greek yogurt, fruit, crumpets and marmalade for everyone?"

"Yes, please." I was famished.

"Please," Reggie added. He had done so much for me that it broke my heart to see him so lost. We were all sick with thoughts about what might have happened or be happening to Elteen, but Reggie was truly scared. There had to be something I could do to at least distract him for a few minutes.

"Karl, can I steal Reg for five? I need his artist's eye for a couple of logo redesigns I'm considering."

Karl nodded and waved us away with a melodramatic sigh. "Go. Take ten. I'll slave away alone, as usual."

I couldn't help but laugh. "Whiny little bitch."

He mimed a drama queen's flouncy exit with a huff, and I dragged Reggie by the elbow to the stairs. "Come on, Mr. Top-of-My-Class-at-ACAD artist. I need your eye."

He didn't struggle, he let me lead him, and just as we started up the stairs he whispered. "Did you just call Karl a whiny little bitch?"

"You betcha."

"Naughty Jubidoo." But he didn't seem angry and even livened up a bit when we got to my room and I opened my laptop and Photoshop.

oOo

Karl and Reggie dropped me off in front of the Calgary Tower at 8:45. Fifteen minutes was more than enough to get up to the fourth floor of the office tower to Dr. Ella's, but once I was inside the building, I dawdled in the lobby. My head was full of such discordant thoughts that I was going to explode and the little bits of Jubilee-fluff would float away on the wind. Except that there was no wind inside the building, and the pending explosion was a result of thinking that my therapist was in collusion with a serial killer who had somehow become my new BFF.

But was I messed up because of my haphazard disregard for my meds, my abuse of alcohol, or the remnants of the crippling trauma? How much was I imagining and how much was real? This was always the point in my confusion when Mom popped in to convince me that it was all in my mind. This was the point that the shadow cast by the gaslight was darkest.

"Fuck it." There wasn't anyone around to hear me in the cavernous, oddly-shaped common area outside the elevators, so I pressed the button and waited, without fear of strange looks or disapproving 'tsk tsks'. I swear a lot, but I try to keep it private.

The elevator arrived, I got in, pressed the button, and when the door closed behind me and the contraption rose for the short trip, so did my anxiety. I could feel my face flush, and perspiration start up. I stumbled down the silent, carpeted fourth-floor hallway, my good hand reaching for the wall, for stability. When I opened the heavy door to the office and stepped into the reception area, Song looked up with her characteristic wonderful smile, but it vanished in a quarter beat. She stood up, ready to help, but giving me space. "Ms. Krawetz—are you OK?"

"Um..."

My indecision moved her and she came around her desk to take me by the elbow and guide me to the big comfy couch. As soon as my ass was safely down, she filled a paper cup at the water cooler and placed it gently in my hand.

"Take a sip. Do you need me to call the doctor out? She's with a patient, but if it's an emergency I can buzz her."

I took that commanded sip, then another. Song's mere presence calmed my foolishness. "I'll be OK. Thank you."

She sat down next to me, at a distance she seemed to know instinctively was perfect for me. I gave her a weak smile and wondered how much of a conversation she was allowed to have with a patient. "Song, how long have you worked for Dr. Ella?" Might as well jump in and ask.

"Five years, three months."

I wanted to ask her things like 'How long had Charlie been a patient?', but I knew I couldn't. I trusted her, but probably because she was worthy of trust, which meant she wouldn't violate her employer's trust by breaking protocol. I wanted to keep her talking for five minutes until my appointment, so I kept it innocuous. Sometimes, too, there were secrets hidden in answers to casual, unimportant questions. "Has the office always been in this location?"

"No. We moved here three years ago from a little place in Banker's Hall that we shared with two other therapists."

I don't know why I asked that, but maybe just to get a feel for their relationship before I hit her with the next question. "Have you ever had an extreme patient, one you've had to call the police for?"

She leaned away and looked at me like I'd just asked for her home phone number. "I think that is a question best asked of Dr. Ella."

"Of course. Sorry. I was just wondering."

She stood up. "It's no problem. How are you feeling? More water?" She held her hand out, I gave her the cup, and she refilled and returned it.

"Thank you." I sipped. It was nice and simple, unlike coffee with its cream, no cream, sugar, no sugar, three sugars... and then there were roast types and filter methods, not to mention the district and country. Water *could* be that complicated, but to me most of the time it's just cold and wet and exactly what I need. Song returned to her desk, leaving me to sip and think.

Although I was still mostly convinced that Charlie was the Butcher, I was becoming less certain that Dr. Ella knew anything about it, and five minutes later, when I was sitting in her office and she was closing the door behind us, I realized how silly her involvement sounded. Silly or not, though, there was dark shit in my life and I needed her help.

Chapter Twenty-Three

"Doctor, have you ever discovered something about a patient that made you call the police?"

"And let's just jump right in with both feet shall we, Jubilee." She smiled and I relaxed a bit, but I still wanted an answer.

"Or does your Code of Ethics forbid it?" I'd read about it online with the lads.

"To answer your questions in order, yes, I have, yes I called, and the Code of Ethics allows us to breach that trust when we believe there's a risk of bodily harm or death to a person or group. We have a bit more flexibility than lawyers and priests, but we don't take such breaches lightly. I've only called the police once because a patient stormed out of here to kill his wife. Why on Earth would you ask this? Have you done something wrong, Jubilee?"

I asked because of Charlie but suddenly realized that there was another unrelated reason for me to ask. "I killed my dog."

"You got another dog since I saw you last?"

"No. I mean that I killed Vivaldidog."

"You told me he died in the accident, Jubilee, and the police report confirms that. You also told me that you don't remember the accident. Has this changed?"

"I remember it all, now" I whispered, and reached for a tissue from the ever-present box on the table beside my chair. Shit. It was one thing to admit the truth to Reggie and Karl who love me and support me, but was I risking more than shame by telling a professional, on the record? A man died in that accident.

"Tell me what you remember."

Fuck it. I told her, step by step, pointing out where reality differed from my nightmares.

"You were texting, too?"

"Trying to. I only had the phone in my hand, but I needed it on the steering wheel."

"Yes, that certainly would have slowed down your reaction time. But you're not a professional driver, Jubilee. You're not trained like the police are, to maintain control after an impact. We all do our best when crap happens on the road, but while you're trudging along carrying the weight of your accident on your shoulders, remember that *he* hit you. *He* started the chain of events that resulted in Vivaldidog's death."

"I was texting." I stared at the carpet.

"You weren't driving as safely as you could have been, but you could just as easily have been reaching for your coffee, scratching your nose, turning the radio down, or even patting your dog's head—all things we do when we drive."

I looked up at her like she'd just admitted something.

"Yes, Jubilee we've all done it. Sometimes we just swerve a bit and catch ourselves, and sometimes it's more serious. But we rarely do it while passing another vehicle on a two-lane road. That takes a special kind of stupid."

I smiled. "That's your professional opinion?"

She grinned back. "Oh, I might dress it up in fancy jargon for a court statement, but yes, the other driver's actions show a self-centred, self-obsessed nature with a complete disregard for people around him. Your accident happened; it wasn't your fault. You are welcome to feel heartbroken for the loss of your beloved dog, and if carrying around a *little* guilt about not reacting as fast as you could have keeps you from distracted driving again, then I'll let you keep that *little* bit of guilt."

That was so kind of her, I thought sarcastically. "You're not going to call the police and tell them I broke the law?"

"Hardly. For one, it's a minor thing, a traffic violation. The heartbreak you're feeling is more punishment than any little fine or demerit points they'll dole out. Secondly, there's no active investigation into your accident. Your actions had no bearing on the other driver losing control after hitting you, swerving off the road and hitting that post in the other ditch."

"If there were an active investigation, you would call?"

"*If* I thought you posed a threat to someone else, yes."

That made me feel better. It also made saying what I was going to say, next, easier. "Thank you. So, if you suspected one of your patients was the Geocache Butcher, you wouldn't hesitate to call?"

"The Geocache Butcher? Jubilee, I hardly think you could be that sadistic misogynist."

"But you would call?" Was she dodging the question?

"If I was reasonably sure, I have friends with CPS I could call, to steer them in that direction, yes. I wouldn't be happy about breaking that bond with my patient, but there would be bigger issues at play."

"OK." I had to tell her. To save Elteen.

"Now, is this all a hypothetical inspired by the news of the latest victim? Did you have a rough weekend?"

"You don't know the half of it." I told her about Mom's blood-fest and Shauna's love-in, for a start.

"Well, that certainly tells us who you need to spend *more* time with and whom to avoid."

"Mom wants to commit me on Wednesday."

"*What*?" There must have been a clock behind me that only she could see because she interrupted herself and held a hand up.

"Your session is almost up, Jubilee but this is too important to just pick up again later in the week. Hold that thought while I speak to Song, about my schedule, please."

"Of course." I was relieved as hell. My mind hadn't been on the time, but I couldn't leave without telling her about Charlie. Just *couldn't*. She stepped out to speak with Song and returned quickly.

"Done." She sat and waited for the door to swing shut and latch behind her. "First of all, you're doing great and hardly in need of an intervention, let alone hospitalization. Some of what you're going through is what we call STUGS—*Sudden Temporary Upsurge of Grief*. Secondly, your mother has no authority to do anything. You're over eighteen and she's not your guardian. We'll take her off your emergency call list as the final disconnection. She would have to have the police accompany her and she'd need proof you're a threat to yourself."

"She thinks I'm imagining my stalker, thinks I'm crazy when I mention the Butcher."

"From all that you told me, I think it's your *mother* who needs the professional help. A serial killer has taken three lives. You'd be crazy *not* to be afraid of an unknown killer."

"But I *do* know the killer." Oh shit. That came out quickly.

"You mean that you understand the profile of a psychopath who would do this? Or do you mean you can identify him from that encounter in the park near the owls?"

"Neither. It's Charlie." Genie-out-of-the-bottle time!

In all my hours in her office, I've never seen the doctor speechless. She'd always been so calm and cool and knew exactly what to say and when, but right at that moment her mouth was moving, but the words were missing. I could tell that she was thinking hard, even if she couldn't express her thoughts. I leaned back in the chair, relieved that I'd finally told her, and I mentally crossed my fingers that I'd made the right decision. I gave her all the time she needed to process my declaration, which turned out to be only a few beats.

"Since I've come to see that you're an intelligent, thoughtful, kind person, Jubilee, I'd like to hear how you came to this quite unexpected conclusion." It was her turn to lean back and wait. She didn't look angry or scared, but rather confused. I waded in.

"It isn't just one thing, it's the sum of a bunch of things. I'm not an alarmist, or paranoid. One: She knows Fish Creek Park intimately—which means nothing on its own, I know. She also knows things like how broken a wrist is without even touching it. I saw her take down that cyclist asshole without even trying. Her reflexes are insanely fast. And she's fearless, facing him down and threatening to hurt him more."

I was on a roll and the good doctor let me ramble. "She's amazing with a firearm, and we don't know exactly how any of the victims were killed. Lastly, she knows details about the murders, about *how* they were murdered, that were *never* revealed in the media. She's also really, really secretive." This last part sounded so fucking lame I wanted to backspace and delete it. I waited for my irrefutable evidence to sink in. She was smart, she would agree.

"Those are all pretty damning facts, leading to a plausible con-clusion, Jubilee. I've seen the police find killers with less."

Ha! I knew I was right!

"But I have facts that you don't, so do you mind if I call Charlie to get her permission to share them? I won't tell her exactly why."

Call Charlie? Shit! "Sure. OK." Was she calling her for backup, like in the movies?

She went to her desk, picked up the phone, and spoke to Song. "Song. Please connect me to Charlene's cellphone. Thank you." After a couple of beats, Charlie must have answered.

"Hello, Charlie. It's Doctor Ella. I'm currently in a session with Jubilee and for the sake of her healing, I would very much like to share your story with her, but just your last year. Yes, I'm sure you were going to, and you can certainly fill in all the details when you see her next, but I'd like to give her the broad-strokes version." She listened, nodding. "Of course. It's all good. Thank you. And on her behalf in advance, I thank you. Have a wonderful day. Thank you, I will." She hung up and returned to her chair, but stopped before sitting.

"Would you like a cup of tea, Jubilee? We might as well relax." She turned toward her electric kettle and tea service. Tea sounded like a great idea, even though I was itching to hear what she wanted to tell me.

"Yes, please. Any flavour at all would be fine."

"How's peppermint green sound?" She turned on the kettle and went about setting up two cups.

"Perfect." And it did. I was a little wound up and it would help.

"So, Charlie knows the parks because she hikes and bikes regularly, as many people do, including my husband and me." The cups and saucers set up, she sat, waiting for the kettle to boil. "Charlie also knows anatomy and injuries so well because she's an Emergency Medical Technician—a paramedic—and a talented one at that. I believe she has received two industry awards in the last ten years. As for the guns—she's a farm girl and grew up around firearms. In fact, I belong to the same association as she does and have even competed against her." She shared with me some of the shooting competitions Charlie had won.

The kettle switch popped, so she got up to fix our cups. She spoke as she poured, as relaxed as if we were chatting in her kitchen. "Charlie is secretive because she's been hurt and bullied, and simply keeps her personal details close to her chest, although I *am* surprised she hasn't already told you all this. She really likes spending time with you. Cream? Sugar?"

"Black, please. I like her, too. I don't like to pry, so maybe she doesn't think I'm interested in her life. That's not entirely true, but we've only just met."

"And finally, what I hope will convince you that not only is Charlie *not* the Geocache Butcher, but she is being really brave talking to you about it at all." She handed me my tea, the string of the bag looped securely around the cup's handle.

Chapter Twenty-Four

"Jubilee, Charlie and her work partner, Delroy, were the first emergency responders on the scene when the left hand of the Butcher's first victim was found cached in the trees on the hillside below Parkland. She knows the details of the murders because she saw the remains herself. EMS was called for the hiker who found the hand and had a stress-related asthma attack. Three weeks later, she and Delroy just happened to be dispatched to the scene of the head of the second victim, where a responding CPS officer had seen the remains, stumbled, fallen, and broken his wrist. Charlie and Delroy saw the remains while they were treating the constable, and although they never actually touched them, all of the first responders there discussed what they'd seen amongst themselves." She took a sip and I let it all sink in.

After a few beats, she continued. "The whole scenario was so horrific that poor Delroy went home and took his own life. The next day Charlie went on leave. She's been my patient ever since. She works light duties around the dispatch office, but the Geocache Butcher's victims aren't just the young women he violates and hides parts of in the parks around the city, they're also the people who have to deal with the horror in person, and their families. So, Charlie isn't the Butcher, she's a *victim*."

Shit! I was so stupid. How could I think such horrid things about such a kind person? "I'm so, so, sorry." The damned tears came hard and fast and I barely set my tea down before the sobbing shook me. I was such a screw-up.

The doctor let me cry, coming over and taking my hands in hers and whispering "It's OK, m'dear. Let it out. It's OK."

o0o

Oh, I let it out all right. I had a full nuclear meltdown right there in her damned office while peppermint steam wafted up from the cup and made it all feel so surreal, so bizarre and off-key.

When I was finally done, she placed the box of tissues on my lap and moved the little wastebasket to my side. I sniffled and dried and blew snot and wiped and she didn't rush me. I threw her an apologetic smile in the middle of it all and she smiled back with that East Coast twinkle in her eyes.

"I think I just used half of your tissues, doc."

"There's more where they came from. How do you feel?"

"Stupid."

That's natural. You had a set of facts and in the stress of the situation, you came to the wrong conclusion. But you know it happens to *all* of us, far more often than we like to admit."

"I know."

"So, you're satisfied Charlie isn't a serial killer?"

"Of course. It all sounds so ridiculous now. I just hope my mother never finds out about it, or I'll never hear the end of it." God, I hope *Charlie* never hears about it!

"She won't hear it from *me*. And to be honest, I think you should just take some time off from your family."

"Agreed. Thank you." A thought bumped into me. "But I still think I'm being stalked. I saw the gold mini-van again yesterday, I think."

"Call the police. You didn't call them about suspicious about Charlie, did you?"

"No. Not yet. Not *ever*, now."

"Good."

"Doctor Ella, I rolled off the wagon last night, and to say that I had a rough one would be falling short of the mark."

"This was a heavy-duty weekend for you, Jubilee."

"No shit." I filled her in on the rest of the weekend's details, including Friday's conversation with Detective Marlin, the pub dinner that didn't stay down for long, right up to my rescue by the lads. She interrupted me only periodically to have me clarify important details, but for the most part, she just let me tell it like I remembered it.

"I'm so very glad that you have such good friends and that you're not afraid to let them in. I agree with the detective that you need to be more cautious, starting with staying with Karl and Reggie as long as they'll have you. But you can't hide inside forever, so I'd like to see you get out more for coffee or a movie or whatever, with friends. Tune your family out and concentrate on the people who truly love you, even the old symphony friends. Your success at your friend Shauna's on Saturday—as emotional as it was—was excellent. As for Charlie, I hope you continue to do things with her now that you know the truth, but the choice is your own. As I said before, she enjoys spending time with you, and even though *I* won't tell her, I think she'd see the humour in your mistaken assumptions about her."

I wasn't so sure about that. "Maybe someday."

"Fair enough. Now, as for your family coming over on Wednesday... I'm glad you'll be staying with Reggie and Karl, but I think you need to send both your mother and your sister a text telling them that you're staying with friends, so you won't be home on

Wednesday, and maybe you can get together for coffee next week. I don't think you *should* go for coffee, but a text like that will forestall any actions they're considering, and maybe defuse them."

"I'll do that immediately so that I don't forget."

"Good. But if you have any trouble, call the emergency number on my card. Do you still have my card?"

Did I? "Probably. On my fridge or in my wallet."

She reached back to her desk and took a card out of the little silver holder. "Here. If you call, you'll get my service, but give them your name and tell them it's an emergency and they'll put you through. As soon as we're done here, I'll call and give them your name and the OK."

"Thank you." I was starting to feel like the ground under my feet was more solid than it had been in a while.

"That's why I'm here, although I don't think your mother will follow through. She's a bully who uses gaslighting to keep you off balance and keep herself in a position of power. I believe that as soon as you push back calmly and firmly, she'll back down."

"You don't know Mom."

"True enough. So, maybe instead send her a text saying you're going up to the mountains to stay with friends and you'll call her when you get back."

"That might work better. There won't be much she can do if she doesn't know where I am and knows I'm not alone."

"Very true. But if none of this works and she insists on being on the offensive, we'll get a restraining order to keep them away. You're not a fragile flower, but at this stage of your healing, you're still vulnerable to her attacks. Over the next few weeks, we'll work on your defence against gaslighting."

"Thank you. Do I get a wand, too?"

"Only if you pass your potions exam. So, how are you feeling *right now*?"

"Solid. Hopeful even."

"Excellent. We can talk some more about the accident if you wish. That's a pretty big realization, your part in it. Don't expect that pain to go away overnight, and I'd rather you not use alcohol to dull it. You need to take your medication exactly as the doctor prescribed them. No more self-regulation, and no mixing them with alcohol. If you can stay sober while dealing with this, then you'll be well on your way to building a solid emotional foundation you can trust not to collapse at any given moment."

I didn't need any more damned meltdowns in playgrounds, that's for sure. Some poor kid probably met up with my vomit on the slide this morning, and that's just *sad*. "Maybe talking about the accident some more now will help."

"Then let's."

o0o

We went over the details again bit by bit as I remembered them, and then we compared the reality with my nightmares and what the extreme differences between them might mean. After probably half an hour of this I was knackered, but my guilt was a smidgen lighter. We both agreed that I still had some distance to travel in terms of healing, but when I said how tired I was and could go 'home' for a nap, she cut me loose with a final hug and an appointment for Friday. We still didn't know how Mom was going to react to not getting her way, so I thought that the anti-gaslight training should start ASAP.

o0o

As soon as my feet hit the sidewalk outside, I texted Mom and Joyce together. I worded it pretty much as the doctor suggested, thanking them for the 'offer' to come visit me on Wednesday, but I'd been invited up to the mountains for a week and would call them when I got back. I even signed it "Love, Jubilee", just to mess with them. I was done responding with anger. It was time to use kindness and distance to disperse the gaslight Mom sent my way.

I thought of turning off my ringer so I wouldn't know if they texted back, but that would have been childish. Besides, the lads might call or maybe even Elteen. I sent Karl and Reggie a quick text to say I was OK, that I was taking advantage of the beautiful weather, that the sidewalks were full of people so I was safe, and that I was walking back to the condo. I promised to pick them up some truffles, too and asked if there was anything else they needed.

Thirty seconds later, Karl texted back that truffles would be more than enough, I was to watch out for gold vans, and they'd see me soon. I replied with a happy face emoji because I felt good and was in a goofball mood, but before I could put the phone away and get down to the business of enjoying the walk, it rang. Detective Marlin.

"Hello."

" Ms. Krawetz, it's Detective Marlin. Can we meet? There has been a development I'd like to talk to you about."

"I'm nowhere near home, detective. I'm downtown, just walking past the Palliser Hotel."

"That's perfect. I'm about ten minutes away, at the Municipal Building. If you go into the hotel and have a seat in the lobby, where you can see the front desk, I'll come in and get you. I'd rather you be somewhere secure."

Uh oh. That didn't sound good. I started up the steps into the grand old railway hotel. "Of course. I'm just going into the hotel now. I'll see you shortly."

"Thank you." He disconnected the call, which was good because it sounded like he was driving.

I found a seat, sent Karl a text to explain my delay so he wouldn't freak out, and I waited. I checked my emails, scanned my Facebook updates, and was about to see if anything was interesting on Instagram when a siren approaching the hotel caught my attention. I looked over at the big brass and glass doors to see red and blue flashing lights reflected in them, but instead of passing by, they stopped. A moment later Detective Marlin jogged into the lobby. I was on my feet before he reached me and he led me back out to the street, to his car.

"Thank you for seeing me."

"Of course. You sounded pretty worried." He sounded *scared*.

"The city is like a dry forest waiting for a single spark, but we've made some serious headway on the case. If you were in danger before, Jubilee, it's even worse than we originally thought. I have an office over on Eleventh Ave where we can chat."

"Uh, yeah, sure," was all I managed to mumble while I buckled up and we were off, having been blocking very busy, one-way, Ninth Avenue. He turned off the flashing lights, I guess because the urgency was in getting to me.

"How well do you know Niko Cardellini?"

Niko? What? "He's someone I met on eRomance-dot-ca."

"Did you ever speak with him or meet him in person?"

"No. Just texting and emails. I was on my way to meet him when I was in the accident."

"How long did you communicate with him, in any form?"

"A couple of months. We connected just after Valentine's Day."

We pulled into a driveway down into an underground parking garage of a building I don't ever recall having seen before, even though I'd lived three blocks away for a few years. He tapped his ID on the reader, the big door rolled up, we entered, he found a spot, parked, and we were out and walking.

"Tell me about your conversations, please."

"Sure." I explained about our emails about dogs and music and Mozart's home in Salzburg, Austria. I told the detective as many details as I could remember about Niko's coarse sense of humour, how he grew up on a farm where they bred Labradoodles and his odd affection for Tchaikovsky's 1812 Overture. While I talked, we entered a secure elevator accessible only with the detective's ID, then we went up to the second floor and a small, simple, utilitarian, computer-equipped office with a south view. I ran out of Niko stories just after we grabbed coffees from the single cup server on his file cabinet, and settled into chairs, his behind his desk.

"Niko Cardellini isn't his real name. His real name is William Watson."

"The missing reporter?" What the hell?

"Exactly. And we're certain now that he isn't investigating the Geocache Butcher, he *is* the Butcher."

Fuck! "How? Why?" I was dumbfounded. What the hell did a blowhard reporter have against three women and *me*?

"When he first went missing, his sister let us into his condo, which revealed nothing about his alter ego. But this weekend she discovered a small file in a kitchen drawer. It contained the title to a property she didn't know anything about, southwest of the city. Inside a trailer on the property, she found a bulletin board with profiles of each member of the Girls of Cache-a-Lot, and bloody work coveralls on the floor of the shower. She stopped exploring and called us immediately. We found the saw, the shed where he probably did his gruesome work, and a desktop computer with an encrypted external hard drive and an internet connection. The eRomance-dot-ca web page was bookmarked. It didn't take our techs long to get into his accounts, though the hard drive is giving them a bit more trouble. One of the eRomance accounts is in the name of Niko Cardellini."

Holy shit! "Watson wasn't there?"

"No. And he hasn't been for a few weeks. We think he's on the run. We haven't been able to find information on any additional properties, but he's smart and could have one or more places hidden in the mountains of British Columbia."

"Then he's not here in the city."

"Again, a bad assumption to make. He might not have another rural property, he could have another condo, or be renting a basement apartment somewhere. We just don't know, yet. I'm hoping the chat I have with the press downtown in an hour will get his photo out everywhere and flush him out of hiding. Stay with your friends, please. We're closer to catching this bastard than we have been since he started killing and I don't want his victim's list to get any longer."

"I was on my way there when you called."

"Then that's where I'll drop you when we're done here."

"Thank you." I was still stunned. "I can't believe that this reporter is the Butcher. You're sure?"

"The Forensics Crime Scene Team is out there searching the property with every piece of tech they've got. It'll be a while before we have the DNA results on the blood we've found so far, but the evidence in front of us so far is pretty conclusive. The pieces are all fitting together quite nicely."

"But why?"

"I think it has to do with that geocaching challenge you and your goddaughter were on last fall. Although he'd done his best to delete them, our techs were able to find online reviews your friends posted trashing the course they did. With a bit of digging, we found that it was *his* treasure hunt and he was livid that they gave it such horrific reviews. They had quite the ongoing online insult war going on with him. The ladies seemed to take some joy in goading him, and he kept taking the bait, getting more and more livid. At this point, it's the only motive we have."

"Three women are dead and my goddaughter is missing because some incel asshole couldn't take criticism?" That was fucking ridiculous!

"That's one of the angles we're looking at, yes."

"Then he better hope you find him first because if he tries to take me, I'll gut him."

"Please don't. Hide. Stay indoors. Don't answer the door. He's fit, fast, and experienced."

"And I'm just a short, crippled musician, is that it?"

"Sorry, but yes. These are all young, fit women he has managed to abduct and murder. Even *I* want backup when we catch him."

"Then hurry. Please." My hands started shaking in my lap. "I'm all talk. A couple hours at the gun range and I think I'm invincible, but I'm..."

"Being scared is OK. Only a fool isn't afraid."

"Then I'm no fool, at least not for that reason." My phone buzzed, probably with a text from Karl wondering how long I was going to be. "Is there anything more I can help with, detective?"

"Not at this time. Let's get you to your friends' and then I'd better get to City Hall to update the media. It will help Calgarians to finally have a face for the Butcher, then they can all relax and stop rolling through the streets like vigilantes."

"Hopefully."

oOo

I texted Karl that we were close and on our way and he was waiting for us when we pulled up in front of the building. "Well, someone got herself a special escort. What's up?"

I waved at the detective as he drove away, then grabbed Karl's arm and dragged him to the front door of the townhouse. "Let's get inside, first. The shit is about to hit the fan."

We practically jogged up the steps where he opened the door and held it for me. "First, *we* have news. Elteen is safe! She just called her mother collect from a payphone in some harbour to say she'd been invited out on a friend's old cabin cruiser photographing orcas north of Vancouver Island and dropped her phone in a sink full of water before they even launched."

The door closed and latched behind us and I felt safe enough to take a breath. "Oh thank, God." My relief was immense, but there was still a serial killer out there with Elteen's and my names.

"Did they catch the bastard?"

"No. But they know who he is and they have a good idea what his twisted motive is."

He led me upstairs, to the living room, where Reggie was sitting, sipping from a mug and reading something on his tablet. He stood up when we came in, smiled past tears of relief, and hugged me. "Jube, she's alive."

"For now." I was safe there with the two of them. "The psychopathic Geocache Butcher is none other than that missing journalism school dropout with the Journal-Times, William Watson."

"*That* angry, opinionated shit murdered three women?"

We sat on the couch. "That's what the evidence says." I filled them in on everything I'd just learned from the detective, and they were as stunned as I was upon hearing it. "He murdered them because they humiliated him online."

"And he's after you, next." Karl looked worried.

"That's what Detective Marlin thinks. I had nothing to do with any of that online stuff, but he had my name written down with Elteen's, so the logical step is to assume Elteen and I are in danger. She's out on the West Coast so that just leaves me."

"Then you stay with Reggie and me indefinitely, and we'll get a message to Elteen to find somewhere safe."

"Thank you." Hopefully, it wouldn't be for long, though. I loved the boys, but home was my home.

"What happened to your theory about your friend, Charlie?"

"Well... let me tell you about how wrong I was there." I gave them the details I had, blushing with shame when I admitted how much of an idiot I was.

"The poor girl," Karl commented when I was done. Reggie just sat in sad silence. "Maybe we can have her over for dinner sometime, if you'd wish, Jube."

I think she'd like the two of them. "Let's just wait until this is all over, please."

"Of course."

My phone bing-bonged with an incoming text. Mom. A simple *Have fun in the mountains. We were so looking forward to having a nice visit with you but can wait until you return. Mom.* Wow. She seemed to have forgotten what the originally stated purpose of her 'visit' was. Oh well. Screw her and the distillery wagon she rode in on. I put my phone back in my pocket without responding. "It was Mom. At the doctor's recommendation, I sent them a text saying I'd be out of town for the week."

"Good thinking."

Just then I remembered my promise to the boys. "I didn't get the truffles. I'm sorry."

"I'll pick some up on my way home from rehearsal." He looked at his watch. "I have to go. Will you two be OK?"

I smiled. "Between the two of us, I think we'll stay out of trouble. Right, Reggie?"

He smiled and nodded. "You betcha. Go rehearse. We'll be good, Love." He even got up off the couch to give Karl a hug and a kiss.

I squeezed Karl's hand gently from where I was sitting. I would have loved to go with him to rehearsal to see everyone, now that I'd taken something of a first step at Nola's, but I wasn't sure I had the emotional energy for that quite yet. Like learning to play the cello, healing was going to take time. Music hadn't been something I was able to do overnight, and even after I went pro each new piece took time and effort to master. As much as I wanted Dr. Ella to slap my forehead with her palm and declare me "HEALED!" it was going to take more than truffles and a few meltdowns.

Karl picked up his violin case from the corner and left. Reggie wandered into the kitchen. "Coffee?"

"Please." It sounded like such a good idea that I didn't even care if it was a generic grocery store instant. Of course, in this household, there was no chance of *that* happening. While Reggie tinkered away, I closed my eyes and leaned back on the couch. A couple of minutes later, Reggie placed a mug of brew on the coffee table in front of me—an Italian light roast, by the scent. He joined me on the couch with his mug.

"Hey, Jubidoo, howyoudoin'?", he asked in his best Joey Tribbiani New York accent. " I get the impression that your detective is a good man and a good cop. Is he married?" He winked.

I flipped him the bird. "Yes."

"Twin brother?"

I laughed. "I don't fucking know, Reggie. I'll text him and ask."

"Good. You need a man... or a dog. A man with a dog would be good."

"That is insulting, mister. I'm offended as a woman and I'm offended as a friend. I have *you* two."

"Yes, you do." He squeezed me.

"Although I *was* thinking about dogs on the ride over. Maybe a little mixed-breed rescue."

"So soon?"

"It might help with all this healing I'm supposed to be doing. It's not like I'll be going back to eRomance-dot-hell to find a soul mate. Oh shit! I forgot to tell you. There was no Niko. It was the Butcher posing as Niko to lure me in or something. Now *that* is sick.

"What? I thought she sounded too wonderful to be real."

"It turns out you were more right than you knew. So, no more online dating. One psycho killer is enough, thank you very much." I took a tentative sip of the hot brew. Mmm. "I'm going to delete my account."

"Probably a good idea."

"Thanks. Then again, what are the odds that another Butcher is hiding in the group of ten men I've been swapping notes with?"

Reggie didn't say a word. He just turned and gave me his dirty look of one squinty eye and a sneer.

"Fine. I'll delete the account."

"Good girl."

"I'm so glad you approve, *Mom*."

"Ouch."

Chapter Twenty-Five

I eventually filled Reggie in on the rest of the session with Dr. Ella while we puttered around in the kitchen and made salad and sandwiches for lunch. He liked the message I'd sent Mom and Joyce and made a really good point.

"Like I said before, you need to have your locks rekeyed."

"Rekeyed? How about I just replace the entire mechanisms with different brands that won't even let the old keys in?"

"Better still. I know you have to get some work done, but my afternoon is open if you want to take care of it. Karl is out until seven, as they prepare for the concert next month."

I flinched a tiny flinch at the mention of the concert. "Let's do it."

After lunch, Reggie grabbed his toolbox from the laundry room and I filled two travel mugs with more coffee, then we were off. I didn't want to stick just *any* ugly locksets in, so we went to all three of the big box hardware stores in my 'hood until we found the perfect sets. One for the front and one for the back, in a nice brushed nickel to match the handles and locks on the storm doors. When we got back home, an Amazon box containing my new camera was sitting on the stoop.

We replaced the back door set first so that if we screwed it up it wouldn't be on the door I used the most. The learning curve was steeper than we expected, but when were done it worked as smooth as silk and looked great. After a short break, we completed the front door quickly, then rekeyed it to match the back door.

Reggie handed me the old lockset and froze, looking over my shoulder, into the street. "Jubidoo," he whispered, his lips not moving. "What make did you say your stalker's van is? Don't turn around, just tell me."

Oh shit! "It's a Dodge Caravan, gold, with tinted windows. Is the fucker behind me?"

"Well, a van like that is parked down the other street about six houses away. I didn't see it until the big truck drove off a moment ago."

"Can you see the driver?"

"I can't see inside it clearly, but I think there's someone in the big evergreens on the north side of the playground."

It was time to end this shit and put the Butcher behind bars. I'd had enough of his fear-mongering. He destroyed those women and now I was going to destroy *him*. I picked up the rubber mallet. "I'm going to go out the back door and sneak around behind him. Call 9-1-1 and tell them we have the Geocache Butcher at my address. I'll go let the air out of his tires so he can't drive away."

"What's the mallet for?"

"Self-defense."

He took his phone out of his back pocket. "You're crazy. You're going to get yourself killed, and then Karl will never talk to me again."

"Would you rather do the sneaking and I'll make the call?"

"I'm six-one. I don't 'sneak' very well. Go. I'll call. Be careful."

This was insane, but we had a chance to catch him and I wasn't about to let the opportunity slip away so another woman could be butchered. I went inside, scooted through the house, and out the back. Through the yard, out through the gate, and into the laneway. Since I knew exactly where he was, I was able to stay out of sight, zip across the road, and get behind the parked cars until his tacky gold van was between me and his hideout in the trees.

As I tiptoed across the road to his van, I resembled a cartoon Pink Panther on a caper. I couldn't see my stoop and Reggie from where I was, but I hoped to hell he was making the call and they took him seriously. With the mallet gripped tightly in my good hand, I unscrewed the valve cap to the front left tire with the two-and-a-bit good fingers of my left hand. I dropped the cap on the street and pressed on the valve stem with my thumbnail. It hissed so loud I nearly pissed myself. I cupped my hand over it and tried again. It was muffled, but it was still louder than I liked. I prayed that the noise from the two nearby intersecting highways drowned out my vandalistic efforts.

It took a helluva of a lot longer than I expected, but eventually, the tire was flat. I shuffled back to the rear tire and was unscrewing the cap when I was interrupted.

"What the hell are you doing to my van?"

I jumped up with a squeak, half-expecting it to be one of my neighbours and I'd seriously screwed up, but it was *him*—clean-shaven now, with his camera in his hand. I had no fucking idea what to do, so I did the only thing I could. I threw the mallet at him.

Having never met a serial killer before, I really had no idea what to expect, but his reflexes were as slow as shit and my lucky throw caught him hard in the forehead, just over his left eye. He went down like he'd been punched by Georges St-Pierre. I kicked the bottom of his foot to make sure he was out cold, watched his chest rise and fall to make sure I hadn't killed him—not that he didn't deserve it—and picked up the mallet just in case he needed another whack for good measure.

The first police cruiser came racing around the corner with its lights flashing but sirens muted. Just one cruiser? For a serial killer? Then a police SUV skidded to a stop right behind me. The next thing I knew I was surrounded by cops, the mallet was pried out of my hand, and a female officer escorted me away from the scene. Reggie appeared at my side and took my other elbow. In the background, I heard another officer call for an ambulance.

o0o

The officer sat me on my couch while Reggie got me a glass of water. I accepted it with mumbled thanks. The shock was setting in. The cop must have thought so, too because she started asking me questions in a soft, calming voice. When did I first notice him following me, how many times had I seen him, and had he ever been carrying a weapon when I saw him?

I answered as best as I could, pausing when I heard sirens approach. She smiled and reassured me that it was the ambulance arriving. Time did a funky tempo-change and I lost track of a few moments here and there while I fielded more questions. After a while, there was a light tap-knock on the front storm door.

"Ms. Krawetz—Jubilee—it's me, Detective Marlin."

"Come in."

He greeted the officer as a friend as she exited, introduced himself to Reggie, and then sat on the other couch, facing me. "You've been busy."

"Just another day of rock and roll," was all I could come up with.

"Your timing is even better than we first thought, Jubilee. The story will be all over the news this evening. My chief has called for a press conference at five."

"'Geocache Butcher in custody, film at eleven'?"

"Not exactly. He's not the Butcher."

Oh shit. "So, it'll be 'Crazy Cripple attacks bird photographer with hammer'?"

"Well, not that either, but we'll deal with that in a minute. The release will say something like "Reign of terror over! William T. Watson, the Geocache Butcher, was killed in a multi-vehicle accident last month on his way to meet his next victim, Calgary musician, Jubilee Krawetz."

My hands started to shake, and my mouth went dry. In my head I was shouting *'What?'* but I was outwardly mute. The detective smiled and Reggie put a comforting hand on my forearm.

"It's taken us this long to connect all of the pieces. It turns out that Zach Grizowski who sideswiped you and then lost control and slammed his car into the post was yet another alias of Bill Watson. They've been holding his remains as a John Doe since his ID didn't check out, but once we logged Watson's DNA in the system we got a match."

"The Geocache Butcher is dead. We're *sure*?"

"Sure enough that my Chief is making a statement this afternoon to tie up the loose ends and take the city off high alert. About twenty minutes after I dropped you off, the rest of the remains of his three victims were found in graves out near his trailer. There was no sign of your goddaughter, I'm afraid."

Reggie sighed, and when the detective looked at him, I explained. "Eileen Kennedy is Reggie's niece, and she's safe. She was out on a boat, up the coast towards Alaska or some such. She just contacted her family this morning."

"That's terrific news! I'll have her Missing Person's Case closed."

"What about the Butcher's accomplice?"

"We've been investigating our butts off, and not found any evidence that he working with anyone. It's over. The Geocache Butcher is no more, thank God. From what we've seen, you were to be the next victim so he could send the geocache coordinates to your goddaughter. It was her he had a serious hate for. She was pretty sharp-tongued in her online take-downs of him. He was going to eliminate the remaining four Girls of Cache-a-Lot, one at a time."

"When he first disappeared, the press said something about his having a sister. How is she?" Trust Reggie to worry about someone he'd never met.

"She's in the hospital. She had a breakdown not long after she found the rural property. Her husband came and fetched her and they returned to Edmonton. She's getting help."

I had a horrifying thought. "Then who did I just concuss with a mallet? Will he live? Am I a *double* murderer?" Oh shit! I'm a *killer*!

"He'll be OK. I spoke with him briefly before I came in. He'd like to speak with you when you're ready."

"Now? He wants to yell at me *now*?"

"Oh, not at all. I think you might even find this funny. They're going to keep him in the hospital overnight, for observation, but his concussion isn't serious. Nice shot with the mallet, by the way."

"Um, thanks? I suppose I should hear what he has to say so they can get him to the hospital."

The detective led the way out to the ambulance. The police vehicles were gone. On the gurney was my one and only, camera-equipped, gold-van-driving stalker. An icepack was bandaged to his forehead and his eyes looked like they were having trouble focussing, but he held his hand out in greeting. I shook it, confused as hell.

"Ms. Krawetz, my name is Mitch LaBelle. I owe you a huge apology for scaring you. I didn't mean to. I'm a private investigator and your insurance company hired me to find out if the injury to your left hand was real and if the damage was permanent and irreversible. I've been wearing disguises and taking pictures and videos as part of my job."

"Insurance company? *What* insurance company?" What the hell was he talking about?

"In 2019 you took out a policy for a million dollars. A policy that would pay out if you had an accident of any kind that would result in your not being able to play cello again."

"Are you shitting me? We got that as a joke. James—my ex—said he was going to cancel it, ages ago."

"He didn't. The premiums have been paid every year. It's current, and after watching you—"

"*Stalking* me."

"Fair enough. After *stalking* you for these few weeks, I'm certain your injuries are catastrophic and debilitating, and I'm going to recommend full payment. I was only here today because the case manager wanted a full twenty days of observations."

I wasn't sure whether to laugh or cry. "Sorry about the hammer."

"Don't worry about it. I'm just glad your bird-watching friend didn't shoot me."

"Good point." He must have followed me to the gun range.

The paramedic interrupted us. "Sorry folks. We need to get Mr. LaBelle to the hospital."

Detective Marlin put a hand on the gurney's sidebar to stop them. "One quick moment, please. Mr. Labelle, if you don't press charges for assault, I'm willing to bet that Ms. Krawetz won't press charges for trespassing or invasion of privacy."

"I was just doing my job."

"We can let a judge decide that if you wish." He looked at me. "Jubilee? Would that be acceptable to you?"

"What? No, of course. I mean I won't press charges. I just want this to all be over."

LaBelle nodded, then winced from the pain the action caused. "It's a deal."

"Excellent." The detective took his hand off the gurney and Labelle was loaded up and whisked away with flashing lights.

"Jubilee, you've gone through Hell the last while. If you feel *any* guilt at all about your involvement in the Butcher's death, just remember the four women whose lives he didn't get to take because you were in *that* place at *that* time."

"Thank you. That does help."

"Good. Now, if you'll excuse me, I have another press conference to prepare my chief and the mayor for." He shook our hands and left. Reggie and I walked back to the house, closed the door, sat on the couch together, and *lost* it. We wept like babies. It was over. It was *all* over. Three women were gone forever, but the Butcher would take no more, including me and Elteen.

After the tears subsided, we locked up the house and began the slow drive back downtown in rush hour traffic. Halfway there Reggie turned off the irritating radio and squeezed my hand. "So, what now?"

"I could use a drink, to celebrate taking my life back."

Reggie sighed. "Another Thorogood?"

"Hell no. Coffee. Black."

Special Thanks to:

Ann Cooney

Adrienne Kerr

Jennifer Rahn

Virginia O'Dine

Shannon Allen

Stacey Kondla

Gary Renshaw

Suzy Vadori

Jayne Barnard

Kate Salter

Craig Venables

Lisa Dutton

T. K.

The When Words Collide Workshoppers

Writing this story took me back into some dark places of my soul, and I am forever grateful for the friends and family who kept me balanced and guided me back to the light.

About the Author

According to CBC Radio, Tim Reynolds is
"Canada's modern-day Aesop".
That's great praise he struggles to live up to, but what
he will admit to is being a prize-winning,
award-nominated Canadian with stories to tell.

Based out of Calgary, Alberta, Tim grew up in Toronto,
earning first a B.A. and then a B.Ed. from
the University of Western Ontario.

He currently remains trapped in his house,
a willing indentured servant to his animals.

Find out what Tim is working on now at:

www.TGMReynolds.com

Also by the Author

The Broken Shield (an urban fantasy)

The Death of God and Other (short) Stories

Waking Anastasia (a ghostly novel about love)

The Sisterhood of the Black Dragonfly (a YA fantasy)

The Gravity of Guilt (a sci-fi thriller)

She Runs with Wolves, He Sits with Kittens
(a romantic comedy)